ANTIQUES LIQUIDATION

Also by Barbara Allan

Trash 'n' Treasures mysteries

ANTIQUES ROADKILL
ANTIQUES MAUL
ANTIQUES FLEE MARKET
ANTIQUES BIZARRE
ANTIQUES KNOCK-OFF
ANTIQUES DISPOSAL
ANTIQUES CHOP
ANTIQUES CON
ANTIQUES SLAY RIDE (e-book)
ANTIQUES FRUITCAKE (e-book)
ANTIQUES SWAP
ANTIQUES ST. NICKED (e-book)
ANTIQUES FATE
ANTIQUES FRAME
ANTIQUES WANTED
ANTIQUES HO-HO-HOMICIDES
ANTIQUES RAVIN'
ANTIQUES FIRE SALE
ANTIQUES CARRY ON *

* *available from Severn House*

ANTIQUES LIQUIDATION

Barbara Allan

SEVERN
HOUSE

First world edition published in Great Britain and the USA in 2022
by Severn House, an imprint of Canongate Books Ltd,
14 High Street, Edinburgh EH1 1TE.

Trade paperback edition first published in Great Britain and the USA in 2023
by Severn House, an imprint of Canongate Books Ltd.

severnhouse.com

British Library Cataloguing-in-Publication Data
A CIP catalogue record for this title is available from the British Library.

ISBN-13: 978-0-7278-5091-1 (cased)
ISBN-13: 978-1-4483-0765-4 (trade paper)
ISBN-13: 978-1-4483-0764-7 (e-book)

All Severn House titles are printed on acid-free paper.

Typeset by Palimpsest Book Production Ltd.,
Falkirk, Stirlingshire, Scotland.
Printed and bound in Great Britain by
TJ Books, Padstow, Cornwall.

In memory of
Dorothy Carolyn Jensen Mull

Brandy's quote:
'When one person is mad and the other isn't,
the mad one always wins'

– Mary O'Hara

Mother's quote:
'Sticks and stones may break my bones,
but words will never harm me'

– old adage

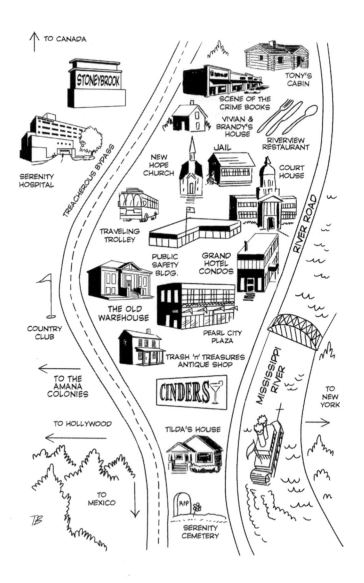

TO CANADA

STONEYBROOK

SCENE OF THE
CRIME BOOKS

TONY'S
CABIN

VIVIAN &
BRANDY'S
HOUSE

RIVERVIEW
RESTAURANT

SERENITY
HOSPITAL

TREACHEROUS BYPASS

NEW
HOPE
CHURCH

JAIL

COURT
HOUSE

RIVER ROAD

TRAVELING
TROLLEY

PUBLIC
SAFETY
BLDG.

GRAND
HOTEL
CONDOS

COUNTRY
CLUB

THE OLD
WAREHOUSE

PEARL CITY
PLAZA

TRASH 'N' TREASURES
ANTIQUE SHOP

MISSISSIPPI RIVER

TO THE
AMANA
COLONIES

CINDERS

TO
NEW
YORK

TO HOLLYWOOD

TILDA'S HOUSE

TO
MEXICO

RIP

SERENITY
CEMETERY

TB

ONE

Button Button, Who's Got the Button

I was shaken rudely from a deep slumber. My art-deco-appointed bedroom was dark, but I could make out Mother's disembodied face floating above me, a ghostly mask in oversize glasses and lipstick.

I was Brandy Borne, thirty-three, blonde by choice, divorced by misadventure, Prozac by prescription; Mother was mid-seventies – exactly how 'mid' a well-guarded secret – Danish stock, widowed, and bipolar.

'Warning lights flashing, dear!' she said, settling into one almost-in-focus image. 'Your help needed!'

'Wha . . . what's wrong?' I asked groggily.

Her response was to pull back the covers, exposing me in my short pjs, and Sushi, my little brown-and-white shih tzu, to the chill of an over-compensating air-conditioning system in August.

I sat up. 'What *time* is it?'

'Two o'clock,' Mother said.

'In the *morning*?'

'Yes. Don't tarry now! Get dressed.'

'What is this *about*?' I demanded, and leaned over to click on the bedside light – a 1939 World's Fair Saturn lamp whose pink glow added a touch of further mystery.

Two in the morning or not, Mother was nicely coiffed, wavy silver tresses pinned back in a neat bun, her makeup perfect, like the Werewolf of London's hair. She was wearing all black, unusual for her . . . unless she was up to no sneaky good.

Her chin rose and her eyes lowered. 'I'll fill you in on the way,' she said.

'Nooooo,' I replied. 'You'll fill me in *right* now.'

The eyes widened, an alarming sight behind those magnifying-glass lenses. 'Don't you trust me?'

'Of course I don't.'

Her sigh began at her toes. 'How sharper than a serpent's tooth it is to have a thankless child!'

Mother – a community theater diva when she isn't acting the amateur sleuth in what passes around here for real life – loves to trot out that Shakespeare line. But I wasn't having any of it. Besides, what could I manage with one lousy tooth against this formidable woman? Now, a whole *mouth*ful, I might stand a chance.

She sat herself primly on the edge of the mattress and took on an air of reasonableness – not her most convincing performance. 'Very well, if we must. It's regarding the auction next week.'

Mother had been talking incessantly about attending that upcoming event with an eye on freshening the stock of our Trash 'n' Treasures antiques shop. But I'd paid scant attention, having put a moratorium on going to any auctions myself, deeming them a waste of time – you either didn't get what you wanted, or paid too much if you did.

She was saying, 'Anyway, the auctioneer is Conrad Norris, and he has agreed—'

I smirked. 'To sell you some things beforehand because you once were "an item."'

Mother splayed a hand on her bosom. 'Brandy! You simply must refrain from itemizing my male friends of a certain age as if each and every one is a former paramour. You have an over-active imagination, child. You seem to think I've spent my life being intimate with every available man in Serenity!'

'Only the straight ones.'

She stared at me, a beautiful older woman with the eyes of a big bug. 'That's not worthy of a response.'

'And yet you just gave me one,' I countered. 'All right. You have some dirt on this Conrad Who's-it and you're blackmailing him to get a jump on the auction.'

Her head tilted and her expression tried for thoughtful. 'Such a harsh word, blackmail. I prefer quid pro quo.'

'You prefer "quid," period. I won't be a part of blackmail, by any name . . . particularly not at two o'clock in the morning.' I gave her a 'so there' look and flopped back on the bed.

Mother stood. 'All right then. But don't hold *me* responsible for what I might buy on the sly without your guiding influence. I'll have to go it alone!'

The second Mother uttered the word 'go' Sushi jumped off the bed, essentially defecting to her side.

At the door, Mother made a Columbo-like pause to turn back and ask, 'By the by, how's our liquidity?'

If she meant the shop's, then, not good – mostly due to a slowdown in foot-traffic during summer's dog days, but also thanks to some poor purchasing decisions on her part. Or perhaps you're interested in a dozen never-used Brownie cameras, a box of old glass insulators, or some old rusty dental tools?

'Oh . . . *fine!*' I said childishly. 'But you'll have to take me just as I am.'

'Don't I always, darling?'

Just the same, I threw on a leopard-print robe over my pjs, and settled my feet into a pair of Minnie Mouse slippers.

With Sushi in my arms, we went out into the humid, sticky night to our new gently used Buick SUV in the driveway. We used to have a more ecologically friendly vehicle, but Mother could never get used to the hybrid, thinking it had stalled at every stoplight. Plus, she liked having some room in back for hauling finds from yard sales and junk shops.

I got behind the wheel, Mother riding shotgun, Sushi on her lap.

With a frown I asked, 'Why are you dressed like that?'

'Like what, dear?'

'All in black like a burglar or a ninja or something. Please tell me we're not breaking in somewhere. And don't say, "Ask me no questions and I'll tell you no lies!"'

After all, we'd once done thirty days in the county jail for just such an offense, a light sentence only because along the way we'd managed to catch a killer. While Mother had a ripping good (her words) time in stir (also her word), befriending other female inmates, I had been miserable, gaining five pounds on the starchy jailhouse fare.

'No, dear, we've been *invited* where we're going,' she replied. 'But it could be dusty, and black is rather forgiving in that regard.'

Frowning, I leaned toward her. 'Is that my new cashmere

sweater?' I'd snagged the off-season luxury item at a discount, online.

'I didn't have anything black,' she replied, adding, 'It's not in my color chart.'

'So those are my *slacks*, too!'

'Possibly.'

Fuming, I said, 'You'd better not get them filthy!'

'Brandy, dear,' Mother said, the voice of reason. 'Let's not keep Mr Norris waiting.'

I started the car. In a bored cabby voice, I managed, 'Where to, lady?'

'The old warehouse on Main.'

I backed the SUV out of the drive, and pointed it in the direction of downtown Serenity.

And now for some back story on our quaint little Iowa town, population twenty-five thousand, give or take a few souls. (Longtime readers may skip to the paragraph beginning with 'Where was I?')

First to settle on the grassy banks of the Mississippi River in the fertile valley between two bluffs were the peaceable Mascoutin Indians. Germans arrived to build lucrative lumber mills, and the Indians politely moved over. Then the Germans grudgingly made room for Scandinavians, who established pearl-button factories by harvesting mussel shells from the river. About the same time, Serenity – one of the stops on the Underground Railroad during the Civil War – offered a safe haven and freedom for runaway slaves, some of whom decided to stick around.

After that came an influx of migrants from Mexico who labored in the tomato and melon fields during the summer; they liked what they found, and everybody moved over, except the wealthy who inhabited East Hill, having helped themselves to the best view of the Mississippi River early on.

The ethnic mix remained the same until the debacle of the Vietnam War, after which Serenity welcomed displaced people of Asian descent, adding one more ingredient to our ethnic melting pot. For a town our size, we have a pleasing array of authentic food from all over the world, with a special nod to the Italians, who showed up some time or other. My sense of history isn't perfect.

A word about the Mascoutins. Every so often, some well-meaning citizen petitions the city council to remove the bronze statue of the chief of the Indian tribe from the river front, or change the name of our community college's Mascoutins baseball team, or rename Papoose Creek. Every time such well-meaning efforts are mounted, Mother puts on the American Indian costume she wore for a teenage stint playing Princess Iowana on a local kids' television program, and goes before the council on 'Citizens Speak Night.' There, blissfully unaware of her political incorrectness, she solemnly approaches the microphone, and, raising her head-dressed head regally, gazes out over the overflowing audience.

'So,' Princess Iowana begins, 'you seek to erase any trace of my people . . .' Always a few titters here, due to Mother's obvious Nordic heredity. '. . . as if we never existed! As if we didn't welcome you with open arms. As if our *bones* are not buried on the very ground you now inhabit.' (There had been several Indian mounds discovered in the city park.)

I don't mean to imply Mother's speech was always the same – she covered various ground (burial ground included) and improvised in a manner combining eloquence with unintentional humor. Which is why she always drew a capacity crowd for these performances, and why the end result was always the same – a standing ovation for Princess Iowana, the now-sheepish do-gooders silenced.

Princess Iowana, by the way, was not a historical figure representing the Mascoutins, but the picture on the Iowana Dairy milk cartons.

Where was I?

Our destination was Pearl City Plaza, a block of restored and refurbished Victorian buildings turned into boutiques and bistros and nightspots, with nice apartments on the upper floors. The warehouse where we were headed was the only holdout, a neglected four-story red-brick structure at the end of the street, a decaying tooth in an otherwise attractive smile.

The warehouse had been built in the mid-1800s by Germans from Hanover who established a wholesale food business supplying mom-and-pop neighborhood grocery stores. According to Mother, the company had survived until the arrival of the big

chain supermarkets, whose own food supply network spelled the
end of the wholesale company and the mom-and-pops they served.

'Who bought the building after the grocery company went
bust?' I asked Mother. We were cruising a deserted Main Street,
lit by faux Victorian lampposts.

'A man by the name of Lyle Dayton. But everyone called
him the Liquidator.'

'Sounds ominous.'

'He *was* a bit of a rascal,' she admitted. 'Ran a business with
the help of his young nephew, Ryan Dayton, buying up unsold
and unwanted merchandise for a pittance – mostly taking advantage of bankruptcies. Used the warehouse for storage, then sold
the items for a tidy profit.' Mother pointed. 'Turn here, dear.'

I did. 'One way to make a buck, I suppose.'

'Yes, if a bit unsavory.'

We were bouncing along a potholed alley.

'What happened to this Dayton?' I asked. 'I never heard of
him. Did he leave town?'

'No, Lyle disappeared eight or nine years ago – here we are,
dear. Pull up next to the loading dock.'

I complied, then killed the engine. 'Maybe the nephew
liquidated the Liquidator.'

I was just making a bad joke, but Mother swiveled toward me
with eyes wide. 'That's what *I* thought – Ryan being Lyle's only
relative. But soon after the disappearance, the nephew closed
the liquidation company, shuttered all but the first floor of the
building, and rented to various business.'

That part of the history I knew – the bottom floor of
the warehouse had been, variously, a dance club, Mexican
restaurant, work-out gym, and the late lamented antiques mall
where Mother and I had rented a booth beginning our Trash 'n'
Treasures venture together, not long after I'd come crawling home
from Chicago after my divorce.

'Still,' I said, 'sounds like the nephew always found a way to
make money out of the position his uncle left him in.'

'Eking out an existence is more like it,' she said. 'The cost of
maintaining the building, and paying property taxes, ultimately
overwhelmed him.' She paused. 'And if Ryan Dayton *had* killed
his uncle – why wait until this *year* before going to court to have

the man declared dead, whereby the nephew would inherit the building free and clear?'

Leave it to Mother to weave a sinister tapestry out of a wisecrack of mine. But I found myself asking, 'What's the statute in Iowa for declaring someone dead who's gone missing?'

'As short as six months in some cases.' She paused. 'But that's rare – such as when some poor soul is witnessed jumping off a bridge, and the body isn't recovered.'

Which had happened from time to time in Serenity, our bridge pedestrian-friendly, but the current of the Mississippi River at times unfriendly.

'No,' Mother went on, still weaving, 'I think Ryan always thought his uncle would return one day, like Enoch Arden.'

'Who?'

'It's a famous poem, dear. Tennyson. Perhaps I should have encouraged you to read more than *Glamour* and *Elle* in your youth.'

'You were too busy reading Rex Stout and Agatha Christie.'

We exited the SUV, Mother transferring Sushi to me, and headed toward a door adjacent to the loading dock.

'Don't tell me,' I said. 'Doug Holden snatched up this place.' Holden was a local developer who owned all the other buildings on the block and had gradually refurbished them.

'Lock, stock, and barrel,' she said. 'I understand he's planning to restore the outside to its original majesty, and transform the inside into luxury condos.'

I didn't see what was majestic about a big crumbling brick building, but Mother was a great proponent of architectural conservation. She once chained herself to the front entrance of the old art moderne Palace movie house to save it from the wrecking ball. The theater died anyway, becoming a parking lot yet giving birth to the Serenity Historical Preservation Society, devoted to preventing other such architectural demises around town.

'Condos would be nice,' I admitted. Holden had a great deal to do with not only revitalizing the downtown, but making quality housing out of an area that had been fairly sketchy for years.

We stood at the back door of the warehouse.

I asked, 'What if Mr Holden finds out about your back-alley deal with the auctioneer?'

She sniffed, 'Douglas Holden will still fare quite nicely, I'm sure. He always does.'

'Not as "nicely" as he would have if you hadn't gone cherry-picking before anything got to the auction block.'

'That's between him and the auctioneer, dear. I am simply a conscientious consumer.'

Wearing black in the middle of the night.

The door was unlocked, and we stepped into darkness. I used my cell-phone light, revealing a back room stripped bare to its studs.

She whispered, 'Seems the little buzzards have already been picking the field clean.'

I didn't whisper. 'Then what's left for the big buzzard?'

She gave me a cunning look. 'You'll see.'

Paint me skeptical that anything left would be worth risking a blackmail charge.

Rather clinically she asked, 'Are you familiar with the term "dead stock?"'

'Sure,' I replied, throwing light onto her face like a glass of water. 'Everything that we haven't been able to sell in our shop that's now stuffed in our garage.'

She guided away my hand with the cell phone shining. 'No, Brandy, dead stock is old unused *new* merchandise,' she said. 'Which can bring considerable moolah.'

I grunted. 'So which is it? Old or new?'

She studied me like a spider does a fly. 'Dear, you could use a little attitude adjustment. Have you been taking your medication?'

'Have you been taking yours?'

She shrugged. Fair question.

Still, usually we didn't reach this stage of rancor until at least halfway through the book, which should alert you to the possibility of a bumpy ride ahead.

'*You kept me waiting long enough!*'

The sudden grumpy voice out of the darkness was enough to make us both jump, and to get a low growl out of Sushi.

As he moved out of the shadows, auctioneer Conrad Norris lit his face with his own cell light. 'We'll have to use our phones – I'm not turning on any lights and risk attracting attention.'

Norris was in his late forties or early fifties, his medium-height and average frame wrapped up in a yellow polo shirt and pressed tan slacks. His brown hair was thinning, his wire-framed aviator-style glasses at least as oversize as Mother's, and he may have been handsome once, but his face betrayed the bloated vein-shot appearance of a heavy drinker.

Norris gave me the fish-eye. 'What's *she* doing here, Vivian? Who's that, your daughter? I said come alone.'

Mother shrugged. 'I didn't imagine *you'd* want to help me transport the goods, Conrad.'

If I'd had any doubt about my role up until now, it had just been made clear.

Norris scowled, 'Not hardly. I hope she can keep her mouth shut.'

He turned abruptly and we followed him into a cavernous area where a long bank of high windows facing the street let in light from the faux Victorian lampposts.

A few ghosts remained of businesses gone by: a disco ball left hanging from a high ceiling beam, a restaurant table and chairs, a weightlift doorstop, and – familiarly – taped outlines on the floor designating where each booth had been when this was an antique mall. Something bad had once happened here (*Antiques Maul*) but *that* tape had been removed . . .

Sushi squirmed in my arms, wanting to run free, as I often allowed – she was good about returning on command.

But I said, 'No, girl,' and hurried to catch up with Norris and Mother, heading toward the ancient freight elevator – a truly dangerous contraption.

There wasn't much concern back in the late 1800s regarding employee safety. The only thing keeping someone from stepping off into a dark abyss was an accordion-like metal gate, meant to stay closed when the elevator wasn't waiting. But no mechanism had ever been installed to keep that gate honest. Once, when Mother and I had been renters, I caught her arm just as she had one foot in midair.

She had said, 'Watch that first step – it's a doozy!' But for once she'd been truly frightened.

The auctioneer pressed a button summoning the elevator. Above, it groaned and moaned with displeasure, arriving with rattle and a big, shuddering *clunk*.

With some force, Norris pulled the rusty gate aside.

'I'll just take the stairs,' I said.

He shrugged. 'Be my guest. But we're going to the top, and a few steps are missing here and there, all the way up.'

I got reluctantly onboard the car, its squeaky, spongy floor welcoming me, and Norris pushed another button. It was a slow, herky-jerky ride, but fascinating to watch through the gate as an empty second, then third floor went by, tall windows letting in just enough streetlight to make shadows out of gray murk.

The elevator came to a bouncy stop on the fourth – *boi-yoi-yoing* – as if reluctant to land. The auctioneer opened the gate and we entered an inky world, leavened by only what our cell lights captured, chiefly the state of the original wooden flooring, with gaps between some boards providing a glimpse of the floor below.

With no windows up here, the air was hot and stuffy, a massive old attic, and I was already sweating in my robe, not anxious to display my short pjs before the male auctioneer. Color me modest.

Norris moved to an ancient wall switch, illuminating the front half of the cavernous room, leaving the rear swallowed in shadows.

I gazed at the conglomeration of stuff before me. The Liquidator had apparently not been terribly discerning in his buying habits over the years. He'd scavenged anything and everything: building materials, machinery, clothing and textiles, plus other indiscernible items packed in wooden crates and corrugated cardboard barrels.

Mother, drawn to a grouping of the latter, gasped. 'Oh, my goodness! So *many*!'

'What's in them?' I asked, my interest piqued.

Mother's head swiveled my way. 'Dear, you'd know if you'd *bothered* to examine the auction listing rather than indulge yourself in such luxuries as cashmere sweaters.'

Like the one she was wearing!

Turning to the auctioneer, she asked regally, 'Would you mind if I enlightened my daughter?'

Our nervous host scowled. 'Yeah, yeah. Make it quick.'

A real charmer.

Mother gestured to the dozen or so containers. 'Pearl buttons, dear – dating back a century and a half, made by the Larsen company.'

The local pearl-button industry's demise had not been due to a private supply chain, like the grocery business, but the popularity of inexpensive plastic buttons.

Mother now crossed to an open wooden crate, where exposed cardboard boxes nestled neatly among excelsior packing.

I approached, and picked up a box, examining the outside, where a logo on the front read: *Peter-Mar Quality Toys, Serenity, Iowa.* The top identified the contents as *NOAH'S ARK*, and below that *BLUE.*

I'd heard about the local company that in the mid-1930s began producing wooden toys – perhaps most famously an ark with Noah and his wife, and animals, two by two. But, a few years later, with a second world war looming, lumber suddenly became limited to government contracts, and Peter-Mar – reduced to scraping for scrap wood – couldn't keep their arks afloat.

Mother was saying, 'Only a dozen or so of these have surfaced, and very few have all the pieces. Plus, while the arks were painted in both blue or green, blue is harder to find.' She paused. 'And the original boxes? Rarer than hen's teeth!'

Do hens have teeth? I'd have to check. Or ask Mother.

She moved to another group of crates. 'And over here are dishes that had been rescued from the Palace Theater before it was torn down.' She turned to me as if I were a customer in our shop who needed schooling in the value of an item. 'During the Depression, this is how movie theater managers enticed wives to spend their husbands' hard-earned money on picture shows! Giveaway drawings for free dishes.'

I knew about 'dish night.' The author Jean Shepherd wrote of a riot that took place at a theater in his hometown during one of these events – after the same gravy boat had been handed out on three consecutive 'dish nights,' the women bombarded the stage with cracking crockery.

Which, come to think of it, could make the likes of that gravy boat valuable – as rare as hen's teeth.

I crossed to join her.

Inside this crate, protected by crumpled rolls of paper, were stacks of cobalt blue dishes – plates, bowls, cups, saucers, and yes, some gravy boats, immediately recognizable as Fiestaware.

'But the Homer Laughlin Company still makes these,' I

said, wondering what about these dishes might make them blackmail worthy.

Mother shook her head, 'Not the same,' and tapped a plate with a finger. 'Laughlin introduced the line in 1936, and cobalt blue was the first color. But women hated it. They wanted bone china with floral designs, and gold rimming. So this first Fiestaware ended up at theaters as giveaways.' She shrugged a shoulder. 'Then the economy improved, and people suddenly saw Fiestaware as modern, the newer, brighter colors cheerful, something that didn't remind them of the Depression.'

Sushi – apparently just as uncomfortable in her fur coat as I was in my robe – wiggled out of my arms, dropping down.

'Stay here,' I ordered, worried she might wander off and fall through to the floor below.

Sushi obeyed.

Norris said gruffly, 'All right, that's enough yakety-yak . . . what do you want of these, Vivian?'

Mother told him – a crate of the arks, a crate of dishes, and a barrel of the buttons.

'Not gonna happen,' said Norris, firmly. 'I can't fudge *that* much on the inventory list.'

Which also told me he was going to pocket tonight's cash transaction. Not a big surprise.

Mother asked, rather pitifully, 'What *can* I have?'

'One set of dishes, one ark—'

'Two arks,' I cut in. 'There are two mouths to keep shut here.'

The antiques business is not for sissies.

The auctioneer glared at me, then at Mother, then back at me.

I turned to my accomplice for support, who seemed surprised I'd gotten involved. I explained, 'I want to give one to Baby Brandy.' My best friend's toddler, named after me.

Mother nodded, turned to the auctioneer and said, '*Two* arks.'

'All right!' Norris snapped. 'All right. But that's all. I can always say the crates ran short.'

'Not quite,' Mother said. 'There's the matter of the pearl buttons. And I *insist* on one full barrel. Good grief, man – look at the trouble we went to, tonight. Yourself included!'

I started to ask what she would want with so many buttons, but Mother waved me silent.

Surprisingly, Norris responded, 'You can have one. *Anything* to get you out of here.'

Mother, bending at her waist, spoke to Sushi, pointed and said, 'Pick a barrel.'

The little furball – probably understanding only that she had permission to move – trotted immediately to one that was closest, circled it, sniffed, then barked. Selection made.

Norris found some empty boxes for the plates and arks, and, while I packed them, he and Mother moved off for a confab, after which I saw filthy lucre exchange hands.

A few minutes later, we boarded the elevator, boxes and barrel loaded onto a flat-bed cart, the ride down smooth and fast, as if the elevator wanted rid of us, too.

Soon Mother, Sushi, and I, along with our ill-gotten goods, found ourselves unceremoniously dumped out onto the loading dock, its metal garage-style door coming down with a *slam!*

'Well,' Mother huffed, dusting herself off as if she'd been thrown through a western saloon's batwing doors. 'He needn't have been so rude!'

'What did you expect? "Oh, thank you, Vivian, for black-mailing me."'

'I wish you'd stop calling it that. Let's consider it paying tribute – rendering unto Mrs Caesar. I merely took advantage of something he did that he shouldn't have.'

I sighed, raised a palm as if in court swearing in. 'I don't even *want* to know. I'm too tired. How are we going to get this stuff down and into our car?' The dock offered no stairs on its either side.

'How are *we* going to get down?' Mother lamented.

The answer to her question was not one we wanted. A police car, lights flashing, came to an abrupt halt next to the loading dock, bathing us in strobes of red and blue.

Busted.

One hand on the holster of her gun, a female officer leapt out assuming we were robbers.

Well, weren't we?

As the woman guardedly approached, Mother chirped, 'Well, hello there, Shawntea. How are your boys, Trayvon, Kwamie, and Zeffross?' Like old friends running into each other at an ice cream social.

The officer squinted, hand moving off the holster. 'Mrs Borne? Brandy?'

Guilty as charged. Or soon would be.

Mother had met Shawntea Monroe a few years ago when she and some of her gal pals made a trek into Chicago to see the Cubs play. Afterward, the ladies got lost leaving Wrigley Field, and their car had a flat tire in a rough part of town called Cabrini-Green. Shawntea, having just disembarked a smoke-belching bus, took pity on the fish-out-of-water ladies, and got her brother – a member of the Gangsta Disciples – to change the tire. But before the grateful ladies drove away, Mother told Shawntea that if she ever wanted to get a fresh start in new surroundings, she'd be welcome in Serenity, giving the woman her address.

A few months later, Shawntea arrived with three little boys in tow. Mother helped secure her a job, and the boys thrived in our small-town school system, Shawntea completing her GED in the evenings. She enrolled in community college, earned a degree in law enforcement, and joined the Serenity police force.

So if we had to be discovered in suspicious circumstances in the middle of the night by an officer of the law, this was a good one to draw.

Mother was saying, 'I know this looks bad, but we bought some things before the auction next week, and thought we'd best remove them from the building.'

'In the middle of the night?' Shawntea asked.

'Brandy here couldn't sleep.'

'It's this gosh-darn insomnia,' I managed.

'Would you like to see the receipt?' Mother asked. 'I have it with me.'

What receipt? Mother hadn't wanted a paper trail of *this* transaction!

Luckily, Shawntea replied, 'No, no, Vivian, of course not.' She gestured to the boxes and barrel. 'Looks like you could use some help.'

Mother said, 'Would you, dear? This lumbago is such a cross to bear.'

Sciatica, axial, radicular – whatever the bago, she had bagged it.

Shawntea helped Mother off the platform, then I handed the officer the boxes, which she loaded into the back of our SUV. But it took both of us to get the barrel in. A button is, after all, as light as . . . a button. But there were thousands of them in that thing.

We thanked Shawntea, and she returned to her vehicle.

As we watched her drive away, I asked, 'What if she finds out what you were *really* up to?'

'What *we* were up to, dear.' Mother was petting Sushi in her arms. 'The only witnesses to the transaction were you, me, and Mr Norris. And none of us are likely to talk. Including Sushi.'

'What are you planning to do with a whole barrel of buttons?'

'I'm going to put it by the checkout counter in the shop, of course – with a scooper, and sell the buttons at so much a bag. Like peanuts.'

She'd had worse ideas.

We got into the SUV.

But something she'd said stuck in my mind. If the only witnesses to the transaction were us and Norris, and a little dog . . . then why did the auctioneer have to summon the elevator from an upper floor?

A Trash 'n' Treasures Tip

Dead stock is unused inventory of any kind that had never sold for a variety of reasons: it fell out of fashion, was stored and forgotten, or became a casualty of bankruptcy. What can make dead stock valuable is the passage of time, its rarity, or a renewed interest in the product. So there's hope for those Brownie cameras, yet.

TWO
I Spy With My Little Eye

A week after Mother's wee-hours shakedown of Conrad Norris, the day of the auction had come.

Normally, business at our Trash 'n' Treasures shop was brisk on Saturday mornings, but we were located within a block of the auction-site warehouse. That would make parking for our customers nearly impossible, so Mother and I decided to stay closed during the proceedings, then open up afterward, to catch any bidders who still had money to spend.

Right now we were at home, seated in our dining room at the Duncan Phyfe table – La Diva Borne attired in a white short-sleeved blouse and turquoise slacks, her vassal in pajamas. We were lingering over coffee after a breakfast of scrambled eggs, bacon, and something called Dutch Cobbler's Cake.

Remember me mentioning that Mother had made some not-so-savvy purchases as of late? These weren't limited to antiques. Seems a recipe handed down from her grandmother called for a package of Holland Rusks. When Mother couldn't find any in the grocery aisles, she ordered six packages online. Or thought she did. But what arrived was six *cases*. Since then, we've been eating anything and everything that calls for a rusk.

Dutch Cobbler's Cake

4–5 tart apples (Mother uses Granny Smith)
¼ cup water (more if needed)
3 eggs, separated
¼ cup butter, softened
1 cup sugar
1 3.5 oz. package of Dutch rusks (Mother uses Reese's)
2 tsp. cinnamon

1 tsp. ground ginger
1 pinch ground cloves
½ cup raisins (I asked Mother to leave them out)
powdered sugar (optional)

Preheat oven to 375 degrees. Lightly grease 9-inch round cake pan. Peel, core, and slice apples, then cook in saucepan with ¼ cup water on medium high heat for about 30 minutes, until apples form a thick puree, adding more water if needed. In medium bowl, using an electric mixer, beat egg whites until they form stiff peaks, and set aside. In a large bowl, beat egg yolks, butter, and sugar, then add crumbled rusks *(NOTE: they had mostly come crumbled!)*, the apple puree, cinnamon, ginger, cloves, and raisins (if you must). Mix to combine. Gently fold in the egg whites. Spoon batter into the greased cake pan. Bake for 45 minutes, or until a knife (or a toothpick) inserted into the center comes out clean. Cool pan until cake can be easily removed, then dust top with powdered sugar. Serves 8. (Also good with whipped cream or ice cream.)

'So why bother going to the auction?' I asked, between nibbles of the genuinely delicious Cobbler's Cake. 'Didn't you already score what you wanted on our midnight ramble?'

Mother's coffee cup was just leaving her lips. 'It was a two a.m. ramble, and anyway, I want to see who buys what. Market research.'

Market research my Aunt Fanny's fanny. Vivian Borne was an incurable busybody.

'And, who knows?' Mother went on. 'I might still pick up a few things.'

Which was what I was afraid of. But not afraid enough to go with her – my allergy to auctions had grown acute.

She was saying, 'I know how you feel about bidding affairs, but I'd welcome your company.'

Actually, she'd probably just as soon as I stayed away. 'Thanks but no thanks,' I said, slipping a piece of leftover bacon beneath the table to a little land shark called Sushi. 'I'm going to see Tina and take Be-Be my ark this morning.'

Christina – or Tina, as I called her – was my best friend, and her daughter Be-Be (Baby Brandy) had just turned two. Tina and her husband Kevin had named the child after me. Certainly that was worth a toy ark, even a vintage one. Mother pushed back her chair, stood, and said, 'Very well.'

'What's the rush?' I asked. The auction wasn't until noon, two hours from now. 'They won't open the doors till eleven.'

Mother smiled. 'The other Pearl City Plaza shops will be open. I'll do a little pre-game shopping there.'

As if, I thought. It was far more likely she was planning to find some way to get into the warehouse early, just to snoop around.

She gazed down at me and at the table with its dirty dishes. 'You *do* know what my solo departure means?'

'Yes. I'm on KP duty.'

Mother nodded. 'Also, since you're staying, our readers will be coming with me. Who wants to be with you while you're washing dishes?'

Good Lord, she was already planning to make a book out of this! And we hadn't even stumbled onto a robbery much less a corpse.

Welcome, my adored, adoring readers! Dearest ones assemble! This is, of course, your obedient servant (as Orson Welles used to say), Vivian Borne.

First of all, I must pause to take issue with Brandy labeling me a 'busybody.' By no stretch of the imagination am I a busy-body. I do *not* meddle in other people's affairs. Admittedly I often do like to *know* of other people's affairs. Being well-informed in the hustle and bustle of this dangerous world is only sensible. And, as it happens, on occasion, I use that knowledge for the greater good. And, yes, sometimes the greater good and my own welfare coincide. But then, a person shouldn't have done what he or she or they did, and will think twice about doing it again if he or she or they know that I know what he or she or they did.

Clear?

Also, because I felt certain that Brandy wouldn't come with me, I could appear magnanimous by inviting her along, thus putting her tender mind at ease knowing I had nothing untoward planned (other than slipping into the building in advance).

Why such subterfuge? Frankly, and it pains me to say this about my grown daughter, she often slows me down, and puts a crimp in my style, baby! (If you will inject a little Austin Powers into that last phrase, your enjoyment will be increased.)

After leaving Brandy, I embarked into an almost chilly morning – a cold front had come through in the night, granting a short reprieve from the heat – and headed to my Vespa, parked in front of the garage. I had, you see, lost my driver's license – well, actually I knew right where it was . . . it just had the word VOID stamped across the front, an unfair response by the authorities to a few minor mishaps of mine. So for the nonce the scooter was my mode of transportation (legally sanctioned mode, that is).

I do admit to having taken the car a few times in the wee small hours of the morning, while Brandy was slumbering, for a quick trip to a QuikTrip to quell a craving for chocolate mint ice cream, a weakness I willingly admit (and frequently give in) to. (Brandy thinks I don't know where she hides that extra car fob – foolish child.) (And yes I know she will read this and find a new hiding place, but I will suss that out as well, so she needn't bother.)

As for using a Vespa rather than that big clunky SUV, why I'm just fine with that! I zip along like Audrey Hepburn in *Roman Holiday*, stylish coiffure ruffling in the breeze, suffering not a pang over the absence of Gregory Peck (but I would stop to pick up Mr Cary Grant any old day).

I tooled down Mulberry Street, taking that tree-lined, gradual descent into downtown Serenity, passing by upper- and middle-class homes, newer ones mixed with old, some owners trying hard to keep their lawns green with sprinklers, others allowing the grass to go dormant (I am of the latter school).

When I arrived at Pearl City Plaza, cars were beginning to hug the curbs, and fifty or so antiques-driven souls had already gathered near the front of the warehouse.

Due to such intense interest, a normal auction procedure had been simplified to this: as each person entered, he or she was handed a large white card with a number representing the available chairs (one *could* pick their seat) (let me rephrase that – *select* their seat). There had been no pre-registration, nor was information taken from attendees, perhaps to avoid human traffic jams at the door or at a table within. Everyone was on the honor system. After the cards ran out, no one else would be allowed in.

The process had been further simplified by selling like-kind merchandise in large lots; for example, all of the crates of arks at once, all of the barrels of buttons, all of the building material, and so on. Clearly, new warehouse owner Doug Holden, who set the rules for the auction, wanted the place cleared out pronto. Which meant bidders had to have deep pockets (or extended credit at their bank); therefore, I determined many of the attendees were here more for the spectacle of the thing. As was I.

I steered the Vespa into the alley behind the warehouse, where signs had been posted warning of steep fines for unauthorized parked vehicles, then stowed my ride beneath the loading dock. On the off-chance that the alley door would be open, I tried the latch – no joy.

About two feet separated the warehouse from its Victorian neighbor, an old fire precaution to keep one building's blaze from spreading to the next. I squeezed along the access until reaching a window-well of the warehouse basement.

Then I eased down into the well – perhaps three feet – and, from the fanny-pack around my waist, withdrew one of my lock picks. The ancient glazed window had an old-fashioned hook latch, and I easily slid the pick through the window's edge. In two shakes of a lamb's tail (or Bob's your uncle, if you prefer), I had it sprung. The panel swung inward, and I went through feet first, dropping down about four feet onto a dirt floor with some impact.

There I waited, while my eyes adjusted to the darkness and my hammer toes stopped aching, and until I felt certain I was alone.

It was eerily quiet. For further ambience, I would love to report that I heard a spooky rustling of rats, but if they were present, the little devils just didn't cooperate. Still, trust me – it was an unsettling atmosphere.

I panned my cell light around the vast high-ceilinged space, which – as far as my little light could project – appeared to have been cleared of any storage, excluding a few basement-type articles such as a pail, and shovel, and bag of rat poison. Which did explain the lack of rat rustle.

As I moved slowly forward – the dirt floor rough and uneven – I stepped into a soft area, nearly taking a tumble, but quickly recovered.

The basement steps looked to have been replaced, and I ascended them to an old wooden door that hadn't been. Trying the round metal knob, I found it locked. A trifling concern. Again, I dug into my fanny pack, this time selected the two small hex wrenches that would allow the picking of a skeleton key lock.

Moments later, I cracked open the door, determined the coast was clear, and slipped on through. Standing at the rear of the first floor, sunlight streaming in the windows, I took in the tableau before me – a cavernous room, its central area with wooden folding chairs neatly arranged in rows and facing a lectern on a riser, where soon auctioneer Conrad Norris would be holding court.

Behind the lectern, and off to one side, was a card table where a woman was busy setting up a laptop – Elizabeth Norris, the auctioneer's long-suffering wife, cashier at his auctions. Her features seemed rather plain, but that might have been due to the lack of even a dab of makeup; perhaps fifty, she had a slim figure ill-served by a drab print dress that perhaps aided and abetted a desire to fade into the background.

Surrounding the chairs, like covered wagons circled to fend off attack – not that Native Americans didn't have a right to object to trespassers on their soil! – the lots being bid upon were numbered and neatly stacked or arranged. (Or it might have been outlaws like the James gang. In my circled wagon simile.)

I was pondering my next move, when Conrad Norris, in a light blue polo shirt and navy slacks, stepped onto the podium, arranged some papers and his gavel on the lectern, then tested the micro-phone – *one, two, one, two*. Satisfied with the volume, he turned the mic off with a *click*. (Or should that be 'turned the mike off with a *clik*?' Oh well, I guess that's what copy editors are for.)

Norris had just stepped down when freshly minted warehouse owner Doug Holden strode out from between lots, and planted himself in front of the auctioneer, as if to block the man's path.

In his early forties, the developer might have been a construction worker in his faded yellow T-shirt, frayed jeans, and scuffed work boots – and once upon a time he had been. On the short side, burly, with close-cropped sandy hair, the once-lean Holden had developed a paunch since forming his restoration company – others did the labor now.

If the mic (mike?) had been hot, I might have innocently overheard their conversation, which seemed one-sided so far, the developer poking the auctioneer's chest with a forefinger, words hissing through gritted teeth, as if Holden was mindful of Elizabeth being within ear-shot.

Norris, his face flushed, finally got a response in, and Holden abruptly turned and headed toward the front entrance. He did not look happy.

Then Ryan Dayton – nephew of 'The Liquidator' and former owner of this warehouse – appeared on the scene. The young man – in his late twenties, with dark hair and nicely chiseled features – also entered a tête-à-tête with the auctioneer, though their exchange was harder to read, as Dayton had his back to me, blocking any view of Norris.

Then the nephew walked away, and Norris glanced behind him at his seated wife, who either had not noticed the two exchanges or was pretending not, keeping her head buried in the laptop at the card table. The auctioneer kept his back to her as he withdrew a silver hip flask and took a furtive sip.

A sudden commotion at the front entrance of the building indicated the doors were open. Soon, people from varied walks of life – farmers in bib-overalls, retired seniors in sensible shoes, executives in business attire, antiques dealers, and the assorted curious – rushed in like water into the hull of the Titanic. Some made straight for the chairs, others headed over for a look at the lots.

I slipped in among those on their feet.

Suddenly realizing I was in need of a numbered card, I followed a young male and female strolling hand in hand. When the female set her card down on the side of a crate to pick up the ark on display, I nimbly acquired the card and moved casually away.

Does this strike you as dishonest or perhaps uncouth? Frankly, no one ever compliments anyone on their 'couth,' and, sad to say, 'honesty' rarely comes up these days. But I was operating well with the 'street legal' sense of the true antiquer (if indoors). Firstly, the woman could share her partner's card, which she really should have been doing anyway, if things had gone far enough for hand-holding. Secondly, should she find herself lacking a chair, *he* could give her his, as chivalry isn't dead or at least shouldn't be, and as a woman over fifty still suffering from the side-effects of hip surgery, I had a landing pad coming more than some hardy young man. Thirdly, handling an auction item on display is a no-no, per signs posted stating so. Naughty naughty!

In the meantime I had spotted a seat of my own, where I could perch in the back row, on the aisle, and thereby get a decent view of everyone in front of me – more than just their backs, a side view as well. I was heading there when I literally (not figuratively) ran into Serenity's top toy afficionado, Dolly Gambol, literally (ditto) not seeing her.

The diminutive woman – who claimed to be in her mid-sixties (ha!) – bore a round fleshy face, curly blonde hair, over-the-top fake eyelashes, circular red-rouged cheeks, and bee-stung painted lips. Frankly, she looked just like one of the vintage dolls she collected.

'Do forgive me, my dear,' I said, gazing down at her. A pity that platform shoes had gone out of style, though of course if we were both wearing them the point would have been moot.

Rather pretty eyes gazed up at me through raccoon-circle mascara. '*My* fault, Vivian,' Dolly said. The woman had a way of inflection that told you she thought the opposite of her words – this time just a hint of question in her cadence.

I gave her a sly smile. 'I'll just bet I know what brought you here today . . . it's those Peter-Mar arks!'

'Guilty as charged.' A pause while Dolly considered if inquiring of my intentions was worth her time. 'And you, Vivian? Thinking a few toys might spruce up your shop?'

To put her mind at ease, I responded, 'Merely an observer this time.' Then, resisting the urge to pat her head, as I might have Sushi, I ladled on a dollop of fake enthusiasm. 'But I'll be rooting for you, Dolly dear!'

'Thank you, Vivian,' she said. 'What a *lovely* friend you are.'

The sarcasm of her emphasis seemed obvious to me. Then Dolly turned and was quickly swallowed up by the throng sans even a burp.

Why the acrimony between us, you ask? I'm glad you brought it up.

Some time back, I starred in a national cable reality TV show called *What Is It?* (Brandy was the Gabby Hayes to my Roy Rogers) (that's what Google is for, younger readers). On our much beloved and fondly remembered one-season show, people brought unidentified possible antiques in for our (mostly my) explication. (The show's cancellation wasn't my – or even Brandy's – fault; without giving too much away, let's just say someone integral to the production died – see *Antiques Swap*.)

Anywho, after much haranguing by Dolly, I invited her to be on an episode to share examples from her vast toy collection. We had scheduled a ten-minute segment of back-and-forth conversation, but she hogged the spotlight (you know the type!).

Then, afterward, Dolly contacted our producer and pitched a show of her own! Hers never came to be, but, still . . . the betrayal stung. Dolly does do a *local* cable channel show once a month – or so I'm told, as I've never watched it myself – and she managed to get on *Antiques Roadshow* with one of her tin toys. (Brandy and I have been turned down several times by the *Roadshow*, perhaps out of jealousy over the attention our accidentally similarly titled book *Antiques Roadkill* got us.)

My selected chair was still open, and I was moving toward it when Sally Wilson grabbed my arm.

A toy-collecting rival of Dolly's, Sally ran an antiques shop in Amana, a tourist area about an hour from Serenity. Younger than Dolly, tall and slender with shoulder-length brown hair, she exuded the kind of nervous energy that made waitresses offer her decaf. Though rather attractive, she was what some back in the day – not *my* day, mind you – might have called a spinster.

Sally, sotto voce, began, 'I saw Dolly speaking to you.' Her eyebrows were up.

To bring them down, I replied simply, 'She'll go to the mat for those arks.'

She twitched a frown. 'Well, she has the money to do it.'

'Indubitably,' I said. Isn't that a wonderful word? Then I added, 'But I'm rooting for you,' meaning it for once.

'Perhaps you'd care to throw in with me?' Sally asked, which was one way she might triumph over Dolly.

And not a bad idea at that! Then another idea popped in my head: the inevitability of Brandy's ire. After all, Prozac could only do so much to calm a girl. Besides, in order for Sally and *moi* to make our money back, we'd have to flood the toy market with the contents of that crate, thereby plummeting each ark's value, at least in the short term. Dolly, on the other hand, could afford to dole the boats out over time, which would likely be her intention.

'Sorry, my dear,' I told Sally. 'No can do. Trash 'n' Treasures just isn't right for moving that kind of quantity of an item.'

But as I'd uttered 'sorry,' Sally's eyes began flitting around, searching the crowd for another possible partner. And before I'd even got to 'item,' she was gone.

As I settled into my chair, I noticed Doug Holden and Ryan Dayton standing off to one side near Elizabeth's card table. Neither current developer nor former warehouse owner brandished a bidding card – perhaps they were here as mere spectators.

As auction time approached, chairs began to fill – but not *all* of them. A dozen or so potential bidders, having just found out that the items were available only in large lots, were heading out the doors, faces blue with disappointment or red with disgust. (This included that hand-holding couple, so you needn't worry about the young woman going without a seat.)

As Conrad Norris stepped up onto the platform, a hush fell over the now sparse audience. He read the rules in a somewhat slurred fashion, and announced that while the contents of the crates had been verified as authentic – and estimated as to the count of the items within – an *exact* number of those items had not been tabulated. In other words, items were sold 'as is,' which should prevent any post-auction complaints about, say, a hypothetical missing set of dishes or two toy arks.

The first lot came onto the chopping block.

Now I happen to know that any auctioneer worth his weight in bids saves the good stuff – garnering, as good stuff does, the

most interest – until last. Norris was no exception. Therefore, to
expedite our story – and not burden you, dear reader, with
boredom-inducing irrelevancies – I will fast-forward the process.
Although, come to think of it, you might have been interested
in the lot consisting of five hundred coolie hats – give or take a
coolie.

(*Note to editor Olivia Adams from Vivian*: Is the usage of
'coolie' politically incorrect?)

(*Note to Vivian from Olivia*: I'm afraid the term, derived from
the word 'guli,' which refers to a low-wage laborer of Asian
descent, is indeed considered outdated and offensive.)

(*Note to Olivia from Vivian*: Oh, dear! Then whatever should
I call them? The pointy straw hats, I mean. They originally
belonged to the owner of a Vietnamese restaurant who planned
to give them out to customers, but then Mr Nguyen decided to
move to San Francisco, orphaning the poor hats. P.S. *He* called
them coolie hats. P.P.S. And perhaps some may have innocently
misinterpreted a 'coolie' hat as a hat that cools one off.)

(*Note to Vivian from Olivia*: I would suggest using 'conical-
shaped straw hat,' to be prudent.)

(*Note to Olivia from Vivian*: I shall henceforth do so, although
I must admit being prudent is not among the many qualities that
have been ascribed to me.)

An hour into the auction, the lots of tools, building materials,
office equipment, and other less than thrilling items had been
disposed of, reducing the already reduced audience by another
half. Norris, sweating a bit, his polo shirt darkened in spots,
announced that the next lot up for bid would be the three crates
of Fiestaware.

Elizabeth came out from behind her table to stand where her
husband could see her, a cell phone to one ear, indicating a call-in
proxy bidder for the vintage dishes.

Now, I had heard that restauranteur Otto Berger – a jovial,
portly man in his sixties, if a little too fond of his own cooking
(but then, as a rule, one must never trust a skinny chef) – wanted
the dishes for his retro-1950s diner. Knowing how many restaurant
plates I'd cracked or chipped in my day, not to mention nights
– and horrified that the beautiful vintage Fiestaware faced a
similar fate – I secretly hoped Otto wouldn't get them.

Still, I needn't have worried. While Otto put up a good fight from the front row, the proxy caller prevailed, and I had a pretty good idea who it was. Or at least who the proxy represented.

The Homer Laughlin China Company
d.b.a. The Fiesta Tableware Company
672 Fiesta Dr.
Newell, WV 26050

Dear Sir or Madam,

Please find enclosed information regarding an upcoming auction that might be of interest: specifically, the sale of three crates of Cobalt Blue Fiestaware manufactured in 1936. It occurred to me that your company might want to preserve these dishes for posterity, just as Patek Philippe often go after their rare early watches.

The odds-on favorite to win the bid is Otto Berger, whose intention is using them in his restaurant. I'm sure I needn't point out that early Fiestaware contains high levels of lead paint, which could leave your company open to lawsuits, as frivolous and unfounded as they might be. Deep pockets, you understand!

Sincerely,

Vivian Borne

P.S. Please bring back Chartreuse! Many of my old dishes need replacing, and the color goes so well with my dining room drapes.

I did receive a lovely response from a representative of HL (which I am unable to share since I didn't acquire permission) saying that they were indeed interested in the scarce dishes, and would be looking into the auction. Also, since the discontinuation of Chartreuse in 1999, there had not been many requests for its return, and perhaps I might want to consider new drapes.

(I thought that last part was a little presumptuous, but the rep did enclose their latest color chart, noting which shades might substitute for chartreuse. Which was nice, except I'd fibbed about having the dishes at all, wanting to end my letter on a light note.

Anyway, chartreuse is a dreadful thing, a mixture of yellow and green – whatever could they have been thinking!)

Onward. Next came twelve barrels of Larsen Company buttons (mine would have made it a baker's dozen), which got off to a rousing start, but then a multi-sided battle quickly devolved into an expensive skirmish between a call-in bidder and Johan Larsen. A blue-eyed, blond-haired forty, Larsen – a descendant of the long-gone founder of the Larsen Button Company – owned the Serenity Button Museum.

I couldn't discern whether the reason other bidders held back was out of deference to Johan's lineage or knowledge of a desire to showcase the barrels at the museum. Perhaps they were perplexed about what to do with all those buttons – one can only make so many collages. At any rate, soon the proxy bidder also dropped out.

Now came the moment I'd been waiting for: the sale of the crates of arks, and final bid of the auction.

Who would prevail, Dolly or Sally? And how valuable would that make the two arks Brandy and I had wheedled out of Norris a week before?

But the crates also generated intense interest from others – locals who knew of the legendary Serenity toy company as well as antique dealers from all around the country, some of whom I recognized, others I did not. And Elizabeth had two cell phones going.

The suspense was accelerating, the bids too, as the entrants charged toward the finish line with lightning speed, making it hard for mere spectators to keep up. Even auctioneer Norris once lost track of the count before climbing back into the saddle again. Then, one by one, bidders fell away, until it was a two-filly race between the toy rivals. At last Sally acquiesced. By the way, wasn't that a lovely extended horse-race metaphor?

As the diminutive Dolly rose triumphantly to her feet, Sally sprung out of her chair, visibly shuddered in rage and disappointment, and galloped out. No winner's circle for her! (Too much?)

While what remained of the crowd slowly began to disperse, winning bidders congregated around Elizabeth's table to settle up and make transport arrangements. I stayed put and, in doing so, witnessed two rather interesting exchanges.

Norris, having left the podium, obviously weary and drenched in sweat, was approached first by restauranteur Otto Berger – most likely unhappy about his failed bid on those dishes – who delivered a few harsh words with the auctioneer. I couldn't make all of them out, but the ones I caught are not printable, at least not in a respectable book like this.

Not long after Berger departed, Johan Larsen buttonholed the auctioneer (see what I did there?). And, while the interaction appeared superficially friendly, a flush in Larsen's cheeks, which hadn't been there before their conversation began, was a 'tell.' I didn't figure he was any happier with Norris than Berger had been.

And I guess we all know that Norris was capable of making under-the-table, beforehand arrangements with unscrupulous parties. Perhaps a promise or two hadn't been delivered on.

When the button-museum owner stepped away, I moseyed over to Norris, hoping to gather some intel.

I was about to say how well the event had gone when the auctioneer snapped at me: 'I thought you could keep your mouth shut!'

And he stomped away.

Puzzled by his rude comment – because, after all, Vivian Borne is not about to betray a secret, especially when it doesn't benefit her – I watched as Norris joined his wife at the card table.

What could he have meant? That I had blabbed about our little arrangement? Or let slip a certain indiscretion of his? I had spilled nary a bean about either one!

But it only made me more curious to know what words had passed between the auctioneer and Doug Holden . . . and Ryan Dayton . . . and Otto Berger . . . and Johan Larsen.

But, more importantly, what in the world was I going to do with five hundred conical-shaped straw hats?

Vivian's Trash 'n' Treasures Tip

Other terms that refer to dead stock include 'dead stock vintage,' 'new old vintage,' and NOS (never off the shelves). Some sellers, avoiding the word 'dead,' tried listing 'livestock' on their internet sites, but too many prospective buyers made inquiries about cows and sheep.

THREE
Wink, Wink, Murder

B randy at the helm again. Everyone all right? Ten fingers, ten toes?

Just to set the record straight about Dolly Gambol's local cable show: Mother is glued to the screen, every episode. She even takes notes, and makes little sounds that cause Sushi's head to tilt to one side, as if the dog has never heard growling quite like that.

Anywho (as Mother would say), after La Diva Borne had departed for the auction, I cleared the dining-room table before going (as promised) into KP mode.

A little about our 1920s-style house: each room represents a different era reflecting that decor and various collecting interests of ours. Upstairs, Mother's bedroom is art nouveau; my bedroom, art deco; and the guest room is '70s psychedelic, ensuring visitors inclined to longer stays do not linger too long. Downstairs, the living room is filled with Victorian furniture and fixtures while the dining room is neoclassical (not my favorite). The library is home to an eclectic collection of dusty old books, rather antiquated but not valuable musical instruments including a creaky stand-up piano and a cornet on which Mother can blast out 'Boogie Woogie Bugle Boy of Company B' if you ask her to (but please don't), plus anything that couldn't find a proper place elsewhere.

The library is also Mother's 'incident room,' wherein she keeps an ancient schoolhouse blackboard on wheels tucked behind the piano (which neither one of us knows how to play), and on which she complies her 'suspect lists.' (The board, not piano.)

Our kitchen is straight out of a 1950s magazine ad with vintage white stove and refrigerator, and even an early dishwasher that works better than most modern ones (I have to question how much energy is being saved these days by a new dishwasher that runs for three or four hours).

Sometimes, however, we didn't have such good luck with vintage *minor* appliances, like the time the toaster oven caught fire or the electric mixer that gave Mother such a shock she couldn't remember her name for an hour, though her hair took on a rather attractive curl. Overall, we prefer the simplicity of these old workhorse appliances that mostly did just one task, but well. Besides, psychotropically medicated women forced to face an appliance offering a myriad of options early in the morning is a recipe for disaster.

Finished with the clean-up, I remembered I'd forgotten to give Sushi her insulin, so I gave her a shot. She never runs from the needle, knowing there's a treat afterward, even though it's the teeniest, tiniest little dog biscuit ever baked.

I trudged upstairs to get dressed, not so much tired from my kitchen clean-up as worried about what trouble Mother might get herself into.

At my 1930s Birdseye maple vanity table with its large round mirror – you could just picture Jean Harlow seated there, brushing her platinum hair – I perched on a tufted stool, applied a little makeup, and, after failing to tame my frizzy hair due to the humidity, pulled it into a pony-tail. Satisfied that this was as good as I was going to look today – all downhill from here – I went to my closet to select an outfit.

I'd been obsessed this summer with a west coast clothing company called Rails, loving its laid-back style. Selecting a boxy, short-sleeved white cotton blouse with tiny palm trees and a pair of tan linen Bermuda shorts, I slipped into them, then ruined the cool California vibe by inserting my feet into some nerdy Crocs.

Be-Be loved those colorful tie-dyed clogs, especially the little charms I'd begun adding to the holes, and I'd inserted a new one for today that I hoped she'd notice.

Finally, a small brown cross-body Coach bag – to free up my hands – completed my ensemble.

Sushi, standing on my bed, had been waiting patiently, knowing we were heading somewhere. But it wasn't until I'd slipped on the clogs that she realized *exactly* where, and excitedly began to twirl, as if chasing her own tail but not really.

Back downstairs, I picked up the box containing the Peter-Mar Noah's Ark and, Sushi trotting behind, went out the front door and headed to the SUV, surprised and delighted by the cool morning air.

Tina, with husband Kevin and toddler Be-Be, lived in a white ranch-style house north of town along River Road, on a bluff with a spectacular view of the Mississippi and beyond.

Before Be-Be was born, nothing was more relaxing to me than whiling away the hours on their back patio with a glass of champagne (which Tina always kept on hand), chatting with my BF. Spring through fall – and sometimes winter, with the gas-fire pit going – we would lazily watch the traffic on the water . . . speedboats mostly, but also cargo-laden barges, heading toward the lock and dam to continue their travel downstream to St Louis and points beyond. Every so often, the *Delta Queen*, an old-fashioned paddle-wheeler, would steam by, its calliope playing old-time tunes ('Put On Your Old Gray Bonnet'), while its passengers gathered at the rail, gawking at our shoreline.

Backstory on Tina and me for newbies (others feel free to skip over).

Christina was a year younger than me, and we became fast friends in high school when yours truly came around a hall corner after classes, finding some senior girls picking on her. I'd let them know how I felt about bullying in the kind of vernacular that would make the most profane rapper blush (and might make you, gentle reader, set this book aside). Later, Tina and I both attended Serenity Community College, and – after our two-year stint – Tina went head-over-heels for Kevin and married the lucky lug, while I met and married a broker in Chicago who was ten years my senior, though neither of us were very lucky.

While I truly had loved Roger, too big a factor in our getting somewhat impulsively hitched was (I am embarrassed to admit) the chance to escape from Mother. Sadly, I was not cut out to be the wife of a high-powered businessman, though I gave it the college try, or anyway the community college try. And our union did produce a wonderful son, Jake (now fourteen), who lives with his father, and often comes to stay with Mother and me on his school breaks. These days the biggest bone of contention between my ex and me is the way Mother has gotten our son caught up in some of her investigations. This reflects an eager willingness to do so on Jake's part, but that's another story. A bunch of them, really.

I pulled my car into Tina's driveway and up to the open double garage, my friend's white mini-van parked on one side, the other empty – Kevin at work no doubt, tending to his thriving insurance business.

Tina met us at the door, looking trim but shapely in a floral sundress and Havaiana thongs, her lovely features framed by natural blonde hair that fell to her shoulders like liquid gold, her wide smile revealing perfect teeth. And yet I don't hate her. You see? I do have some good qualities . . .

Sushi greeted our hostess with a perfunctory little bark before trotting inside to find Be-Be.

Tina's blue eyes widened as they landed on the Peter-Mar box in my arms. 'Oh my! . . . Is that what I *think* it is?'

A connoisseur of vintage collectibles herself, Tina had often gone antiquing with me, though she was much more selective in decorating her home, sprinkling in old among the mostly new.

'Do you think she'll like it?' I asked, suddenly uncertain about the old-fashioned toy in an era when everything must 'do something.'

'Be-Be will *adore* it,' Tina assured me. 'Come . . . she's playing in her bedroom.'

I stepped into the large foyer, then trailed behind my friend, passing by a beautifully appointed living room on the left and a formal dining room on the right, and finally down a hallway to the toddler's bedroom.

Toys were everywhere, scattered across the alphabet rug and flung on the Peanuts bedspread – Peppa Pig, Bluey, Paw Patrols, and Disney princesses galore – along with wall shelves crammed with stuffed animals. Despite Tina's assurance, my ark seemed suddenly inadequate.

Be-Be, in a pink Joules dress I had given her (and you thought I only bought clothes for myself!), was down on the floor, flinging her little arms around Sushi. She was giving the dog a bit-too-hard of a hug, which Sushi put up with as the price of admission.

Baby Brandy caught sight of me, squealed with delight, and my heart filled with so much love it nearly burst.

Releasing poor Sushi, my namesake ran over to me, arms extended. I set down the box, and picked the toddler up, holding her, smelling the scent of her curly blonde hair, feeling the softness of her skin. Then I gazed into the cherubic face with its brown eyes, button nose, and mischievous smile.

My face.

You see, Be-Be was mine, and Kevin's.

Get your mind out of the gutter! Before you go raking me over the coals, let me explain. Four years ago, after Tina had cancer treatments that left her infertile, I offered to help her have the baby she and Kevin so desperately wanted. And with the blessing and support of both, I had done so, via artificial insemination.

Gently, I lowered Be-Be to the floor.

'Winnie Pooh!' she cried, pointing to the new charm on my Crocs.

'That's right,' I said, then added, 'Brandy brought something.'

'Brandy *bought* something?' she said. I loved the way Be-Be had been repeating what was spoken to her, as if trying the words out, often revising those words with slight malapropisms that were more appropriate than the original.

'It's a boat with animals,' I said.

'Boat with any mules?'

I laughed. 'Mules and more.'

Tina interjected, 'Let's take it outside. I'll get us some lemonade.'

I let Be-Be slip from my arms and picked up the box.

On the patio, with a cool breeze coming off the river, I set the present down, then removed the toy from its carton – the ark looked as new and fresh as it would have on unpacking decades before.

But when I held it out for Be-Be to see, she reached for the ark and I let go of it too soon, and the toy dropped to the cement.

I held my breath for the toddler's reaction, expecting hysterical crying. But instead, Be-Be pointed to a little chip in the blue paint on the ark's bow and said, 'Needs a Band-Aid.'

Tina, watching wide-eyed, replied as carefully as if re-inserting a pin in a grenade, 'Yes, honey. We'll get one for it later.'

Crisis averted.

I added, 'That will make the ark special, sweetie. No one else will have one exactly like it.'

'Yay!'

Down on the ground, Be-Be and I explored the ark, which was essentially a houseboat on wheels. Stored inside the house part, under a removable roof, were the animals, two by two, plus Noah and his wife of course. Also included was a little plank to assist in the boarding process.

Be-Be really appeared taken with her new toy – at least for the moment – immediately becoming engrossed in examining each animal, completely forgetting the real one by her side. Sushi frowned at the toy, as if thinking, 'What does that hunk of wood have that I don't?'

Sushi got over that quickly, however, because Tina appeared with a tray holding two flute glasses, a tippy cup, a pitcher of lemonade, and a small plate of petit fours. Food trumped toddler any day.

Pouring the sweet cool drink into the glasses, Tina said, 'We can pretend it's champagne.'

She and I clinked glasses, then took sips.

Yum! Almost as good as bubbly. Well, *almost* . . .

'Where did you get the ark?' Tina asked. 'I know those things are rare. Hope you didn't spend a small fortune on it.'

'Not really,' I said. 'Mother got two of them in advance of this morning's warehouse auction.'

'Well, your mother is a crafty, canny gal,' Tina said. 'Because you can bet Dolly Gambol will be there, and snag the rest of them.' She paused, then frowned. 'Interesting thing . . .'

I waited.

'Kevin ran into that unpleasant woman a few days ago, and, figuring the same thing – that she'd buy all of those arks? – asked her if she'd like to have them insured, considering their value.'

'And?'

'Dolly told him a policy wouldn't be necessary, because she wouldn't have them very long.'

The toy collector must have had a buyer in mind, or maybe was planning to dump the arks on the market to drum some cash up quick. Unless Dolly was strapped for some reason, the latter seemed unlikely.

Sushi scratched my leg and I gave her the last bite of my little cake. Even a diabetic dog has to live a little.

Our conversation veered to topics ranging from movies to books to clothes to home repair to the two men in our lives (you'll meet mine later). As our conversation began to wind down, and knowing Kevin would be arriving home for lunch, I could tell something was bothering her.

I asked quietly, 'What is it, Tina?'

Be-Be was helping the elephants up the plank into the ark.

My friend smiled wanly. 'And here I thought I was hiding it pretty well.'

'Not from me,' I said. 'I know you better than myself.'

One corner of her smile climbed a little. 'I feel the same way about you.'

I waited to learn what she'd wanted to keep from me. But I was afraid I already knew – there'd been too many doctor's appointments for Tina of late. Just preventative testing, she'd said.

'It's back,' she said, then corrected herself. 'No, it never left . . . it was just under control.'

It.

Tina had one hand on the table, and I added mine to hers, saying with conviction, 'And you'll get it under control *again.*'

Her eyes met mine. 'Yes. Yes I will.'

'I'm here for you, day or night. You know that.'

I withdrew my hand as Kevin entered the patio.

'And how are the three most beautiful girls on the planet doing?' he asked, that dazzling smile of his trying a little too hard.

He knew.

Kevin was a handsome hunk with sandy-blond hair and eyelashes I'd kill for. He wore a lightweight grey suit, not too flashy – that would've been bad for his insurance business. How could clients feel they were getting a great deal from a guy wearing Armani?

'We're doing great,' Tina responded, as Be-Be made for her father's arms.

'Yes,' I chimed in. 'We're having a lovely time.'

Tina enthused a bit about the ark, and Kevin pretended to be interested.

When I got to my feet and said, 'Duty calls,' there were protestations. Couldn't I stay for lunch?

I smiled and shook my head. 'Mother's off at that auction and the shop won't open itself.'

'At least let me walk you to your car,' Kevin offered. 'Seems I rarely see you anymore.'

'I'll stay with Be-Be,' Tina said. The toddler had gone back to her ark, making the toy animals dance.

I gave Be-Be a kiss on the top of her head, then gathered Sushi.

Kevin and I walked silently to my SUV, where we stopped and turned to each other. Sushi was panting in my arms, the coolness of the morning having evaporated.

'She told you?' he asked softly.

'Yeah. I had to dig a little, but . . . yeah.'

'Tina didn't want you to worry.'

And I *was* worried, if a little hurt that my BF hadn't confided in me sooner. Yet, in her place, wouldn't I have done the same? Tina and I had always been two loners whose friendship was based on giving each other plenty of space.

I said, 'I'm not going to tell you – or her – that everything's going to be OK, because no one knows. I hate empty words like that.'

'Understood.' There was more than concern in his eyes – fear.

'But what I *do* know,' I said, 'is that you and I are going to do *whatever it takes* to help Tina through this.' No matter the outcome. 'And I'm well aware it's going to be the hardest on you.' Not that watching helplessly from the sidelines wasn't hard enough.

Kevin nodded.

I touched his arm. 'I promise not to be such a stranger.'

'Thank you, Brandy. I really *do* get it.'

'Get it?'

'That being around Be-Be is as difficult for you as it is . . .'

'Wonderful?'

He nodded. 'I know you go out of your way to find the balance between being supportive and being too big a part of little Brandy's life.'

I swallowed and nodded. Speechless for once.

I got into the car, and waved goodbye. I didn't cry till I pulled into our driveway.

Our antiques store is (as I write this) located at the end of Main Street in an old house at the base of West Hill, the area of town where all the lumber barons, pearl-button manufacturers, and bank founders had long ago built their mansions. The higher you climb, the grander the structures got, each trying to outdo the other, captains of industry sailing their fancy land-bound ships.

Mother and I had been able to buy the somewhat-dilapidated two-story clapboard on the cheap, because during the 1950s an unsolved Lizzie Borden-type axe murder took place in the parlor like a particularly nasty game of *Clue*. Over the years, an array of owners quickly fled, claiming the place was haunted; but at that price, the idea of ghosts didn't bother either of us. In fact, it just added some color. Still, as a precaution, Mother had asked Father O'Brien of St Mary's to bless the house, even though we were members of the Protestant New Hope Church.

And there *had* been a few strange occurrences when we first opened – an antique rocker rocking with no one in it, for example, and once I felt a rush of cold air and thought something brushed by me. But after Mother and I solved that long-ago murder (*Antiques Chop*), there hasn't been anything out of the ordinary around Trash 'n' Treasures.

Except Mother.

Guiding our SUV into the downtown, turning onto Main Street with the picturesque river front a block away, I could see cars still parked around the warehouse. A few spaces between vehicles indicated some bidders had left, and that the auction must be winding down.

In an alley behind our shop-cum-house, I parked in a spot that had once been a short driveway, gathered Sushi, and went in through the back door. I stepped into a mud room lined with old crocks, then entered the kitchen, setting Sushi down on the red-and-white-checkered linoleum floor.

Just as our rooms at home had a theme, Mother and I had

decided to stock each room of the shop to reflect its original purpose – all of our kitchen antiques in the kitchen, bedroom sets in the bedroom, linens in the linen closet, bath fixtures and paraphernalia in the bathroom, steamer trunks and old doors in the attic. Downstairs, formal furniture was in the parlor, dining sets in the dining room, books in the library, and 'mantiques,' like beer signs and tools, in the basement. Even the knickknacks were placed where one might expect to find them.

During business hours, the wafting aroma of freshly baked chocolate-chip cookies would often lure patrons to the kitchen, where they were welcome to sit at the yellow-and-white boomerang-print laminated table and partake of the free goodies, along with a hot cup of joe – no purchase required.

Customers often claim that shopping at Trash 'n' Treasures gives them the vague sense of visiting an elderly relative – a grandmother, perhaps, or kindly old aunt (pronounced like the bug, thank you) (a linguistic pet peeve I share with Mother). Only here you didn't have to wait to inherit something that might catch your eye; for the listed price (or maybe a haggled-over lower one), you could walk out with a treasure right now.

The first thing I did – still in the kitchen – was to get the cookies baking (peanut-butter today) and coffee (hazelnut) percolating. Then I walked down the center hallway to the foyer where we had installed a checkout counter and, from a large drawer, selected two flags from a stack of three – one with a big 'B' on it, the other an 'S,' representing myself and Sushi respectively, leaving 'V' for Vivian behind. Customers could see the flags flapping at a distance from our front porch and know that 1) the shop was open, and 2) who was there. No flags flying meant we were closed.

The idea had come to Mother a few months before when we traveled to London to meet our new editor (*Antiques Carry On*) and, en route in one of those wonderful black taxis, had glided by Buckingham Palace. She recalled that when the Queen was in residence, a special flag always flew. Well, if the Queen had a special flag, so could Mother. Fair being fair, Sush and I got our own flags, too.

Flags flying, I got behind the front counter and fired up the laptop, then returned to the kitchen to check on the cookies and coffee. Sushi hadn't moved from in front of the stove. No need for a timer – that canine's nose knew exactly when the cookies were done, her bark better than any bell.

I removed the cookies, and while they cooled, set up the coffee station using our Jadeite Fire King creamer, sugar bowls, and mugs (no messy condiment packets, or Styrofoam cups, for us).

Then, when transferring the cooled cookies to a Jadeite platter, I 'accidentally' dropped half of one on the floor for Sushi.

(*Mother to Brandy*: Dear, you're putting everyone to sleep with this needless blather! Do try to follow my example and stay on point.)

(*Brandy to Mother*: Are you kidding? Anyway, our editor said we're supposed to add a few more pages to the next book. And this is the next book.)

(*Mother to Brandy*: Well, there must be a better way to do it. Such as . . . **Get on with the story!**)

I returned to the checkout counter where a small stack of children's books had been left to be added to our inventory list. Generally, juvenile books made poor sellers for us, so we had to be selective. But one caught my eye: *Children's Party and Parlor Games*, circa 1965. Thinking it might be useful in entertaining Be-Be, I flipped through the book's wonderful illustrations showing how to play each game, along with the origin of each. Many I recognized as something I'd played, in some variation or other, as a child.

Did you know that Ring a Ring o' Rosies, which I knew as Ring Around the Rosie – where we held hands, danced around a (usually pretend) rose bush, and then fell down – was a song about the black plague? One sign of the disease was a ring of rosy color on the skin, and a pocket full of posies was supposed to disguise the smell.

(*Mother to Brandy*: Brandy! First you put our readers to sleep, and now you're scaring them to death! On with it!)

Since the auction had concluded by now, I figured it would be OK to bring the barrel of buttons out from behind the counter where it had been hidden beneath a sheet. The corrugated cardboard barrel had a metal bottom and lid, and I removed the top with the help of a flat screwdriver. This action released a surprising amount of button dust stirred up from all the jostling. While the smell wasn't unpleasant, I sneezed just the same – Sushi did, too, nearby, keenly interested in what I was doing.

Sun rays from the entryway window, falling across the pristine small pearl buttons, made for a diamond-like sparkle and shine. I positioned the barrel at one end of the counter, inserted the tip of a silver scoop into the buttons (as Mother had dictated), and placed some little brown bags nearby.

Mother decided that 'a scoop' would go for ten dollars. And, because these gleaming buttons had been harvested from the shells of mussels – now an endangered species and protected – she had directed me to add a proviso to the sign (I had yet to make) assuring one and all that a TBD percentage of each sale would be donated to The Protection of Mussel Shells Foundation (which I doubted existed). This supposedly would ease the conscience of any ecologically inclined person considering a purchase of buttons, assuring them these had been harvested before any restrictions had gone into effect.

I know.

But, for now, I just hand-printed **$10 A SCOOP** on a piece of paper, and stuck it on the front of the barrel. A few days ago, I'd brought out a box of vintage Halloween collectibles from storage; with the holiday only two months away, I busied myself arranging the items inside a glass curio cabinet near the front door where we showcased the good seasonal stuff.

Included in the display was an antique paper-mache jack-o-lantern made in Germany; a vintage die-cut cardstock skeleton with movable limbs; several mid-century Ben Cooper children's masks (werewolf, witch, vampire); and a half-dozen or so Halloween greeting cards.

The little bell above the door jingled, and two women entered, in mid-conversation.

'I'm surprised Conrad could finish the auction, as drunk as he was,' Mrs Fusselman was saying. A retired teacher, she'd flunked me in Algebra. I'm not quite over it.

'And did you see the daggers fly between Dolly and Sally?' offered Mrs Crumbly, an aging socialite and a town gossip almost rivaling Mother.

Sushi, who'd been sleeping in her leopard-print bed behind the counter, trotted out to stare at the women; she didn't like them either. She trotted back.

I paused in my work to paste on a smile about as friendly as the jack-o-lantern's. 'Ladies, how was the auction?'

They giggled, as if sharing a secret.

'All right,' I said. 'I'll bite.'

Then Mrs Crumbly said, 'You'll *never* guess what your *mother* bought!'

'Oh,' I replied casually, 'then she won the bid.'

Mrs Fusselman frowned. 'You *know*?'

'Of course,' I lied. 'She texted me.'

Mrs Crumbly, deflated, asked, 'Well, what in the *world* are you girls going to do with five hundred coolie hats?'

You know the sound a submarine makes when it dives? That's what went off inside my head: *Ah-OOG-Ah! Ah-OOG-Ah!*

But somehow I kept the smile going, replacing her question with my own: 'Is there something I can help you with?'

Crumbly said, disingenuously, 'No . . . we're just going to look – *oh!* You already have one of those barrels of buttons! I thought *Johan Larsen* got them all.'

Looking rather pop-eyed, she was clearly waiting for me to provide an explanation. Right then – absolutely on cue – Mother blew in.

All eyes went to her.

'What did I miss?' Mother asked, looking a little disoriented, as on those rare but memorable occasions at the Playhouse when she came on stage and promptly forgot what play she was in.

I said, sweetly, 'Mrs Crumbly was just inquiring about how we happened to have a barrel of the buttons . . . already.'

And I left her to explain, heading back to the kitchen, where I poured myself a cup of coffee and sat at the table, smirking. Let her get out of her own jam.

After a short while, Mother joined me.

'Well, they're gone,' she said. Her shrug was as casual as a blink. 'And our town gossip seemed to have accepted my explanation about having had those buttons for quite some time. From an entirely different source.'

'The truth will out, you know,' I groused.

'What truth would that be, dear?'

'How you blackmailed Conrad Norris.'

'Who, me? *You* were right there *with* me. Wanting that ark for

Be-Be.' With a toss of her head, she added, 'You'll just have to stick to my story.'

'*Your* story?' I countered. 'What "story" is that?'

'I'm sure one will come to me. And I'll share it with you. Anyway, let's not let such an insignificant matter devolve into a spat. Not when we have more important things to talk about.'

I smirked. 'Like what to do with five hundred coolie hats, for instance?'

She leaned back in her chair, folded her arms. 'So those blabbermouth hens told you. Well, we mustn't refer to those Asian chapeaus in that fashion, dear – it's politically incorrect. A better designation is conical-shaped straw hat.'

'A better *destination* would have been a dumpster! Whatever they're called, what are we going to do with the stupid things?'

'We'll start by removing the hats from the warehouse by five o'clock. As I assured Conrad I would.'

It was now a little after three.

'"We" didn't assure anybody anything,' I said.

Her grandiose shrug was impressive to behold. 'I made an executive decision.'

I sighed; I knew how Atlas felt with that globe on his shoulders. 'OK. Then let's go ahead and close up. Any after-auction traffic should have happened already.' I paused. 'By the way, any thoughts about where to store five hundred cool hats?'

'Dear . . .'

'I said "cool" not "coolie."'

Mother's eyebrows rose and then she did. 'Let's worry first about getting the hats in the SUV. And since I have my Vespa, the front seat will be free for extra hauling space.'

I could just see me behind the wheel, Sushi on my lap, surrounded by conical-shaped straw hats blocking my view.

While Mother brought in the flags, I unplugged the coffee pot, powered down the laptop, and stored the half-emptied Halloween box behind the counter. A short, unprofitable day, unless you consider five hundred straw hats profitable. Then I gathered Sushi, shut off the light, activated the security system, and out the back door we trooped.

The alley behind the old warehouse was littered with debris – pieces of broken wood, various packing materials, and a trail of buttons, as if one of the barrels had spilled. Other bidders had already hauled off their winnings, the only remaining vehicle a silver Lexus parked next to the loading dock.

'That's Conrad's car,' Mother said.

I pulled up next to it and we got out. With Mother holding Sushi, we entered the warehouse through the back door.

The activity of the past few hours – the auction, the removal of so much old merchandise – had filled the air with particles of dust that hung like smog, or the special-effects of a fog machine in a movie.

The vast first floor was once again empty . . . except for a mound of stacked hats . . .

Mother said, 'I must find Conrad before we start loading.'

I frowned at her. 'What for? You've settled up, haven't you?'

'It's not that, dear. It's something he said to me.'

'What did he say?'

Her hands went to her hips. 'He implied that I had been indiscreet about an indiscretion of his!'

'Had you been?'

'No! How can you say such a thing?'

I let that pass. 'So what? Indiscreet about those early sales, you mean?'

'Heavens no. His romantic indiscretion.'

Oh. So he'd had an affair. 'That kind of thing is bound to come out some time,' I said with a shrug. 'I mean, at least *one* other person knows! What difference does it make?'

'It makes all the difference, dear! If word gets out I can't be trusted with a secret, who could I ever blackmail again?'

Suddenly the 'blackmail' word came readily to her lips. Still, the combination of Mother's hypocrisy and the dusty air was giving me a migraine.

'All right, all right,' I said, hands up in surrender. 'We'll go find Conrad.'

Since the auctioneer wasn't on the first floor, we walked over to the waiting elevator.

As we drew nearer, Sushi, still in Mother's arms, began to bark. The dog was looking upward, as if trying to tell us the auctioneer was on an upper floor and not in the basement.

After I slid the accordion-type metal gate to one side, we

stepped on and I closed us in. Pushing the UP button, the elevator began its grinding, grunting oh-so-slow ascent. But while we made a thorough search of it, Norris was nowhere to be found on the second floor, nor the third or fourth.

Back on the first floor, we exited the elevator.

Mother was frustrated. 'He *must* be in the basement.'

Frowning, she passed Sushi to me. 'I want to try something, dear. Just a hunch.'

I hadn't yet closed the gate. Mother, standing just outside of the elevator, reached one hand in and pressed the second-floor button, sending the elevator up by itself.

'What on earth are you doing . . .?' I began, then, 'Mother be *careful*!'

She was peering over the edge of the floor, looking down into the shaft.

Suddenly, she drew back. 'Well, he didn't fall down there.'

'Can we *please* just get those stupid hats and go?' I was starting to feel uneasy.

Mother called the elevator back. 'You can start loading,' she said, 'while I go down myself.'

Good. If Norris *had* met with a bad end down there, I had no yen to have a look at him. I had enough images of dead bodies floating around in my head, thanks to Mother's amateur sleuthing.

She stepped onto the elevator, closed the gate, pushed the basement button, gave me a little wave, and descended from view.

And then coming *into* view was the roof of the elevator car, on top of which Conrad Norris lay, sprawled and twisted and obviously very dead.

A Trash 'n' Treasures Tip

The best place to find dead stock is online at sites such as eBay, Etsy, and Market Publique. To assist in your search, input the item of what you're looking for, e.g. 'dead stock sunglasses.' If you are interested in dead stock conical-shaped straw hats, please write to us in care of our publisher.

FOUR
Tug of War

First to arrive at the warehouse were two male blue-uniformed paramedics, who left their bright orange EMS vehicle double-parked in the street, lights flashing.

While I stood numbly by, holding Sushi, Mother welcomed the pair at the front entrance as if the two were latecomers to a party.

'No rush,' she told them, cheerily businesslike. 'The poor man is already dead.'

The thinner EMT, whose last name ATKINS was embroidered on a shirt pocket, said patronizingly, 'That's up to us to determine.'

Mother flipped a hand. 'Just trying to provide a little context and prevent you wasting energy.'

The heavier-set one, whose tag read THARP, asked, 'Where is he?'

'This way,' Mother said, leading the way with a quarter-bow and a flourish, as if she were the maître d' in a fancy restaurant showing them to their table. The two EMTs, who seemed never to have encountered Mother before (but had undoubtedly heard of her), exchanged frowns.

I tagged reluctantly along as she escorted the pair to the elevator shaft, where the metal gate had been pulled back.

The medics stood at the edge, and peered down.

Atkins muttered, 'Well, that's a new one . . . falling on top of an elevator.'

Tharp said, 'I don't suppose it has a manual control, so we can bring it up part way . . .'

'It does not,' Mother replied. 'But I've been thinking . . .'

'If you don't mind, Mrs Borne,' Atkins said, '*we'll* do the thinking.'

They'd heard of her, all right.

Mother shrugged. 'As you wish . . . I just thought you might want to take care to preserve the crime scene.'

Atkins took a step toward her. 'You think this is a crime scene? A *murder*?'

'Indubitably.' She liked that word.

'You've called the police?' Tharp asked.

'Of course.'

That she'd done so was soon confirmed by the arrival of Officer Munson. Tall, gangly, with a long oval face, he reminded me of the actor Fred Gwynne on the old *Munsters* TV show. The officer had been with the PD long enough to know Mother and me all too well. You could tell by the way his eyes glazed over at the sight of us.

'Dispatch said someone reported a body,' he told our little gathering. 'Would that happen to have been *you*, Mrs Borne?'

Mother replied, 'Obviously. These paramedics didn't just stumble in on their own. I gave my name – the dispatcher should have told you that.' She looked behind him. 'Oh! There's Hector Hornsby now!'

Trudging toward us came the county coroner, a stout, bald, bespectacled man in a raincoat carrying an old-fashioned black doctor's bag.

In a high-pitched, irritated (and irritating) voice, Hornsby said, 'Vivian, there *is* a proper protocol to follow whenever you find a body! And calling me at home is not it!'

'Just expediting matters,' Mother said. 'Skipping a pointless step or two might bring a murderer to justice all the sooner! Have you lost weight, dear? You look positively slim.'

He hadn't, and didn't.

'Bringing murderers to justice, Vivian,' the coroner said, his reddened face bringing a radish to mind, 'is not your job.'

'Well, *someone* has to do it,' she said blithely.

Sushi gave me a look as if to say, 'You better get her out of here.'

'Hector,' Atkins said, 'we've got to get down to that man. Any ideas?'

Everyone began talking at once, with the exception of myself, and then an ear-splitting, fingers-in-your-mouth whistle stopped everyone mid-sentence.

Tony Cassato strode toward us.

Approaching fifty, with graying temples, steel-gray eyes, a bulbous nose, barrel chest, and a commanding presence, Tony was the chief of police. And also my fiancé.

'Sitrep, Munson,' the chief said sternly. 'Now.'

Tony was attired in his usual office garb of light blue shirt, navy striped tie, gray slacks, and brown Florsheim shoes, his badge attached to his belt. His presence meant one thing was certain: the dispatcher had mentioned Mother's name, all right.

Officer Munson turned to his boss. 'I was just trying to ascertain that, Chief.'

Tony's granite eyes shifted to the paramedics.

'Sir,' replied Tharp, 'we have a body down the shaft on top of the elevator car, which is on the basement level.'

Atkins added, 'We need to get to him ASAP. We've yet to determine if he's alive.'

'I assure you he is not,' Mother interjected, not hiding her exasperation, 'judging by the way his neck is twisted. Which is why I called Hector directly – the paramedics were a mere formality.'

'Vivian,' Tony said, tightly but with remarkable patience, 'that is *not* your determination to make.'

'Must I remind you, Chief Cassato, that I am myself a representative of law enforcement?'

'You are an honorary Deputy Sheriff, which gives you absolutely no right to behave in such a highhanded manner.' He looked at me for an explanation of our presence.

'Mother bought some hats at the auction this morning and we came to get them,' I said, like a child trying to explain a broken cookie jar. 'I discovered Conrad Norris when she took the elevator down to the basement. As it descended, I saw him lying on the top.'

He came over, his expression softening. 'You all right, Brandy?'

'Yes.' No.

'This isn't about your mother sticking her nose in where it doesn't belong?'

'No.' Yes – or anyway, it soon would be.

Sushi, in my arms, stretched toward Tony, and he acknowledged her with a quick scratch on the head. What she really wanted was to sniff his clothes for any scent of Rocky, Tony's dog – the unrequited love of her life.

'It seems to me,' Mother was saying, a finger on her cheek, 'that the conundrum is how to remove Mr Norris without disturbing the crime scene. Because dollars to donuts the man was murdered.'

She always used that expression in the presence of the police, whether to get a rise out of them or not, I couldn't say.

Mother went on: 'Now, if I might suggest—'

The chief raised a warning finger accompanied by a stern look, and Mother made a 'zip' motion across her lips. The last thing she wanted was to get thrown out. A murder scene was Christmas morning to her.

Tony crossed to the elevator shaft, looked down, then got his cell from a slacks pocket and punched at the screen.

A moment later he said, 'I need someone S & R with rappelling experience . . . Ah-huh . . . only about eight feet down . . . How fast?' Briefly the chief explained 'the conundrum.'

Originally, Search and Rescue had been used for boat accidents on the river, or drownings in many of the water-filled gravel pits just outside the town; with the growing interest in rock-climbing at the area's many limestone bluffs had come a need to address occasional mishaps.

'Calling S & R was exactly what I was going to suggest,' Mother whispered to me, irked she hadn't been given the opportunity to voice that.

The chief ordered Officer Munson outside for traffic and crowd control, dismissed coroner Hornsby for now, and asked the two paramedics to stand by.

Then he eyed Mother and planted himself before us.

'What makes you think this man was murdered?' he asked her. 'He might have twisted his neck in an accidental fall, after all.'

She waved that away. 'Conrad had his share of enemies, many of them in attendance at the auction this morning. It's highly likely one of them tried to make this look like an accident . . .

as if the poor man hadn't noticed the elevator car wasn't there – emphasis on "as if!"' She took a deep breath. 'You see, I have it *all* worked out. What the killer did was—'

I interrupted, hoping to nip this in the bud. 'Tony, two auction attendees, who stopped by the shop, were talking about Norris – they'd said he'd been drinking at the auction.'

Mother glared at me.

'Is that right, Vivian?' he asked.

'I am not one to gossip,' she said.

Tony and I exchanged looks, and I said, 'Apparently he'd been sipping from a flask all morning.'

If I'd been standing closer to Mother, she would have given my shin a good swift kick.

'A *small* flask,' she said, then to me, 'Anyway, dear, you weren't even there! How many times have I advised you not to go around spouting hearsay!'

'Pot meet kettle,' I said, 'kettle meet pot.'

'The auction this morning,' Mother said, on the verge of raving, 'was *teeming* with potential suspects in what is *clearly* a murder!'

Tony made a calm-down motion with both hands. 'All right, ladies, that's quite enough. I'll take Vivian's concerns into consideration.'

Mother put her hands on her hips and leaned into him. '*Concern*s? Since when is murder a mere *concern*?'

Tony raised a palm. 'Rest assured, Vivian, I'll have our forensics crew take a good, hard look around.'

That hardly appeased Mother.

'A look *around*?' she asked. 'Are they going shopping or trying to find a killer?'

The vein on Tony's temple began to throb.

She was going full throttle now. 'As the former sheriff, I'll want to see the preliminary examination report!'

Mother had indeed been elected sheriff of Serenity County (*Antiques Wanted*) last year, although her reign turned out to be short-lived. But that brief tenure was why she wound up carrying that honorary badge.

When Tony hesitated, she quipped, 'I *do* have my ways of getting it.'

Mother had more moles in city hall than an old tugboat had barnacles.

Perhaps sensing she'd gone too far, as Tony had that look a bull gets right before it charges the fool poking swords in him, Mother said, disingenuously, 'But, of course, I'd much rather *not* resort to such tactics . . . being a believer, as I am, in going through proper protocol.'

Tony's smile was every bit as disingenuous. 'I'm glad to hear that, Vivian, because the proper protocol will be through *me*, when I determine when and if you should see a report figuring in an active investigation.'

Her eyes flared maniacally. 'Then you *do* consider this a murder investigation!'

'No, Vivian, I—'

Interrupting at her own peril, Mother said, 'I'll go on record saying I intend to conduct my own inquiry into the possible suspects.'

'Absolutely not.'

'Discreetly, of course.'

'No.'

'A few questions.'

He shook his head.

She said, 'One question of each suspect: where were you at such-and-such a time.'

He pointed toward the front entrance. 'Out. Before I arrest you for obstruction of justice.'

'But I wanted to see them bring Conrad up,' Mother protested, like a child denied an ice-cream cone. 'I want to see the S & R team in action! I'm a great afficionado of rock climbing!'

'Go!'

A last-ditch effort. 'Brandy and I need to load up our conical-shaped straw hats.'

'They'll keep. Leave.'

We left.

Hatless.

Happy not to be swamped in straw, I drove home with Sushi while a glum Mother followed on her Vespa. Once in the house, she made straight for the Victorian couch in the living room, and plopped down facing at – and staring out – the picture window, giving me the silent treatment. Once again I had sided with Tony over her.

That was fine with me, because I was too tired at the moment to handle the argument that was sure to come. But not too tired to prepare dinner in the kitchen.

Crab Meat On Rusk Sandwiches

¼ cup softened butter
8 oz. cream cheese
1 tbsp. minced onion
1 tbsp. lemon juice
1 tbsp. Worcestershire sauce
1 can crab meat (chunk, if possible)
6 American cheese slices
6 tomato slices
6 bacon slices, precooked
6 rusks

Mix together first 5 ingredients. Blend in crab meat. Place mixture on rusks, adding slices of cheese, tomato, bacon. Bake at 325 degrees for 20 minutes.

At the Duncan Phyfe table, a few minutes into the meal, Mother – summoned from the couch by the bell of the oven and smell of warm food – broke her silence. At least I'd had time to get something into my stomach before the fur began flying, even if it included rusks.

'How *could* you take that man's side?' she huffed.

I knew not to answer, even if 'that man' was my fiancé. I chose to consider that a rhetorical question, and anyway nothing could have quelled the diatribe to follow.

'How many times have people willfully ignored Vivian Borne's insights?' she lamented in the third person. 'How many times have the police carelessly disregarded her theories? And how many times has she been right? Why, if it weren't for Vivian Borne, how many murders would have gone unsolved in this community? Killers left on the loose, to roam free, to kill again at will!'

Say, these rusk sandwiches aren't bad!

'If only you had bothered to attend the auction, dear, you would have witnessed Conrad being confronted by one person after another who had some kind of bone to pick with him. The first one was . . .'

Tomorrow, at the shop, I'd finish putting the Halloween decorations in the curio cabinet. Plus, replace the hand-written button sign with a better one, including Mother's proviso.

'. . . shortly after that, Conrad was approached by . . .'

Was Tony upset with me? I hoped he saw that I'd done the best I could to shut Mother down.

'. . . and then, when the arks came up for bid, there was quite the kerfuffle between . . .'

Would Be-Be play with her ark today? Or had she already lost interest in the toy? Kids moved on so quickly from one enthusiasm to another.

'. . . and, after the auction, two more people corralled the poor beleaguered man . . .'

I really should order some more clog charms – Be-Be just loved those.

Mother had stopped talking.

'Well?' she asked. 'What do you have to say about all that?'

I blinked.

What I had to say was this: 'You're imagining a murder where there isn't one because you want to investigate another case, and want another book to write. And you don't give a hoot how many people might get hurt in the process, how many lives could be upended, and how many aspersions you cast upon innocent people.'

But I didn't. Because I'm a coward. Because I would do just about anything to avoid confrontation. That's why I betrayed my husband rather than tell him how unhappy I was, why I didn't fight for custody of my son, and why I continue to let Mother dominate my life.

I replied, 'There's some valid points you've made there. But why not wait for the autopsy report before getting tied in knots over it?'

Mother grunted. 'Spoken like somebody who's about to tie the knot with the chief of police.' She studied me, pondering the point I'd made. 'Very well. I admit that's not an unreasonable suggestion. The report *will* give me more to go on.'

And it well might conclude that Norris was legally drunk at the time of his death, leading to an inquest verdict of accidental death.

'How about some dessert?' I asked, changing the subject.

Rusk Pudding

1 8 oz. box rusks, rolling-pinned into crumbs
¾ cup sugar
¼ cup butter, melted
1 tsp. cinnamon
1 package of cream pie filling (I used lemon)
whipped cream for topping optional

Mix together first four ingredients to form a crust, and press into an 8 inch pie tin. Cook cream pie filling as directed on the package, then pour into pie tin. Cool.

After clearing the table, I left Mother in the kitchen for clean-up – her turn for KP – and trod upstairs. Sushi would remain with Mother until the last morsel of food had been stored away, and then, and only then, would she reluctantly eat her bowl of dry dog food.

I flopped on my bed, exhausted, and though it was early evening, decided to call it a day. I was even considering not bothering to get out of my clothes or brushing my teeth when my cell sounded on the nightstand.

Tony. 'You OK?'

'Yes.'

'And Vivian?'

'Contained for the moment.'

'Thank you.'

'Tony?'

'Yeah?'

'Nothing.' I was going ask, what if Mother was right, and Norris *was* murdered?

'Get some rest,' he advised.

'OK.'

'Love you.'

'Love you.'

My unbrushed teeth and I drifted off in my clothes and soon I was dreaming of being chased by a shadowy killer with my only path to escape crossing a river using stepping stones made of rusks that kept dissolving in the water.

Mercifully, my cell woke me.

Caller ID said: TINA.

Since she almost always texted, a call from her – especially in the middle of the night – could mean nothing good.

'Tina, what is it?' I asked, alarmed. Be-Be, the cancer, Kevin, the house on fire? Odd, how the mind arranges things in order of importance when nighttime phone calls come in.

'Sorry to disturb you, Brandy,' she said. Her voice sounded calm – or was she just trying to put me at ease?

My BF went on, 'Seems we've had a prowler. The police are here.'

I swung my legs over the side of the bed. 'Is everyone all right?'

'Yes, yes. We're all OK. Whoever it was didn't get inside.' Her laugh was small and forced. 'Be-Be has slept through the whole thing.'

'I'm coming over,' I said, expecting a protest.

But, instead, Tina replied, 'Might be a good idea. Officer Monroe responded to the call, and, well, she'd like to ask you some questions.'

Shawntea.

'I'll be there in five,' I said, and ended the call.

Questions? What kind of questions? Despite the warmth of the room, I felt a chill.

The clothes I'd slept in were damp from perspiration, but I didn't bother to change, and my poor teeth remained unbrushed. Sushi, sprawled outside the covers at the foot of the bed, stood, stretched, considered following me, decided against it, and lay back down.

I crept out of my room, not wanting to wake Mother in hers, in case she'd want to come along. Make that *of course* she would have wanted to come along! But I needn't have worried about the unwanted company, as she could be heard across the hallway, snoring to beat the band.

(*Note to Brandy from Mother*: I do not snore! And certainly not enough to beat any kind of band. I may, however, upon occasion, when I'm very tired, whistle through my nose.)

(*Note to Mother from Brandy*: Any particular tune?)

Downstairs, I grabbed my purse, then slipped quietly out.

The drive along River Road, so scenic and serene by day, took on sinister aspects in the middle of this dark night. To my left, shadows cast by tall pines that grew precariously on the slopes reached down with monstrous clawing fingers. To my right, the river was churning, restless and angry, a strong wind whipping at the car, requiring me to steer with both hands. Veins of lightning crackled through the gathering storm clouds, as if in warning of what awaited me at Tina's.

At the top of a crest, my headlights caught the shape of a dead deer in the road, and I swerved to the left, then over-compensated, returning to my lane, nearly colliding with a metal guard rail that had been installed after several vehicles had plunged into the river.

Rattled, I continued on, but at a slower speed.

Tina's house was ablaze with lights. In the driveway sat a single squad car, its lights flashing. I parked next to it.

Kevin, in a T-shirt and jeans, his sandy hair flattened on one side from sleep, met me at the front door.

'Thanks for coming,' he said.

I nodded and followed him into the living room.

Tina, wrapped in a white robe, was seated on the couch, while uniformed Shawntea stood in front of her, a small notepad and pen in her hands. Both looked my way as I entered.

'What happened?' I asked, my question directed to whoever cared to answer first. Kevin did.

'I wasn't able to sleep,' he said. 'So I went into the kitchen for something to eat. I hadn't turned on the light when I saw something move, out on the patio.' He paused. 'We have a lot of deer out here – sometimes they come right up to the patio doors – but this didn't look like a deer, or move like one, either.'

Tina said, 'We have a motion security light in back, but it kept turning on and off all night, what with the deer and raccoons. After that bright light kept waking us up, we disabled it weeks ago.'

Kevin picked up again. 'Anyway, before I could do anything, whoever-this-was ran off. My first thought was to check on Be-Be – her bedroom is right next to the patio.'

Tina, previously composed – too well, I thought – burst into tears, choking, 'And her window was open!'

I rushed to my friend's side and sat next to her, clasping her hand in mine. 'Don't worry, honey . . . Be-Be's all right. Nothing happened. It's OK.' Was I trying to console her or myself?

'But something *could* have,' Tina sobbed. 'It could have.'

The looming Shawntea turned to Kevin. 'Was the prowler male or female?'

'I couldn't tell.'

'Did you get an impression? A feeling?'

Kevin shook his head. 'No. Sorry.'

'What about clothing?'

Another shake of his head. 'It was just too dark.'

Shawntea sighed. 'Probably wore black.' The officer consulted her notepad. 'So the prowler was spotted at about two fifteen. You saw or heard no car either arrive or leave . . .'

This had been covered before I arrived.

'. . . the prowler never entered the house . . . and only one thing is missing from the premises, a toy ark that had been left out on the patio.'

Now I knew why Shawntea had wanted to talk to me – the officer must have noticed what she'd helped Mother and me load into our car last week.

Tina looked at me. 'I'm so sorry, Brandy! I forgot to bring the ark and the box inside. They were still out on the patio.' Her eyes were tearing up again.

'Tina, it's just a *toy*. I never meant it to be anything more.'

'I know,' she said. 'It's not that. Be-Be will be looking for it in the morning, and . . .'

I leaned closer. 'Please, Tina, don't be upset by this. I can get her another one.' And I could: Mother's. I looked pleadingly at Kevin for help.

He went to his wife, gently drew her off the couch and wrapped her in his arms. 'We'll take care of it, sweetheart.' Then, over his shoulder to Shawntea, he asked, 'Is that all, Officer? I'd like to get Tina back to bed.'

Shawntea closed her notebook. 'Yes, that's all for now. Thank you both. I'll see myself out.'

As Kevin walked Tina from the room, Shawntea signaled me to follow her.

Outside, we stood next to the squad car, its lights bathing us in alternating red and blue.

'Wanna tell me about that ark?' the officer asked flatly.

'We got it and another one from Conrad Norris that night you helped us – along with all that other stuff, for not much money because Mother had something she could hold over him.'

'Such as what?'

'Something personal.'

Shawntea raised an eyebrow.

'You'll have to ask her.'

'Oh, trust me – I will.'

Mother's capital with her had just gone bust.

The officer was asking, 'Do you think that ark was what the prowler was after?'

I deflected her question with another. 'Or was the ark taken because that's all the intruder had time to get?'

Her eyebrows drew together. 'If getting the ark was the point, can you think of anyone who would be motivated to steal it?'

Did I really want to plant suspicion on the two rival toy collectors? Or hadn't I made enough trouble already?

Prudently, I answered, 'Anyone who knew its value.'

'Which is?'

I shrugged. 'A couple of hundred dollars.'

Shawntea frowned. 'Hardly seems worth the risk.'

'You don't know collectors.'

The communicator attached to Shawntea's shoulder beeped – a call from the dispatcher about a domestic disturbance – which ended the interrogation.

Shawntea was getting into her car when I felt emboldened

enough to ask, 'Is there anything you could tell me about the preliminary report on Conrad Norris's death?'

At first I thought she was going to ignore me, or even scold me – she knew, like every cop in town, of Mother's propensity for inserting herself into murder investigations. And I was that crackpot pest's daughter, right?

But then, as she settled behind the wheel, her door still open, the officer said, 'The buzz is there was something in the report inconsistent with injuries being caused by a fall . . . And that's all you get, Brandy. You *and* your mom. Your good will with me is just about used up.'

The car door slammed, she backed out of the driveway, and sped away in a fashion that might have got a civilian pulled over.

A clap of thunder directly overhead made me jump, and the sky ripped open, rain pouring down, drenching me in seconds.

I dashed to my car, clambered in, then just sat there while the deluge pounded on the roof and slapped at the windshield, as if a poltergeist was trying to get in.

I looked toward the house.

The prowler was my fault. I had put this in to motion by asking for the extra ark for Be-Be.

What if Kevin hadn't come into the kitchen when he did, and scared the intruder away? What if the toy hadn't been left outside? Would that burglar have come in through Be-Be's open window? And what if the child had woken up? What if, what if, what if . . .

My concern, fear, and guilt turned to anger with myself. *I* had put Tina and Be-Be and Kevin in danger. *I* had caused my friend further turmoil at a time when she was already stressed with the return of her illness.

I wanted to go back inside and check on Tina when the house lights began shutting off, one by one, as if asking me ever so politely to leave.

The drive back in the downpour was harrowing, but at least it kept my mind off of further 'what if's.'

At home, I went directly to the library with only one thing on my mind: to make a suspect list of possible prowlers. I had turned on a small table lamp, and was in the process of wheeling out the old blackboard from behind the stand-up piano, when a searing pain in my side sent me collapsing on the floor in a quivering pile.

A Trash 'n' Treasures Tip

Another type of dead stock is older items with their original tags, purchased by a customer but never used, sometimes referred to as PNU (purchased never used). My closet is full of PNU – clothes a size too small for when I lose those ten pounds. I refer to them as WOM – waste of money.

FIVE
Hike and Seek

E ven as I lay writhing on the floor of the library, I knew
what had happened. I just knew it!
Mother had tazed me!

And it wasn't like it hadn't happened before. When she first
got hold of the protective device – having lost confidence in her
rape whistle (her words not mine) – Mother was trying to figure
out how to use it, when the thing fired off 'accidentally,' and I
'happened' to be in the way.

When the pain let up, Mother was down on her knees, looming
over me in her blue shoulder-padded vintage chenille robe; her
eyes were wide, compensating for her middle-of-the-night lack
of glasses.

'Brandy!' she exclaimed. 'Goodness gracious! Whatever were
you up to?'

'I *live* here, remember!'

'I'm afraid I took you for a burglar.'

'Do I *look* like a burglar?'

'Frankly, dear, meaning no offense . . . you rather do. You're
decked out in black, your hair is all stringy, and then of course
you were skulking around.'

'I was *not* skulking!' I sat up and, to her credit, she helped
me. 'I just didn't want to wake you.'

'Well, thank you for your thoughtfulness, dear.'

I took stock of my injury as she scurried off and up the stairs,
after her glasses. Luckily, only one prong had found its
target, and wasn't embedded in my skin very deep, easily
extracted with a tug and a grimace.

'Would you like me to take you to the hospital?' Mother asked,
upon her return, her eyes even bigger now behind the glasses.

'Just get me an antibiotic,' I said, 'and a Band-Aid.'

'We aim to please!' she said and off she went to fetch them.

I was glad her aim wasn't any better.

Meanwhile, Sushi trotted over.

'Some accomplice you make,' I groused. 'Couldn't you have stopped her?'

I swear the little mutt hung her head in shame.

'Never mind,' I said, giving her a hug. 'I'm afraid I did look like a burglar.'

Mother reappeared with ointment and a Band-Aid large enough to cover half of my side.

'What in the wide, wide world of sports,' Mother asked, tending to my wound, 'were you doing down here in the middle of the night?'

I gave her chapter and verse: the call from Tina, the prowler, the missing ark. And yes, also what Shawntea had mentioned about the auctioneer's preliminary report.

'So,' she said, 'something was inconsistent with injuries from a fall, was it? But *what*?'

Even in the dim light of the table lamp Mother's eyes glowed like a demon's. I had unleashed the Kraken.

(*Note from Mother to Brandy:* Watch the mixed metaphors, dear!)

'Either way,' she whispered, 'we now know one thing . . .'

'Which is what?'

'I was *right*!' she shouted, making me flinch, which really hurt, thank you. 'Conrad *was* murdered.'

I got to my feet, with Mother's assistance. A little wobbly, but not any worse for wear than the aftermath of the time I'd stuck a knife into our vintage toaster to remove a Pop-Tart stuck in there.

Mother was asking, 'There must be a connection between Conrad's murder and that missing ark, don't you think? That the killer and prowler are surely one and the same?'

I shrugged the shoulder on the opposite side of my wound. 'Maybe. Or two skulkers with different agendas.' I paused. 'And maybe Tina's prowler wasn't after the ark at all, but just saw a movement through the glass doors onto the kitchen . . . and snatched the ark up because it was handy, and all that could be had.' Patio furniture being a little hard to haul off in a hurry.

'Well,' Mother mused, roused and ready to go, 'as long as we're up and awake . . .'

She was moving toward the blackboard, when I stepped in front of her. 'Nope. This time *I'm* doing the list.'

Her eyebrows went up and so did the corners of her mouth, forming a smile of parental pride. 'Very well, dear. It's nice to see you taking the initiative.'

'It was my best friend's house that was almost invaded, and Baby Brandy who was put in harm's way.'

'Not to mention the loss of the child's ark, which short of Dolly Gambol's unlikely largesse would be almost impossible to replace.'

Outside of you giving up yours, I thought, but didn't go there.

While I positioned the blackboard, Mother settled into my usual place on the piano bench, Sushi curling up at her feet.

Chalk in hand, facing Mother as teacher to pupil, I said, 'There should be three lists this time: first for Conrad's killer, second for Tina's prowler, and third for suspects capable of being both.'

Mother clasped her hands. 'Excellent, dear. But you'll need my input, as you weren't giving me your fullest attention at the dinner table earlier.'

Strangely enough, I actually did remember everything she'd said, perhaps having gotten stored in the back of my mind and brought forward by the tazer.

Turning toward the board, I said, 'I'll start with suspects in the killing, people you determined had a grudge against Conrad.' I began to write on the left side. When I had finished it looked like this:

KILLER SUSPECTS

Name	Motivation	Opportunity
Doug Holden	?	?
Ryan Dayton	?	?
Dolly Gambol	?	?
Sally Wilson	?	?
Otto Berger	?	?
Johan Larsen	?	?

I turned to Mother.

'Splendid beginning,' she said. Rare praise.

'Should I add Conrad's wife, d'you think?' I asked.

Mother shook her head. 'If Elizabeth had wanted him dead, over his philandering and drinking, she could have gotten rid of him long ago. And wouldn't have had to resort to homicide to do so.'

'Maybe. But you never know when that kind of thing might come to a head.'

'Excellent observation, dear. Hope for you yet.'

I ignored the left-handed compliment and moved to the right side of the board for the second list, which was short.

PROWLER SUSPECTS

Name	Motivation	Opportunity
Dolly Gambol	toy arks	?
Sally Wilson	toy arks	?

Mother was frowning. 'It makes sense that only Dolly and Sally of this group would be interested enough in the arks to kill for a crate of them. But why home-invade for a single ark? And how would either Dolly or Sally know you had given one to Be-Be?'

'No idea,' I admitted. 'I certainly didn't tell anyone.'

'Perhaps Tina did.'

'No,' I said, 'I didn't mention to her what *kind* of toy I was bringing. I suppose she might've gone out later or told someone on the phone.'

'Easy enough to check.' Mother was studying me. 'What is it, dear? Something troubling you? We sleuths have so much to keep track of.'

'Well . . .' I tossed a hand, '. . . the night we met with Norris at the warehouse, I sensed someone else might have been there, too . . . on the top floor.'

She leaned forward intently. 'I'm listening.'

I reminded her that Conrad had to summon the elevator down to take us up.

She looked as pleased with me as ever I'd seen her. 'Dear, you are turning into a quite the detective!'

'Thank you.'

'And from such unpromising material.'

Mother giveth and Mother taketh away.

She went on, 'And if you recall, you *did* mention in front of Conrad that you wanted an ark for Be-Be.'

I had at that!

'Which means that if someone else was there,' I deduced, 'he or she may have heard me, as well.'

I added 'unknown warehouse person' to both the prowler and suspect lists.

I suggested that the third compilation – the crossover between murder suspects and prowlers, destined for the flip-side of the board – was too premature to make. Mother concurred.

So I replaced the chalk on the lip and asked, 'What now?'

Mother stood. 'Now, we get some shut-eye. Then I want to see the preliminary examination report. We can't do anything more until we know the time of Conrad's death . . . and what specific inconsistency Shawntea vaguely alluded to.'

I said, 'Well, it's Sunday. So I don't know how you're going to do that with the morgue closed.'

Mother gave me an unnerving grin. 'You just leave that to me.'

But I was too tired to question her and I needed my rest. Getting tazed takes it out of a girl.

I awoke to the aroma of coffee mingled with other delicious smells. My Frank Lloyd Wright bedside clock read nine fifteen, but I was still dog-tired. I almost just rolled over and played dead, but my stomach said to get up, overruling me.

The real dog with a right to be tired was Sushi, who'd been curled against me; but she was already gone, likely disappearing the moment Mother began clanging pots and pans in the kitchen, which may have been another factor in waking me up – it explained why I'd been dreaming about a one-man band.

Downstairs, the Duncan Phyfe table was set for two – but not with the usual Jadeite Fire King dishes. No. Mother had brought out the good stuff – her wedding dishes, the Haviland Limoges rose pattern, made in France, along with delicately etched long-stemmed water glasses, and her rarely used sterling silver flatware, Grande Baroque by Wallace.

That, combined with the aromatic promise of a feast worthy

of breaking any fast, could only mean one thing: I was in for it, today.

But right now, I was hungry, well aware that Mother was on the runway already in mid-takeoff. There was nothing to be done about it, so I took my place at the table, her one-woman fatalistic crew.

(*Note to Brandy from Mother:* Excellent unmixed, extended metaphor!)

Mother, dressed in one of her Breckenridge top-and-slacks ensembles, entered from the kitchen carrying a platter, Sushi trailing behind like a furry shadow.

'And how are we this morning?' Mother asked in a sing-song suspicious way.

'And what,' I asked, 'might the fare be this morning?'

She set the platter in front of me. Arranged on a white paper doily (!) were steaming pancakes, crisp bacon, and browned sausages.

'Buttermilk pancakes?' I inquired.

'No, dear,' she said.

Rusk Pancakes

1 cup finely ground rusks

(*Note to Brandy from Olivia*: Sorry to interrupt, but while this is all quite lovely, I do believe the rusk recipes are wearing a bit thin.)

(*Note to Olivia from Brandy*: That may well be, but we have five more cartons to use up.)

(*Note to Brandy from Olivia*: A friendly suggestion: perhaps you might offer any further ruskian recipes on your website.)

(*Note to Olivia from Brandy*: OK. This one is really good, though. Especially served with fresh strawberries and whipped cream.)

(*Note to Brandy from Olivia*: Noted. But do please consider the website option.)

*   *   *

After a delicious breakfast of rusk pancakes – the recipe can be found on www.BarbaraAllan.com (if I remember to put it there) – Mother instructed me to get dressed in something very casual. I selected jeans and a plaid shirt accordingly. Also, she suggested I cover my hair with a bandana, which gave me a clue as to her motive. As Mother said, my sleuthing skills were improving.

To placate Sushi, who was not going with us, I put the last sausage in her dog dish, and Mother and I made a quick getaway while the pooch was laser-focused on the meat.

Behind the wheel of the SUV, I asked, 'To the hospital, I presume?'

'Your deductive abilities grow by leaps and bounds!'

Such forced compliments were no longer working, now that the meal was in me. I started the engine. 'Why couldn't *I* be the doctor this time?'

'Because you simply don't look like a doctor, dear. For one thing, you don't look old enough. For another, you look . . .'

'Not bright enough?'

'I was thinking more that you look like you make a fine cleaning woman.'

'Only because of what I'm wearing,' I protested. 'And *you* were the wardrobe mistress of this little extravaganza!'

'Why, I'll have you know I haven't been anyone's mistress in years.'

A pretty good joke, coming from her, considering how limited her sense of humor was.

Grunting, I backed the car out of the drive.

The county morgue was located on the basement floor of Serenity Hospital; this was where preliminary autopsies were performed by Tom Peak, staff medical examiner. Since Conrad Norris had been killed on Saturday afternoon, with the prelim report done shortly thereafter, Peak might not have sent it to the coroner's office in City Hall yet, the building not being open weekends. But even if he'd already emailed it over, Mother must've been figuring he'd likely held on to a hard copy.

Vivian Borne had recently been banned from the hospital

basement, and all other areas, other than those instances when she'd been admitted as a patient herself. This had been a result of her disruption of an autopsy (*Antiques Fire Sale*), hence the need for subterfuge.

I steered the car behind the hospital into the staff parking area, then – per Mother's instructions – parked in a spot where we would not be caught by a security camera.

'The ditty bag, dear,' Mother said.

She loved that term.

I reached for the black duffel in the back seat, brought it forward, and tossed it on her lap.

She unzipped the bag, then extracted her doctor's costume: white smock, stethoscope, headband with mirror, and clipboard. The smock, stethoscope, and mirrored headband came from the prop room at the Playhouse, of course; however, the mirror had been replaced with a piece of cheesy silver paper after blinding other actors on stage during the premiere performance of Mother's modern-day musical version of Dr Jekyll and Mr Hyde, *Is There a Doctor In the House?*.

(Turned out the Playhouse needed one, because a woman in the front row had a heart attack in the second act, and Mother never forgave her for ruining opening night, though the play-wright/director considered the unfortunate event demonstrative of her skillful 'fear effects.')

The only authentic ditty in the bag was the clipboard, which she'd swiped for possible future use on her last hospital visit; attached had been the X-rays of a Mr Von Holten taken before he'd undergone gallbladder surgery. She'd brought this along for (as she put it) 'verisimilitude.'

'Where are *my* props?' I asked.

She reached in the bag and pulled out a hand Swiffer.

'That's it? A duster?'

Mother shrugged, the pseudo-mirrored headband bearing down on me as if this were a bizarre medical exam. 'Best I can do in the cleaning lady vein. Couldn't very well fit a mop and bucket in ye ol' ditty bag.'

We donned white surgical masks, then exited the car, and made our way to a staff entrance protected from unwanted entry by a keypad.

Mother, finger poised before the pad, said, 'The code is changed every Monday . . . so this should still be good.'

I didn't ask who she had pried it from. Or what she promised that person – a part in a Playhouse production, perhaps, or a (forged) autographed photo of George Clooney back in *ER* days.

She punched four numbers, the door lock clicked, and we entered into a wide beige corridor greeting us with a strong antiseptic odor.

'No one will be down here this morning,' Mother said, not bothering to whisper.

'Why, doesn't anybody die on Sunday?'

A woman in green scrubs crossed the T at the far end of the hall, pausing with a stare.

Quickly, Mother consulted Mr Von Holten's X-rays, while I absurdly dusted the nearest wall.

The woman shook her head and continued on her journey.

'Let's get this over with,' I whispered.

'Indubitably.'

'Stop saying that.'

'Saying what?'

We approached a door with a plaque that read:

COUNTY MORGUE/AUTOPSY ROOM
Thomas Peak, Chief Medical Examiner

This was a standard lock-and-key door, and Mother produced two picks from her leather case, which she'd tucked in her right smock pocket, then nimbly set to work. In less than thirty seconds we were inside, the door locked behind us.

The windowless chamber was white with stainless-steel touches, and could have been mistaken for an operating room. But several abnormalities alluded to the chamber's function – a row of stacked coolers along a wall; a central examination table with a perforated drainage-system top; and a small sink with faucet at one end, along with other unidentifiable equipment.

Thankfully, the exam table was vacant, as were several gurneys at the ready, sheets neatly folded.

I shivered, not entirely from the cold temperature.

'Security cam?' I asked.

'Activated only during an autopsy,' Mother replied.

She moved to a small desk with office chair, tucked in a corner like an afterthought. Just enough for a place from which to write up a report.

I joined her, and frowned. 'Wouldn't Peak talk into a recorder, and have it transcribed?'

Mother set the clipboard on the desk. 'He does . . . But Tom Peak is old school. He likes to read from – and hold on to – a copy written in his own hand, in case there's a mistake.' Her hands were leafing through some papers. 'Ah! Here it is. Camera, dear.'

With my phone, I took several photos of the report, after which Mother replaced the single page in the stack, and together we headed for the door. Easy peasy.

I was reaching for the handle when, from out in the hall, came the unmistakable sound of a clanking cleaning cart, enhanced by a squeaky wheel. Rather more cleaning power than a single Swiffer . . .

'Not to worry,' Mother whispered. 'Probably won't make a stop here.'

But then the cart clanked to a halt.

Next came the sound of jangling keys.

My eyes grew wide, as in, '*What should we do now?*'

'Hide,' Mother commanded, sotto voce.

Hide? Where?

But she was already on the move, heading toward the body coolers, whose many doors opened like those of a big file cabinet. Mother tugged at a drawer, found it empty, crawled up on the empty tray, and stretched out. Then, using her hands along the top, closed herself in with an ominous *klik* (or click, if you will).

Had she meant to shut it completely?

There was a folding screen in a corner I could use to hide behind, but I didn't have time to reach it, so I jumped up on a gurney, its wheels thankfully in braked mode, and covered myself with the sheet.

The clanking cart rolled in, then stopped.

Deathly silence.

'HR is going to hear about *this*!' came a female voice that pinged off the walls. 'There are not to be *any* bodies out of the cooler when we clean!'

For a moment I thought this was a conversation, and perhaps a two-person cleaning crew had invaded; but then it became clear our new friend was just talking out loud to herself.

The body the cleaner referred to, of course, belonged to yours truly, under that sheet. And 'sheet' was *almost* the word that I said to myself, silently. I held my breath, so my white coverlet wouldn't move and give me away.

From across the room, from behind stainless steel, came a sneeze. Must have been pretty darn chilly in that locker to produce that from Mother so quickly. Nonetheless, that was my cue: slowly I began to sit up, moaning a bit under my sheet, making a ghost of myself. Or maybe an ass.

Or both.

In any case, the cleaning lady screamed, the cart jostling, as if she'd backed into it. Imagine how she'd have reacted if I'd said, 'Gesundheit!'

Then I could hear the door open and her hauling the cart out with her – had to hand it to her, having presence of mind to bring it along, perhaps for protection. The door opened, slammed shut, and I could hear her shrieks echoing down the hallway as she pushed the cart before her.

I got out from under the sheet.

'Let me out of here!' came Mother's muffled yell, and she began knocking from within the drawer where she'd filed herself away. She had locked herself in, and I might have taken my time freeing her if making haste hadn't been a factor. That cleaner could return with security staff at any moment.

I pulled the drawer open.

Mother climbed off the slab, shivering, and sputtered, 'Just as I planned. My sneeze frightened her off!'

'It was me sitting up under that sheet,' I said, 'and you aren't kidding anybody – that sneeze was the genuine article! You gave yourself a real chill this time.'

'That's your opinion.'

'No,' I said, 'my opinion is we need to get out of here *right now.*'

Mother grabbed her clipboard from the desk, and we left.

Unfortunately, neither one of us noticed she was missing one Playhouse head-mirror.

We got home around noon, exhausted from our little road company Three Stooges production. Sushi, unhappy we'd snuck off when she was busy with the last sausage, had presented us with a little sausage of her own in the front entryway – her little commentary on being deceived.

In the library, I downloaded the photo of the preliminary report from my cell to my email, then printed a copy.

Mother, seated at the dining room table, gestured impatiently for the paper, which I gave her, then peered over her shoulder.

It was a standard, simple, one-page analysis, with columns for name of decedent, address, sex, age, height, weight, length, hair color, as well as time of death, probable cause of death, marks and wounds, and disposition of the case. Also included was a depiction of a human form, front and back.

Under 'Time of Death,' Peak had written 'between 2 pm and 4 pm.' Under 'Probable Cause of Death,' he had written 'Accident.'

And yet, in the column headed Disposition of Case, the medical examiner scrawled, 'Autopsy requested.'

The basis of his decision – and what Shawntea had meant – was in his own hand beneath 'Marks and Wounds': 'Laceration to side of skull inconsistent with injuries acquired from the elevator shaft fall. Further analysis may be warranted.'

On the drawing of the back side of the human, Peak had marked an 'X' to where he was referring.

'There's no mention,' I said, 'of high alcohol content in Conrad's blood.'

'No,' Mother replied. 'But Tom would have taken a BAC sample, with results not available for several weeks.'

'So he's hedging his bet.'

'It would appear so . . . if Norris was legally inebriated, accidental death is more likely.'

'But if Norris *wasn't* drunk, murder becomes a stronger possibility.'

She nodded. 'Particularly if Tom had heard from our coroner that Vivian Borne suspected homicide.' Then she pushed back her chair and stood, announcing, 'To the library!'

'To the Batcave,' I said, almost echoing her.

This time, Mother played the role of teacher while I took the bench as her student, with Sushi curled up at my feet.

'We now know the time of death,' Mother said, 'and that there was a wound suspicious enough for the medical examiner to make a note of . . . along with a request for an autopsy.' She paused, picked up the chalk, and turned toward the board. 'I will now fill in a motive for each suspect based upon what I observed during the auction.'

'Using gossip as glue.'

'Don't underestimate its stickiness.'

Mother was blocking the board, so I couldn't see the results until she'd finished and stepped aside.

KILLER SUSPECTS

Name	Motivation	Opportunity: 2–4pm
Doug Holden	pilfered stock	?
Ryan Dayton	blackmail victim	?
Dolly Gambol	arks	?
Sally Wilson	arks	?
Otto Berger	wife's affair with Conrad	?
Johan Larsen	buttons	?
Unknown warehouse person	?	?

Skeptically, I commented, 'Some of the motivations seem pretty thin. I can't imagine either Dolly or Sally killing Norris over those arks. Or Johan being *that* upset with the auctioneer after finding out that he didn't get every single barrel.'

Mother shrugged. 'Your logic is undeniable. But a collector can be . . . what is the term?'

'A whack job.'

She pursed her lips. 'There are more appropriate appellations you might use.'

She would know.

I asked, 'Just what kind of blackmail are we talking about with Ryan Dayton?'

'Dear, these motives are mere placeholders – we have to start somewhere.'

'OK. But do you know for sure that Doug Holden found out Norris had been pilfering the stock?'

'Speculation. A reasonable guess.'

'What about listing Norris having an affair with Otto Berger's wife? Is *that* what you had on him?'

I took Mother's silence as a yes.

Which she confirmed by saying, 'That's why I'd place my bet on Otto Berger.'

I wasn't so sure. 'Maybe he didn't care about the affair – the way Elizabeth Norris apparently put up with her husband's philandering.'

Mother replaced the chalk on the board's lip. 'Enough speculation. Time for action.'

As if the Morgue Follies hadn't been active enough. But I knew this was coming, and suggested, 'Why don't we investigate the prowler, first.'

Her eyes widened. 'Finding Conrad's killer is a higher priority.'

'Not to me it isn't.' My chin was quivering and my eyes were hot and wet.

'Yes, dear . . . I can see that. Very well, we'll solve that dilemma first. After all, Be-Be *is* my granddaughter, in a way.' She paused. 'But we *must* get to the other suspects ASAP. Once the preliminary report is filed, its contents are bound to get out, even before the police finally get around to conducting an actual murder investigation. And that will give the suspects a chance to solidify their stories.'

She shook her head and leaned close.

'After all,' Mother said, 'some people just can't be trusted with a secret.'

Trash 'n' Treasures Tip

Dead stock is becoming ever more difficult to obtain, due to chains like TJ Maxx, Marshalls, and Ross buying off-season, overstocked merchandise. Estate sales, where unused items have been squirreled away in an attic for years, will become an even more valuable source for unused vintage items. Speaking of squirrels, we got rid of one in our attic by trailing a row of gourmet pecans (Priester's honey glazed) out a window, which slammed shut by a trip wire when the varmint went out.

SIX
Rock, Paper, Scissors

The first of the two suspects in what Mother insisted on calling the Case of the Missing Ark was Sally Wilson, who lived an hour away in Amana, largest of seven small colonies spaced several miles apart in a circular pattern at the northwest edge of Serenity County.

A general misconception about the colonies was that they were founded by the Amish; but the first inhabitants were actually Lutherans who had come to the Midwest after suffering religious persecution in Germany. The small villages, however, soon attracted the Amish and Quakers, who found both literal and figurative common ground in their communal ways, religious freedoms, and simple lifestyles rejecting the encroachment of modern ways.

But the advancement of those modern ways – horses to tractors, candles to electricity, horse-and-buggies to cars – had caused many an Amish farm to either perish or cast aside its religious beliefs in order to survive. Some had, and some hadn't. The latter group supplemented their waning income by sending womenfolk into the villages to sell homemade wares, such as beautifully woven woolen blankets, wonderful baked goods, and tasty meats like chops and sausages to the locals.

Fast-forward to today, where the shops now catered to out-of-town tourists who craved an old-world feeling. This was maintained through strict codes protecting the original buildings and retaining the 'German angle' (as one proprietor crassly put it) by importing merchandise from abroad to supplement locally made items.

But a few shops had stayed true to the old ways, and among those was The Toy Box, whose owner was Sally Wilson. According to Mother, who filled me in on the hour-long trip, the Wilson woman had been a kindergarten teacher who developed strong opinions about what toys a child should be given. She believed the more a toy could do, the less the child would do. And so, her store – which sold both new and old – contained nothing that required batteries, or even mechanical parts, even if it meant the old-fashioned winding-up of a toy to watch it perform.

After sharing this view, Mother concluded with, 'Would Frank Lloyd Wright have become the most renowned architect in the world if he hadn't been given a set of building blocks? Or would Wilbur and Orville Wright have invented the aeroplane without their father giving them a toy glider?'

We arrived in Amana around noon. I guided the SUV down the main thoroughfare, where the buildings bordering both sides of the street were either original to the village or made to look as such, each tended with care and enhanced by an array of welcoming flowers in window boxes and pots.

The sidewalks were alive with mostly older folks wearing an assortment of summer clothes, enjoying a nice, non-blistering sunny Sunday afternoon. The tourists were smiling and laughing as they went in and out of the various specialty shops that had just opened their doors.

I craned my neck as our vehicle approached the Ronneburg Restaurant on the right, one of several eateries serving authentic German cuisine, and my stomach made its needs known – the early morning lavish bribery of a breakfast already a distant memory.

'We'll grab a bite later, dear,' Mother said. 'Let's catch Sally before she gets busy with the after-lunch rush.'

Off the main drag were several short streets containing a combination of shops and old structures that had been converted into residences, strictly regulated as to what could and could not be changed.

'Turn here,' Mother said, gesturing to the left as we neared a side street.

I obeyed, immediately spotting a wooden sign in the front yard of an old log cabin – Sally's shop, which Mother informed me had originally been built as a one-room schoolhouse. We took an angled parking place in front and headed up a step-stone walk leading to a wooden stoop whose railings were entwined with purple clematis; window boxes on either side of the front door sported a mixture of other bright summer flowers. The sign in the door said the shop opened at noon and it was a quarter past that, but when I tried the door it was locked.

Mother and I glanced at each other, wondering if we'd made a pointless trip, when the door came open, its little bell announcing us.

In the doorway, Sally Wilson gave us a startled deer look. The Toy Box proprietor was a tall, almost skinny woman, her mousy brown hair brushing her shoulders, her thin long face flushed. I knew her a little and found her nervousness contagious.

'Why, Vivian . . . Brandy,' she said, smoothing one side of her hair. 'So nice to have you stop by the store. Afraid I'm just opening up – church got out late.'

She stepped aside for us, holding the door open, adding, 'Would you girls mind watching things for a moment? I brought some new items from home and I need to get them out of the car.'

Without waiting for an answer, she disappeared into her store, almost as if she'd been swallowed up by it.

Mother called out, 'Happy to help!'

'She's jumpy as a cat,' I whispered.

'What a terrible thing to say,' Mother said, 'about a cat.'

The Toy Box interior was larger than I expected, the room bisected by a central checkout counter. The front area had book-cases displaying modern toys, chiefly favorites from yesteryear still being made, like the Erector Set, Tinker Toys, and Lincoln Logs. Newer ones had been selected as decidedly educational, such as puzzles, and children's tea sets. A display of dolls did little but stare at you, some unsettlingly so; and hanging from a rustic ceiling crossbeam were an array of wooden puppets, heavily leaning toward clowns, hovering almost eerily.

The section behind the counter – the back half of the cabin – was reserved for Sally's antique toys, housed in a suspect line-up of tall locked glass-shelved cabinets to both show off and protect the precious, often rare items from sticky fingers of all ages. No prices on anything, just occasional cards saying, INQUIRE.

In one cabinet – there among the brightly colorful enameled steel cars and trucks, the Rose O'Neill doll, a pull-along walking dog, and Howdy Doody board game – was a green Peter-Mar ark and all its animals. Mr and Mrs Noah, too.

In a minute or so, Sally sallied forth (so to speak) from a curtained corner near the row of cabinets, a cardboard box in her arms. We followed her to the central counter, where she set the box down.

'Sorry to impose,' she said. 'You shouldn't have to stop by a shop only to be asked to watch the till!'

Her vehicle must have been parked behind the cabin.

'Don't be silly,' I said, signaling to Mother that I was taking the lead – we'd agreed on the way I'd be the one who dealt with Sally, as Mother and our hostess had clashed from time to time. 'It gave us an opportunity to admire your wonderful selection of toys.'

'Thank you,' she said, glancing around proudly at her domain. 'A great deal of thought goes into each item I select, whether new or old. Are you ladies just out enjoying the day, or is there something I can do for you?'

I knew Mother was in agony staying silent, and I have to admit I took some guilty pleasure in that. Well, somewhat guilty.

'I'm looking for something for my best friend's toddler,' I said, adding, 'A two-year-old.'

'Such a fun time.'

Did I mention Sally had no children of her own?

'Well,' she said, moving away from the counter, 'I could show you some things appropriate for a child that age. Or do you have something particular in mind?'

'As matter of fact, yes.'

She glanced at Mother. 'Sounds like your daughter knows what she wants.'

Mother's lips were pressed together and her eyes needed no magnification by those glasses to look big.

'I do,' I said. 'A Peter-Mar ark.'

Had Sally's face drained of color? Or had the flush from her entrance merely receded?

'You see,' I went on, 'I gave her one as a gift just yesterday, but then last night . . . it was stolen by a prowler.'

Her expression was one of immediate sympathy – genuine? Maybe.

'How awful!' she said.

'Awful's a good word for it.'

She gestured nervously toward the rear. 'I do have a Peter-Mar ark back in a case. But that's for display only. And, anyway, it's green not blue.'

'I hadn't mentioned the stolen ark was blue.'

Backpedaling, Sally said, 'I mentioned the one I have is green, *if* a blue one was what you're after.' She continued, 'Also, if I did decide to part with the green ark, I'm quite sure you wouldn't want to pay a collector's price for a toy going to a toddler.'

Now I was the one who was flushed. 'Why? Because a cheap, poorly made toy is fine for a child, but an antique should be reserved for an adult? Someone who can appreciate and take care of the precious thing?'

That came out a little harsh, I admit. But the joy I'd seen on Be-Be's face when she was playing with that ark couldn't possibly be matched by any melancholy adult trying to relive a childhood.

Not really meaning to, I had rattled our hostess, who said, 'I'm sorry, Brandy. Maybe there's something else I could help you with.'

'You could answer a question. A pretty simple one.'

'All . . . all right.'

'Where were you,' I blurted, 'at two o'clock last night?'

She reared back, eyes flaring. 'Are you accusing *me* of stealing that ark?'

Mother stepped forward. '*Of course not*, dear.'

Sally's eyes fixed on her; her chin was up. 'Well, it certainly sounded that way.'

Mother patted the air with both palms. 'You must forgive Brandy. Her little godchild was endangered in the wee hours this morning, by this prowler who purloined the ark.'

Yes. Mother said 'purloined.' I wish I had it on tape to prove it. In her defense, she's always had a weakness for alliteration. And Edgar Allan Poe.

'You can understand how upsetting it would be,' Mother went on lightly, 'to have given the child such a special gift – a perfectly preserved ark, in its original box, with all of the pieces, including Noah and his wife.' She leaned conspiratorially close to Sally. 'Why, the girl is asking simply *everyone* where they were at the time of the crime.'

My face had reddened well past the flushed stage now.

Mother took Sally gently by the arm and walked her away toward the displays of non-vintage items. 'Now, perhaps you could show *me* something that would please the little angel.'

Looking somewhat appeased, Sally said, 'I *do* have a wooden farm animal set that would be appropriate.'

'Splendid!'

The women moved to a bookcase while I stayed behind, hoping to regain my poise.

A few potential customers came in and went back out while Mother selected the toy farm set. As Sally was handwriting up the bill in a receipt book – no modern computer set-up for her – Mother ventured, 'Sally, do let us know if anyone comes in wanting to sell a blue Peter-Mar ark.'

'You know very well, Vivian,' the toy collector said, 'that Dolly Gambol bought a crate of them at the auction, yesterday morning. And she probably intends to sell them to a third party. So a seller might offer me a blue ark and I could contact you ladies.'

Suddenly I was wondering what might be in the cardboard box on the counter.

'That would be lovely,' Mother allowed.

'But,' Sally said rather smugly, handing across the sack with the farm set to her, 'how could I know whether it came from Dolly's lot or is the one snatched away from Brandy's little goddaughter?'

'You'll know,' I said, answering the question addressed to Mother, 'because there's a little chip on the bottom of the ark.'

Sally's smile disappeared. Like the prowler had. And the ark.

As she helped a few more customers, we slipped outside, heading to our car, Mother asking, '*Is* there an identifying chip?'

'There is. Be-Be dropped the ark . . . or rather, *I* did, giving it to her. At any rate, if Sally *is* the thief, she won't risk selling or displaying the toy. So I get some small satisfaction out of that.'

'Perhaps. But it doesn't help get the toy back.'

I stopped in my tracks. 'I thought I did a pretty good job interrogating that woman. Really let her have it.'

We had reached the car.

'That's one way of looking at it, dear.'

I looked over the hood of the SUV at her. 'Yes – till *you* stepped in, anyway.'

She looked back at me. 'No – till you stepped *in* it.'

I opened my mouth for a retort, but Mother made a shushing sound, then said, 'Let us not quibble here, where Sally may be at a window watching. I'll give you my notes over lunch.'

'Your notes! Ha. Of my performance, you mean?'

'*Précisément,*' she said.

That was the only thing worse than when she started speaking in an English accent: when she lapsed into French.

I drove the short distance to the Ronneburg, named for a castle in Hesse, Germany, that had sheltered the ancestors of Amana residents dating back to the religious persecution of two hundred years ago. Inside the old stone structure, we were greeted by a forty-something hostess attired in a dirndl – white blouse, black bodice, red skirt – who asked pleasantly, 'Lunch for two?'

Mother said, 'Yes, lunch for two. But may we be seated somewhere private? We have a funeral to plan.'

This was an old ploy Mother trotted out when she wanted privacy for us to discuss a case . . . with the added value of getting special wait-staff treatment. Usually, if need be, the excuse given was that we'd just gotten word that Aunt Olive had died – actually, Olive had been dead for years, her ashes entrusted to Mother, her closest relative, in the form of a glass paperweight that rested in one piece on a bookshelf at home.

But planning a funeral, rather than commiserating over a recent death, was a new wrinkle. Why someone would want to engage in such a solemn conversation while consuming hahnchen schnitzel was (and is) beyond my comprehension. Still, any excuse Mother came up with was better than diners seated in close proximity overhearing murder talk.

The dirndl-clad woman's expression turned sympathetic at Mother's somber request. 'Certainly. I can put you in a separate area.'

'That would be lovely, dear,' Mother replied, then nudged my foot with hers.

'Yes, thank you,' I added dutifully. 'Most thoughtful.'

We followed the hostess to an anteroom, likely reserved for

private parties, and were shown to a table whose red-and-white cloth seemed sure to cheer us mourners up. We were seated next to a lace-curtained window with a view on couples and families strolling the sidewalk on this pleasant day. Given menus, we were told Emily would be with us momentarily. The woman departed, red skirt swishing.

I asked, 'So – whose funeral are we planning? Aunt Olive's? Does she really need another?'

Mother certainly didn't – she'd planned hers years ago, right down to the casket (white); her wardrobe (vintage 1940s dress with shoulder pads); and the music to be played (Benny Goodman, Glenn Miller, Duke Ellington, in honor of her late husband, who'd been ten years older). She had even written speeches for people to give. I'd read mine. Turned out she was the warmest, funniest, most caring mother a girl could ever have, and I'd made a fine Watson on our murder cases.

This latter I resented. I was pretty sure *she* was Watson. But I guess that's up to you. If you decide that I *am* Watson, please don't make it the befuddled Nigel Bruce one from the old Basil Rathbone movies.

Mother was studying the menu. 'Actually, we're planning *your* funeral, dear.'

'Why, am I not feeling well?'

'No, it's simply a thoughtful thing to do so as not to burden your loved ones. And a way to have a say in it. I'm quite sure no one asked Olive's permission to turn her into a paperweight.'

Our waitress, Emily – young, pretty brunette, perhaps still in high school – arrived crisply attired in a simple white button-down shirt and black slacks. She looked to have had enough spine to balk at a dirndl.

Still, her expression was one of sweetness and innocence, not yet jaded by the deceptive likes of Mother. And me.

Emily respectfully addressed the elder at the table, who ordered the hahnchen schnitzel, adding, 'With iced tea, no sugar.'

Emily's brown eyes came to me. 'And you?'

What I wanted was an assortment of delectable side dishes – potato dumplings, spatzle noodles, pickled beets, and sauerkraut. But Emily had no pad, no pen, no tablet, and I feared if she got my order wrong, it might cost this kid a much-needed summer job.

Waiters and waitresses need to learn that taking a customer's order without writing it down is incredibly unnerving to that customer. You sit wondering just what you'll be served – you might as well be at a carry-out window getting handed a paper bag that holds all sorts of nasty surprises when you get home. Then, if the food arrives wrong, and you request correction, you have to wait even longer, plus who *knows* what indignities the replacement food might suffer in the kitchen. So, I say, wait staff – stop showing off your supposed great memory.

Good grief, I'm becoming Mother!

'Same as her,' I replied glumly, nodding to Mother.

As the girl was leaving, Mother asked me, too loud, 'Now, dear, which do you prefer? Cremation or embalming?'

As if, 'Mashed or French fries?'

I whispered, 'Will you *stop* that. No more fake funeral talk.'

She shrugged. 'As you wish. But I *am* a Method actress.'

'The only method to your acting is madness.'

Her chin came up and her eyes looked down. 'Let she who is without medication cast the first aspersion.'

Elbows on the table, hands clasped under my chin, I said, 'OK, let's have the notes. Fire away.'

Mother settled back further in her chair. 'You began satisfactorily enough,' she said, 'by telling Sally you were looking for just the right toy for a little girl, establishing yourself as a customer, lowering her guard.' She paused. 'I even admired – let's say, found *interesting* – the choice you made in revealing that the ark you had given the toddler had been stolen. An excellent opportunity to gauge the woman's reaction.'

'So I did good,' I said, lowering my arms, and my guard.

'No. You tipped your hand too early, putting Sally immediately on the defensive. That was bad enough, but then you became emotional, the most unforgivable *faux pas* a detective can commit.'

French again.

'You're right,' I admitted. 'I just couldn't help it.'

Mother nodded. 'I do sympathize. But when trying to pry information from a suspect, you must keep your feelings in check.

Remember, your job is to convince *them* to talk . . . make them show *their* hand. You must *get* information, not give it.'

'I did catch her on the blue color, though.'

She granted me another nod. 'And I admit that was bold. Sally recovered fairly well, however. So, I would judge that stage of the contest at best a *draw*.' She shook her head, rather gently, her smile surprisingly understanding. 'Brandy, my darling child, you've accompanied me on many visits to the homes of suspects, helping beard them in their dens. Frankly, I'm surprised you haven't picked up more, watching me in action.'

She had a point. 'I guess all I do is just sit around taking in the scenery – looking at the person's taste in decor and clothes, and wondering if we're going to be offered something to drink or eat.'

Maybe I *was* Nigel Bruce.

'Nonsense,' Mother said cheerily. 'Studying the living quarters and manner of dress – and for that matter the *manners* of a suspect – can tell you much about that suspect's character . . . perhaps even a hint of their guilt or innocence.'

'Thank you.'

She raised a forefinger. 'But . . . let's go back to you mentioning the ark had been stolen. What did you profit in return for this information?'

'Not a lot. Sally's face didn't register anything except sympathy.'

'When you take a risk like that, dear, you must interpret the person's entire body language, not just their facial reactions.'

I leaned forward. 'Why? Did you pick something up?'

'I did – a slight tightening of her shoulders indicated you had struck a nerve.'

'Then you think Sally was the prowler?'

'I do. And that leads me to think *she* was the unknown suspect on our killer list, who was hiding in the warehouse the night we met with Conrad.'

'Hiding from you but not Conrad,' I said. 'She might have been there to make her own deal with him – maybe for all of the arks.'

Mother liked that observation. 'A deal that, if struck, means she was betrayed by the late auctioneer. Or that her offer was rejected, paving the way for Dolly outbidding her. Either one only strengthens her motive for killing Conrad over the arks.'

We fell silent.

Then I said, possibly fishing for more praise, 'At any rate I made the right move saying Be-Be's ark was stolen.'

'Yes.'

I smiled. 'Good.'

'But at a cost.'

'What cost is that?'

'Sally now knows we've focused on her.'

I shrugged. 'How is *that* a bad thing?'

'If she *is* the killer, as well as the prowler, it makes her all the more dangerous.'

Emily arrived with our food.

Mother's appetite was fine. Mine wasn't.

Dolly Gambol lived on a large farm about ten miles outside Serenity. I'd had never been to Dolly's before, but Mother had, and – in and around giving me directions – she filled me in on the drive from Amana.

Dolly saw herself as a homemaker and toy collector, and had played the farm wife well while husband Orville worked the fields, growing corn and soybeans. But when he died from a heart attack some years ago, Dolly sold the land 'toot sweet' (as Mother put it), all but a few acres that included the house and barn.

I pulled off the country gravel road and down a winding dirt lane buttressed by dense trees and foliage. Then, suddenly, Tara came into view. Or anyway a decent facsimile for this part of the world.

'*Not* what I expected,' I said, peering through the windshield at the immense white Colonial structure whose impossibly thick columns supported a second-floor balcony as wide as the edifice itself.

'The house was Dolly's domain,' Mother replied. 'Everything else was Orville's kingdom.'

'Good Lord,' I said. 'Is the structure pre-Civil War?'

'No. Very much post. Dolly always fancied herself a Southern belle, and bought the house after it had fallen into disrepair. That

Gone With the Wind look you've no doubt noted was quite intentional in the remodeling.'

'What does she do with all those rooms?'

Mother smiled knowingly. 'Patience.'

I pulled our car up behind a late-model baby-blue Lincoln sedan parked in the semi-circular gravel drive.

Mother was saying, 'Dolly used to host quite a few parties, and even allowed tours of the home . . . until a rare white Steiff teddy bear went missing.'

Toys again.

We abandoned the car, walked to and up the wide steps of the expansive front porch, where groupings of antique white wicker furniture waited for no one in particular. At the massive door, Mother reached for a chain, tugged, and an attached bell above us went *CLANG!* No camera doorbell for Dolly, not about to ruin the aesthetics of the old mansion.

We waited.

Mother tugged again.

Another *CLANG!*, and we waited some more.

Mother, miffed, muttered, 'Dolly has only the one car, so she *must* be here.'

'A friend could have picked her up.'

'She has very few of those.'

'Maybe she knows it's you.'

That didn't register on Mother, who was already on the move. 'Let's look on the back patio.'

We descended the steps, then made our way past a pre-Civil War lawn jockey (metallic flesh painted white, as if that was enough to dispel the tastelessness) along a stone walk to the rear of the house, where I noticed that, across the lawn, the doors of a rustic barn stood open.

'Bet she's in there,' I said, pointing.

Shortly, we were entering the barn, which was virtually vacant of anything – including Dolly – but for two large wooden crates that had been opened and emptied.

'I should have known,' Mother said. 'She's sold the arks already.'

I said, 'Probably had a buyer in place when she bought them.'

'Precisely.'

Let's see Nigel Bruce top that deduction.

Mother was on the move again. 'Let's find out if the back door of the house is open.'

Normally I might have objected to such an illegal approach; but this time I was onboard. This time it was personal. Like *Jaws 2*.

I trailed her and – when we passed a still-smoldering backyard fire pit – I stopped in my tracks, and called out to her: '*Mother!*'

She turned and came quickly back.

Using a stick to retrieve what had particularly caught my attention, I knocked it out of the ashes next to my feet. Then I bent and picked up a scorched giraffe, flicking off the ashes, coloring my fingertips gray and black.

Mother shrieked like a wounded animal. 'My Lord! Dolly didn't *sell* the arks! She *burned* them!'

I stared at her, incredulous. 'But *why?*'

'That's elementary, dear! To keep her *own* handful of Peter-Mar arks valuable.'

'Oh . . . my . . . God.' Nigel Bruce couldn't have been more flabbergasted. The burnt giraffe fell from my fingers.

Mother, infuriated, bolted toward the back patio, where a glass sliding door waited, and had it not been unlocked, I swear, she would have shouldered through the glass, shards flying.

I hurried after her, through an enormous kitchen with every modern appliance a good cook might desire, gleaming and winking at us like co-conspirators, before we proceeded down a long floral-carpeted hallway. Mother was well ahead of me and already out of sight.

Then I could hear her calling out to Dolly, but couldn't tell from where.

I passed a formal dining room, a well-stocked library, a Victorian parlor, and a ballroom with parquet flooring. Scarlett O'Hara would have been envious. Then I was standing in the large foyer where a huge grandfather clock gazed down at me disapprovingly while a wide staircase curved upward to the second-floor balcony, daring me up just as noises floated down . . .

I bounded up and stopped to listen.

Silence.

The hallway led to half a dozen closed doors, and when I

opened the nearest one, a thousand clowns stared back at me. The next room contained teddy bears, hundreds of them; the one opposite it, tin toys; and the next, model trains, a table set up with an elaborate town and shelves lined with unopened vintage Lionel boxes.

The last door was already ajar. I went to the doorway and stood there, as if eager to take in the disturbing tableau and add yet another entry in my mind's scrapbook of murder scenes.

Surrounded by dolls on shelves, with a prized few in little chairs here and there, sat Dolly in a rocking chair, her head back, eyes as vacant and unblinking as the little figures around her, a sewing basket at her feet. She had been mending a sock of indeterminate color because it had turned red from the blood that had run down from below her chin, where a pair of scissors had been thrust.

Mother was standing in front of the woman, and looked at me so placidly, that for one, long, horrible moment I thought she might have killed Dolly.

'No, dear,' she said, reading my mind.

Of course not. She didn't commit murders – she collected them.

'It's obviously too late,' I said, 'to do anything for her . . .'

'Much too late, but then with an attack like that, no amount of time would have helped. I'd estimate Dolly has been dead about six hours, judging by the dried blood, and the lack of rigor mortis.'

I felt the hahnchen schnitzel climbing my esophagus, and put a hand over my mouth.

'Dear, if you're going to be sick, there's a bathroom next door on the left. But be forewarned – the shelves are home to dozens of Speedy Alka-Seltzer figurines.'

'I'm . . . I'm all right,' I said, lifting my hand in assurance.

Mother lurched toward me, grabbed that hand, and stared at my fingers.

'What?' I asked.

'I noticed that same discoloration on Sally's fingers when she showed me the animal farm. It came from those ashes!'

I withdrew my hand. 'Then you think . . .'

'I *don't* think, dear – I *know*. We have to go back to that toy shop, *now*.'

'Bu-bu-but . . . what about *Dolly*?'

'She's past helping. We've established that.'

'We can't leave the scene of a crime!'

'We've done it before.' She shrugged. 'I'll call the sheriff on the way back to Amana. This is his jurisdiction.'

'No! It's not right . . .'

Her gaze was steady and firm. 'We have a clue indicating who our murderer is. And my deputy sheriff's badge authorizes me to take the next step.'

Really?

She took me by the arms, firmly yet somehow gentle. 'There's nothing we can do to help the poor woman . . . except catch her killer.' Mother let go. 'Now, come along. Or would you rather I drive myself and you stay here with the lady of the house?'

The Toy Box had a CLOSED sign on the door when we arrived back at Sally's shop. Her Sunday business hours were listed on the glass as noon till six, and it wasn't close to six.

Mother used her picks on the lock.

Inside, the room was bathed in semi-darkness, the lights switched off, with the sun – which earlier had shown through the windows – descending behind the surrounding tall trees.

Otherwise everything appeared as it had before. Except for one addition to the array of puppets hanging from the central crossbeam. One of those puppets could not have been brought to life by even the most skilled puppeteer.

Because Sally Wilson, with that single thick string, only *looked* like a puppet.

A Trash 'n' Treasures Tip

When acquiring vintage toys – whether to sell, or keep as an investment – buy what appeals to you personally, because you might wind up stuck with it. Like Mother's collection of Cabbage Patch Kids, most of which weren't worth any more than when she bought them years ago in anticipation of eventually selling them for a lot of cabbage.

SEVEN
Double Double This That

While Mother grabbed Sally's dangling legs, doing her best to hoist the woman up, I snatched scissors from the counter, righted the chair that had been knocked over beneath Sally, hopped up on it, and – with some effort – cut the rope around her neck with one hand, holding onto her by the waist with the other.

But Sally was heavier than I had anticipated, judging by her slender frame, 'dead weight' being more than just an expression, and – gravity working against me – she slipped through my arms, and out of Mother's, making a rather grim landing on her back on the floor.

Mother knelt, then felt for a pulse on Sally's rope-burned neck.

'CPR?' I asked. I had once witnessed Mother successfully revive a man who had just hanged himself.

'No, dear . . .' She stood. '. . . We're too late.' Gesturing to the woman's discoloring ankles, she said, 'Lividity tells the tale.'

And it did. I knew that blood begins to settle at the lowest point of the body several hours after death. Sally must have decided to take her life shortly after we'd left her shop.

Mother removed her cell from a pocket and punched in a familiar number, then put the phone on speaker. 'Sheriff Chen? . . . Deputy Borne, here.'

Charles Chen had been promoted from deputy to the top slot when Mother 'retired.'

'*Where exactly is* that, *Vivian?*' came his sharp reply. '*And why aren't you here?*'

'Well, where are *you*?' she asked, obviously stalling.

'*At Dolly Gambol's! When you called this in, I assumed you'd stay around and wait for me.*'

'As I recall, that didn't come up. You said don't touch anything, and I . . . we, Brandy is with me . . . didn't.'

'*Why didn't you stay put?*' Chen was normally unflappable. But he was sounding decidedly flapped.

'Because,' Mother said, 'I was hoping I might prevent another death.'

Not strictly speaking true – she'd been hoping to take Sally into custody, testing the limits of her honorary deputy's badge.

'But,' she was telling the phone, 'I was too late.'

Confusion and alarm colored his response: '*Prevent whose death?*'

'Sally Wilson.'

'*Who the devil is Sally Wilson? Vivian, where* are *you?*'

'The late Sally Wilson was proprietor of the Toy Box in Amana. Which is where we are. The Toy Box. In Amana.'

The phone seemed to just look at her.

'*I'll be right there,*' Chen's strained voice came. '*Don't you* move. *And don't touch a damn thing!*'

'You or a trusted deputy,' she said, filling the silence, 'other than myself of course, should come to the shop at Amana, ASAP.' At least she didn't say 'toot sweet.'

'Language, Sheriff,' she said, and disconnected.

'Is it my imagination,' she asked me, with the tiniest frown, 'or did Sheriff Chen seem a bit uncharacteristically slow on the uptake?'

I didn't have an answer for her. I was standing, turned away from Sally, who lay on her back, staring up at those puppets. Had I caused this death? Why had I allowed myself to get caught up in Mother's mania? Only, I'd been the one spinning out of control this time . . .

Mother, all business, was saying, 'Knowing Chen, he'll come himself . . . which means his ETA will be about thirty minutes. So that's how long we have.'

'Have for what?'

'Searching the crime scene, of course.'

'Looking for what?'

'*Clues*, dear! Snap out of it!'

'Couldn't we . . . cover her up first?'

Mother tossed a hand, impatient, the clock ticking. 'Be my guest.'

While she headed to the checkout counter, I went in search of something suitable, a coat or sweater perhaps. But the only cloth I found was a long gingham cotton curtain suspended by a tension rod, which Sally had used to section off a back corner.

I removed the curtain, revealing a storage area with a free-standing four-shelf metal rack of business supplies, along with some toys. And one of those toys was a boxed blue Peter-Mar ark, with a chip on its bow; a faint, sticky residue indicated where Tina had indeed administered a Band-Aid.

And perched on a high shelf was a white Steiff bear.

Were these other toys Sally had plundered?

Disgusted, I replaced the curtain – someone else could provide the woman a shroud – and gathered the ark and bear and took them over to Mother behind the counter, who was thumbing through Sally's receipt pad. She was wearing latex gloves, which she'd taken to keeping on her – coat pockets in fall and winter, slacks pockets in summer.

Great, I thought. *I'm the only Borne leaving fingerprints at the crime scene.*

'Look what I found,' I said, placing the items in front of her like purchases. 'Be-Be's ark, and possibly that bear stolen from Dolly's home a while back.'

Mother put the pad down. 'Ah . . . good work, dear. That box she carried in has half a dozen valuable toys that she helped herself to after impulsively killing Dolly.'

'Impulsively? Not premeditated?'

'Not premeditation, no. That was an explosion of sudden rage at Dolly. Sally killed her longtime rival toy collector after discovering what Dolly had done with those crates of arks, which to her was a crime far worse than murder.' Mother indicated the ark and the bear. 'In any case, we have the evidence needed to establish Sally as a thief. She was undoubtedly the prowler at your friend Tina's house.'

'Enough to label her Dolly's murderer?'

The puppets dangling above seemed to lean forward, eavesdropping.

Mother said, 'Forensics will confirm as much when they compare the ashes of the fire with those under Sally's fingernails.'

A siren growing nearer made the arrival of the sheriff imminent.

I shuddered. 'I don't want to be here for this.'

Mother smiled sympathetically, rested a hand on my shoulder. 'Why don't you wait in the car, dear? Or take a walk? It's cooled off and made this an even more lovely day. I can handle Sheriff Chen.'

Only Mother could think that a day with a murder and suicide in it could be lovely. But that was her way of dealing with unpleasantness – she worried only about the things she could do something about. That and pondering why waitresses insisted on saying, 'No problem,' as if asking for a coffee refill was a problem.

I went outside and sat in the car with the windows rolled down.

And tried to tell myself that I hadn't been responsible for Sally taking her own life. Tried to convince myself that Sally was a horrible person, a thief, a murderer, and wasn't worth crying over.

Then why was I?

The following Monday morning, Police Chief Tony Cassato and Sheriff Charles Chen wanted to see us at nine o'clock at the police station, where, no doubt, the city's top cop and the county's ranking law-enforcement officer would grill us about our actions.

In Serenity, the wheels of justice turned in the center of the downtown, where a combination police and fire department station sat next to the county jail, with the county courthouse across the way. A perp could be booked at the police station, walked across the street for his or her arraignment, then escorted back across the same street to the county jail to await trial. Doesn't get more efficient than that. I should know, as Mother and I had made that walk of shame several times before, as punishment for 'bending' the law while solving a murder.

Shame in my case, that is – Mother doesn't seem to know what that is.

I pulled the SUV into the side lot of the station, in a slot designated as VISITOR. Mother, turning toward me in her seat, said, 'Let *me* do the talking.'

'What if I'm asked a direct question?'

'I'll give you a sign if you're to be forthcoming.'

'. . . Oh-kay . . . What's the sign?'

'I'll scratch my nose.' She demonstrated.

'What if your nose itches and you just *happen* to scratch it?'

'I'll scratch it and say, "Darn this itchy nose."'

'Is *that* a sign?'

'It's a sign that my nose itches.'

'OK. What if I'm to be evasive?'

'I'll adjust my glasses.' She put a finger to the eyeglasses bridge, pushing them up.

'And if you don't want me to answer at all?'

'I'll yawn.'

'What if you just *happen* to yawn?'

'Good point. I might just happen to yawn, as those two men do tend to go on. In which case, say, "Mother, am I boring you?" Isn't that clever?'

'Not particularly, but OK.'

'So. Have you got all that?'

'Sure.'

Do *you*?

After exiting the car, we walked through the front plaza with its metal benches, ornamental trees, and row of large cement planters with flowers – all very attractive, but in fact designed as barricades should some drunken and/or disenchanted citizen decide to ram his vehicle into the building.

We entered the modern one-floor red-brick structure through a glass door, passed through metal detectors, then another glass door, and into a small, rather depressing waiting room with beige walls and flooring. A half-dozen uncomfortable plastic chairs were lined up against one wall as if facing a firing squad, the only decorative touch a large banana tree plant, its limbs twisted toward sunlight streaming in a single window.

Straight ahead waited a Plexiglass panel behind which a female clerk – as nondescript as the room – sat in profile at her computer screen. This used to be the domain of uniformed dispatchers until they got themselves dispatched to a new communications center in the basement after the police, sheriff, and fire departments consolidated into one state-of-the-art control center for efficiency's sake.

Mother used to regularly chat up these various dispatchers while in the waiting area, discovering and then exploiting their personal weaknesses to access confidential police information. But now that conduit had closed, with Mother herself to blame, having campaigned for sheriff promising implementation of a new communications center. She came through on her promise, thinking she'd be sheriff for a long time, privy to even more intel in those improved circumstances.

Not how it worked out.

While I remained near the door, she strode up to the clerk, who swiveled toward her. 'Vivian and Brandy Borne to see Chief Cassato,' Mother announced through a small circle of perforated Plexiglass. 'We're expected.'

The woman replied brusquely, 'I'll let him know,' and immediately returned to her work.

I heard Mother grunt. She was aware, as was I, of a sign posted on the other side of the Plexiglass saying DIVULGING CONFIDENTIAL POLICE INFORMATION TO VIVIAN BORNE WILL RESULT IN IMMEDIATE DISMISSAL. Word was the police union had adopted this policy too.

Mother and I took our usual chairs on either side of the banana tree plant. From our bags, she got out her cuticle scissors, and I some bottled tap water, and we set to work on the plant, her trimming the dead leaves – still we had no bananas, we had no bananas today – me giving the tree some much-needed water.

The poor thing would have died without us, and the number of times we got summoned to the station made us the ideal caretakers.

I whispered across the plant. 'Remind me – if I'm to be forthcoming, you'll adjust your glasses.'

'No!' Mother said. 'I'll scratch my nose.'

'And if I'm to be evasive, you'll yawn?'

'No! I'll adjust my glasses.'

'And if I'm not to answer, you'll sneeze?' I asked.

'No! I'll yawn.'

'Got it. Forthcoming, nose; evasive, glasses; not answer, yawn.'

The steel-plated door leading to the inner sanctum opened, and Chief Cassato – in his standard plainclothes office attire – filled the space. He gestured with two curled fingers for us to follow him, his face as stony as a statue's.

For newbies who have never met Tony, I'll provide a little

back story. Others may skip to the paragraph beginning, 'Mother and I trailed . . .'

Tony Cassato arrived in Serenity to fill the department's just-vacated chief-of-police position about five years ago. We had thought it was because he'd had his fill of being a big city cop out east, and the less stressful, smalltime position was appealing. Tony had a different reason for maintaining a low profile, however – he'd testified against the New Jersey mob, who'd put a contract out on him (*Antiques Knock-off*).

Not that it was love at first sight with Tony and me – far from it; his irritation with Mother, over continually sticking her snoot in police business, came seriously between us. But when my life – and that of the unborn Be-Be I was carrying – were put in danger, he and I called a truce. And, thanks to Mother, who got the New Jersey Godfather to call off the hit (*Antiques Con*), Tony was no longer in danger, and the relationship between us could progress, with various steps forward and the occasional one backward.

Mother and I trailed Tony down a long beige-tiled corridor whose tedium was broken by walls lined with group photos of policemen of bygone days. Mother paused to straighten them as she went.

One picture in particular always gave her trouble. As soon as she'd right it, it would go wrong. This time, Mother was ready – she stopped, dug into her purse, brought out a stick of gum, unwrapped it, gave the Wrigley's a few chews, then stuck the wad beneath the frame, and pressed it to the wall.

Tony, picking up on the slowdown, looked back and, I swear, the big lug uttered a Charlie Brown sigh before pressing on.

I figured we were headed for Tony's office at the end of the corridor, but instead he stopped in front of the conference room and gestured for us to enter. We did, taking seats opposite each other – to facilitate Mother's signals – at an oval table that could accommodate eight.

Sheriff Chen was already there, standing sternly at the wall-mounted whiteboard. In his thirties, he was the first-generation American son of Chinese parents who had come to Serenity on a sister-city tour and decided to stay.

Tony closed the door – the tiny click (*klik?*) might have been a pistol cocking.

'I don't suppose there's any chance of coffee?' Mother asked genially.

'Not a bean,' the chief said, setting the tone for the inquiry.

'Pity,' Mother said. 'My memory is so much clearer with a good ol' cup of joe.'

Now she had set her own tone.

Tony's jaw clenched. But he capitulated, going over to a small coffee station, pouring some coffee in a Styrofoam cup, then setting it in front of Mother. The liquid sloshed but didn't quite spill over. Like Tony's temper.

When she opened her mouth, he raised a warning finger. 'Ask for sugar or creamer at your own risk.'

'I was merely going to say "thank you." I happen to *prefer* my coffee black.'

Not hardly. Cream, or milk if you must, and three packets of fake sugar.

The chief, having moved to the head of the table, standing next to Chen, said, 'Before I turn the interview over to the sheriff, whose jurisdiction covers both the murder of Dolly Gambol and suicide of Sally Wilson, I have a few questions for you about something that took place on *my* patch.'

Rut-roh.

'Proceed,' Mother said with a regal wave of a hand.

'Do you know anything about a break-in at the morgue yesterday morning?' His eyes went to me. 'Brandy?'

I looked across the table at Mother.

She scratched her nose, which meant I was to be forthcoming.

'I, uh, do know something about that,' I replied.

'My nose itches!' Mother said.

Tony goggled at her. 'Well, thanks for sharing, Vivian.'

'Not at all,' she said, then frantically adjusted her glasses.

Tony prompted me. 'What exactly do you know about that break-in?'

'Nothing exactly,' I said.

Tony put both hands on the table, and leaned forward. 'Well, what *do* you know?'

Again I looked at Mother, and she yawned.

Tony straightened. 'I hope this isn't boring you, Vivian.'

'No, not in the least,' she said, then to me, 'Well, dear, why don't you answer the question?'

Was I mixed up on the signals, or was she? The pellet with the poison and the chalice at the Palace and the vessel with the pestle . . .

'Yes,' I admitted, 'we, uh, stopped by the morgue yesterday morning.'

Doesn't everyone on a nice Sunday morning?

'But,' Mother interjected, 'the door was *unlocked* . . . so you couldn't really call it breaking in. Entering, yes – breaking, no.'

'Is that right, Brandy?'

'Yes. The door was unlocked.'

Unlocked by Mother with her picks.

'And in my mind,' Mother said, 'that meant we were free to enter.'

This applied to any unlocked door – residential, business, or church. After she'd unlocked it.

'And why,' the chief asked, 'were you there?'

'I was hoping to find Tom Peak to see how he was progressing. I'm an interested party, after all.'

'Hoping to find Peak at work on a Sunday morning.'

Mother summoned an innocent expression. 'I'm afraid I don't really keep track of what hours city officials maintain. I know *you* seem to work seven days a week, twenty-four hours a day, Chief Cassato, dedicated public servant that you are.'

Clenching and unclenching a fist on the tabletop, Tony said, 'You two scared that cleaning woman half to death with your antics.'

If he thought that would shame Mother, he was wrong. Me, on the other hand . . .

But Mother merely shrugged. 'I *am* sorry she mistook us for corpses that had come alive. But we heard something suspicious in the hall and thought someone really *was* trying to break in. So we secreted ourselves.'

'Under a sheet? And in a cooling locker?'

Mother gave him a cheery little smile. 'One catches as one can, as they say. Is it our fault if that woman has an over-active imagination? So common today. You can blame that on everything from violent video games to horror movies. Everywhere you look these days, zombies, zombies, zombies.'

Tony winced. I could tell he had a headache. Poor baby. He gestured to Chen. 'All right. Now the sheriff has some questions. Do try to be more forthcoming.'

'Lock and load,' Mother said.

To my relief, Chen's inquiries were directed entirely to Mother.

Sheriff: *Why did you leave the scene of a crime?*

Mother: *I could see no purpose in remaining with Dolly, once I'd determined she was dead, and notified you of it. I am, as you know, a former sheriff and current deputy.*

Sheriff: *Honorary. Why did you go directly thereafter to call on Sally Wilson?*

Mother: *I determined that Sally had visited Dolly Gambol earlier. They were rival toy collectors. Sally discovered that Dolly had burned two crates of rare antique wooden arks, became enraged, and took the woman's life.*

Sheriff: *And how exactly did you determine that?*

Mother: *Actually, Brandy here gave me the clue, when she discovered a piece of one toy animal in some smoldering ashes at Dolly's. I recalled that Sally's fingers had the same ashy discoloration when we visited Sally's shop a few hours earlier.*

Sheriff: *So, you thought the Wilson woman might harm herself?*

Mother: *I hoped to take her into custody, as an ex officio sheriff. I did suspect she might do herself harm, and hoped to prevent that. Should she feel things were closing in on her. Which they were.*

Chen appeared to have run out of questions. Tony, his exasperation worn down, just seemed tired.

Mother sat up straighter; her expression of compliancy turned to one of defiance.

'Gentlemen,' she said, 'do you know what *I* think?'

'I'm sure you'll tell us,' Tony said.

'I think Brandy and I have been treated quite shabbily. Here we've solved a murder-suicide for you, including establishing the identity of the prowler at Tina and Kevin's, all within a few hours . . . and this is the thanks we get?'

A Sherman tank couldn't have been on more of a roll.

She went on: 'Do you know how much money we have saved both the police and sheriff's departments in man-hours? The debt owed us by the taxpayers of the city of Serenity and the county of Serenity?' Mother paused for a much-needed breath. 'I ask you, have we broken any laws that might justify two public-minded citizens, *moi* a former sheriff and an honorary deputy, being given the Third Degree like common criminals?'

Well, shall we count the ways? Posing as hospital employees, picking the lock on the morgue, taking an image of an unreleased medical examiner's report, fleeing the scene of a homicide, speeding, picking another lock, and rummaging through Sally's shop (also a crime scene) without permission . . .

I'm not sure if defacing police property with a wad of gum would also count, so let's just overlook that.

Tony was saying, 'We appreciate what you and Brandy have done.' He delivered that without a hint of sarcasm, which was a remarkable accomplishment for him. And us.

Mother clearly would have liked more thanks than that, but when it didn't come, she tilted her chin back and said rather grandly, 'Apology accepted.'

Tony asked, 'Anything else you'd like to share with Sheriff Chen and myself, Vivian?'

'Well . . . if the extensive post-mortem on Conrad Norris proves the man *had* been killed prior to any fall, Sally would be the likely suspect in his murder.' She paused. 'However, that is a moot point now, considering the woman is dead, and can no longer be prosecuted.'

'Then,' Tony ventured, 'you're finished with this investigation?'

Mother's eyebrows climbed above her glasses, which was a genuine feat. 'Well, I don't see any *point*, do you?'

'No, no I don't,' Tony replied quickly. And to Chen, 'Do you, Sheriff?'

'No,' he responded. He had a bit of a whipped puppy look. 'I think Vivian has tied everything together quite nicely.'

Mother patted the table with both palms. 'Then, gentlemen, I think we're done here.' She stood. 'Sheriff, why don't you walk me to the car – I'd like to find out how the department is getting along without me these days.'

She'd also like to find out later what Tony would say to me privately.

Mother and Chen were moving toward the door when Tony said, 'Oh, Vivian.' She turned as he approached her.

I don't know where it came from – like a mallet behind Bugs Bunny's back in a cartoon – but Tony handed her the phony head mirror that she had left behind in the morgue, 'Property of the Playhouse' visible on the inside of the band. He'd known darn well it was us before he even asked.

'This is yours, I believe,' he said.

Mother didn't flinch. 'Why, thank you, Chief Cassato. I'll be needing that prop for our upcoming production of my original *Doctor Who* musical. It's been established the doctor can be played by a woman now, you know.'

'I didn't know that,' Tony admitted.

She started out, but he spoke again: 'Just one more thing – the hospital would like Mr Von Holten's X-rays back – they're fussy about their records.'

Mother gave him a curt nod, then whirled and left, Chen following her through the doorway, pausing just long enough to flash Tony a grin. Small victories.

And now I was alone with the chief.

He sat on the edge of the table, looking down at me, making me feel small in the chair, the big bully.

And coward that I was, I was prepared to tell him anything he wanted to know.

But Tony simply asked, 'Do you think she meant it?'

I frowned. 'Meant what?'

'That she was done with any further investigating.'

'I don't see why not. It's all wrapped up.'

He sighed. 'Then for once we got off easy.'

I wasn't sure he was referring to himself and Chen, or him and me, or all three of us.

'Will there be any charges brought against Mother and me?' I asked.

'No.'

I nodded. 'Good.'

'Brandy,' he said, 'I've come to expect the way Vivian behaves, but that doesn't mean you have to go along with her. And look how dangerous Sally Wilson turned out to be. Do you want to wind up with scissors in your throat?'

'No,' I admitted. 'Who does? But who else besides me is going to keep an eye on Mother? And anyway . . . this time I had a vested interest.'

He nodded. 'Tina's prowler.'

'Yes.'

'I understand. I do.'

Officer Munson appeared in the doorway. 'Sorry to interrupt, Chief, but the mayor is in your office. Wants a word.'

'Be right there.'

I stood. 'We could continue this conversation over dinner tonight, if you like.'

'I'd like. But no continuation necessary. My cabin. Seven.'

'I'll bring dinner,' I offered.

'Fine. Oh, but, uh . . . fine, as long as it has nothing to do with rusks.'

Mother was waiting for me in the car. I slid in behind the wheel, then started the engine to get the air conditioner going. Unfortunately, even though the control was set on high, nothing much would come from the vents until the car itself deemed it cool enough. But even a blast of hot air is better than sitting in a sweltering vacuum.

Then a different kind of hot air from my right gave me second thoughts about that opinion.

'Well?' Mother asked.

'Well, what?'

'Don't be coy, dear. How much trouble are we in?'

'If you mean will there be any charges, the answer is no.'

Mother huffed, 'I should hope not. Once again we hand everything over to them on a silver platter.'

I backed the car out of the slot, then steered it into the street.

After a few blocks, Mother couldn't take the silence anymore. 'What *else* did you two talk about?'

'Tony and I are going to have dinner tonight.'

'That's it?'

'Pretty much.' I changed the subject. 'Why did you scratch your nose when you wanted me to be evasive?'

'Like I said. It itched.'

'And why did you yawn when you wanted me to be forthcoming?'

'I couldn't help it. I've been a busy bee, you know. A girl gets tired.'

She wasn't about to admit she'd gotten her own signals crossed.

I said, 'Let's just agree not to have signals anymore.'

She nodded. 'Perhaps that's for the best. When I wiggle my nose, it means "no signals."'

We were tooling out of downtown and along Mulberry Avenue, a main artery where the lawns of well-maintained homes were burnt to a crisp despite last night's rain, even those of owners who had been watering.

Soon I was pulling up to our standalone, over-stuffed garage.

Mother said, 'Why don't you go see Be-Be and take her *my* ark, since the one you gave her will be in the evidence locker for some time.'

'You'd let me? Mother, that's so *generous* of you . . .' Of course, I was going to take it anyway.

She twisted toward me. 'Dear, you cut me to the quick! Of *course* I would.'

'OK.' And I could fill Tina about her prowler.

I asked, 'What will you do for the rest of the day?'

She yawned. And it wasn't a signal. 'I'm going to take a nap. And then probably watch FlossTube.'

No, that's not a site about flossing your teeth, but a YouTube channel featuring cross-stitching. Mother had a dozen WIPs (works in progress) languishing in a drawer, all of which needed frogging (goofs requiring her to 'rip it, rip it, rip it').

She went on, 'Don't you worry about me.'

Why should I?

After all, Mother had said she was done investigating.

And, since I wanted to believe her, I did.

This, in a certain kind of book, is where the author says, *Little did she know . . .*

A Trash 'n' Treasures Tip

Buying old toys generally carries an emotional aspect not seen in other areas of collecting. People want what they used to have as a child, or wish they had gotten for Christmas. A thoughtless mother might throw out a collection of Barbie dolls after her daughter marries and moves to Chicago, even though I told her to keep them for me.

EIGHT
Ding-Dong Ditch

Vivian here, taking over the narrative duties. No need to thank me – even Brandy admits this part of the tale must be told by she who experienced the . . . experiences.

First, however, I must defend my long-ago actions regarding Brandy's admittedly true disclosure that once upon a time I threw out her collection of Barbie dolls. While I admit this may seem an unusual course of action for one renowned for her expertise, re: collectibles, my reasons were thus: the dolls had been moldering in a cardboard box in the attic for fifteen years; lacking their original packaging, they had been mistreated terribly by Brandy in her childhood, thus making them worthless, from fright-wig hair to occasional missing limbs; and in her teens I had repeatedly asked her to get rid of the fractured figurines. So, when she didn't, I did. Suffice to say, every parent with an adult offspring who thinks his/her/their former home should be maintained as a storage locker for childhood memories stands with me in this demonstration of tough love (and good housekeeping).

Secondly, I must address an unrelated matter, which is the relatively current change in the (American) pronunciation of two words: 'aunt' and 'tour.'

For decades, perhaps centuries, 'aunt' was pronounced like the bug, and 'tour' rhymed with 'sewer.' But now, people drop their chins and contort their mouths in some silly affectation, rhyming 'aunt' with 'flaunt,' and 'tour' with 'tore.' Haven't we better things to do than re-invent the longstanding pronunciations of perfectly serviceable words? Not to mention what such mangled mispronunciations can do to a person with loose dentures. (Not that I'm not speaking from experience.)

(*Note to Vivian from Olivia*: While I understand and even share your frustration – we have had similar phonological permutations in the UK – I do think it best to continue with the story at hand.)

(*Note to Olivia from Vivian*: Splendid idea, although it's come to my attention that you good people across the pond have been pronouncing 'aunt' and 'tour' incorrectly for some time. Not that I want to tour my UK cousins a new one! Or make a mountain out of an aunt hill. (And Brandy claims I have no sense of humor!)

And, yes, by all means, let's get back to our story.)

My intention had been to purposefully mislead both Tony and Brandy into thinking I was hanging up my figurative deerstalker cap and Inverness cape, in an effort to clear them from my investigative path. Granted, I did feel a teensy-weensy bit guilty sidelining the dear girl, as for once she was showing some enthusiasm about a murder inquiry.

While I had no doubt that Sally had killed Dolly – and felt confident forensics would back me up – clearly Sally could not have killed Conrad Norris. The receipt pad at her store, and time-stamped credit card receipts as well, revealed in her own handwriting that she had made sales throughout the afternoon of the auctioneer's death. This meant that Sally, after her failed bid on the arks, traveled from Serenity back to Amana, and opened up her shop.

Additionally, I was not convinced that Sally had taken her own life. Murder by hanging is one of the easier suicides to fabricate. This was more a gut feeling than anything else, substantiated only by the theory that Sally had almost certainly been the hidden presence during our meeting with Norris, learning of Brandy's intent to give Be-Be an ark. Therefore, who could say what else Sally might have heard or witnessed that night?

After returning home from the police station, I went straight up to bed to feign a nap, waiting for Brandy to exit with Sushi to take Be-Be my ark (a necessary sacrifice), after which I threw off the covers.

In the kitchen, for sustenance, I had some cold leftover meatballs eaten over the sink while drinking a cup of coffee. (The life of a crime solver is not pretty.)

Rusk Meat Balls

(*Note to Vivian from Olivia*: I believe we agreed to dispense with further rusk recipes.)

(*Note to Olivia from Vivian:* I signed off on no such agreement. With all due respect, what passes between you and my daughter binds only you and my daughter. Anyway, this is my *first* rusk recipe – while Brandy has offered several already. Plus, it was *moi* who make the mistake of ordering so many rusks. Hello? It's a short one.)

(*Note to Vivian from Olivia*: Very well, but this is the last of them.)

Rusk Meat Balls

½ lb. ground round steak
¼ lb. ground pork
¼ lb. ground veal
6 slices rusks (crushed)
3 tsp. salt
3 tsp. nutmeg
3 eggs (lightly beaten)
1/3 cup Half & Half

Mix together the meat, and add all the other ingredients, combining thoroughly. Shape into balls. In a frying pan, melt 1 tbl. of shortening and ½ stick of butter, then add meatballs browning them on all sides. Reduce heat to simmer, cover, and cook for half an hour.

Leaving behind my cell phone 'accidentally,' I went to my Vespa where I proceeded to examine the scooter stem to stern, in search of any tracking device Brandy might have been foolish enough to conceal. I doubted she had learned of the futility of such efforts, despite her last failed attempt to monitor my movements (I'd removed the bug from the undercarriage and transferred it to a random vehicle).

The first time I'd done this, Brandy had planted the device – a gizmo designed to help locate wandering Alzheimer's sufferers which, adding insult to injury, she'd ordered from my AARP magazine – inside the lining of my coat. That one I left beneath a seat on a bus to go round and round our fair city.

So imagine my surprise when – routinely checking the clothes I had on – I came upon a tracker she'd slipped into a pocket of the cardigan I was wearing, among some similarly sized wrapped cough drops. I'd been wearing this item of winter apparel around the house due to the overactive air conditioning and on unseasonably cool days like today.

How disappointing. Had I taught the child nothing? It was as if the girl wasn't even trying! Or did she really think I could be so easily fooled? Of course the effort had taken *some* slight sleight of hand. Credit her that much.

Tracker in palm, I returned inside.

Since I couldn't just set the gizmo anywhere – in case this one could monitor my movements from room to room – I attached the device to my Roomba, and sent the robot vacuum on its merry way to make Brandy think I was keeping busy downstairs.

Back outside, I fired up the Vespa and roared off (well, purred off – scooters aren't really much for roaring).

My first stop on my information-gathering expedition was downtown at the Riverside Café, where I knew the ROMEOs (Retired Old Men Eating Out) would be having their usual Monday lunch.

Now you might think that a group of noshing women would reign supreme in gathering and dispensing all the new and old dirt on everyone in town, but you'd be wrong. I had joined the JULIETs (Just Us Ladies In Eateries Talking) making the same assumption, and whoo boy, was *that* a waste of time! Who wants to hear about grandchildren, vacation condos, and plastic surgery? Additionally, they always gathered at the most expensive restaurants in town and then, after dining, nobody ever picked up my check. Strictly separate tabs! A bunch of cheapskates, if you ask me.

The ROMEOs, in comparison, preferred Blue Plate Specials, and places that offered coffee that kept flowing, and where the

waitresses tolerated a bit of harmless if politically incorrect flirting
(after all, the old goats had to keep up with their moniker). Sure,
you may hear a word or two about the family, or a great fishing
trip, but it was never hard to steer them in my conversational
direction. And I never picked up my own check!

Now, the only problem with the men, aside from the clacking
of their plates (and I'm not talking about dishes), was that the
group kept decreasing in number due to extended illnesses or
death, which meant that a lifetime of information went
with them. (The JULIETs somehow just seemed to go on
forever.)

I entered the river-themed diner with its wall-hung pictures of
boats and barges (to clarify, I didn't enter with the pictures – they
were already there) and spotted the gents at a round table for six
in back, then weaved my way through the noisy lunch crowd.
(Note to younger readers: best fire up Google now.)

Luckily there were but four ROMEOs today – they had finished
their Blue Plate Specials (I prefer not to watch them eat) and
were enjoying bottomless cups of joe all around.

'Hello, boys,' I said, in my usual Mae West-ian manner.
'Mind if I sit down and see you some time?'

Two of them (never mind who) gave me four wolf eyes, which
at my age I didn't mind; I'm in that category where being called
a 'girl' isn't offensive, it's a compliment. And as the queen of
double-entendres once said, 'It's better to be looked over, than
overlooked.'

Most females of the species were discouraged for even considering joining in with this group; but I had long since become an
exception, much as Shirley MacLaine and Angie Dickinson had
been welcomed by the Rat Pack.

Today's group included . . .

Harold, ex-army sergeant somewhat resembling the older Bob
Hope right down to the ski-ramp nose, jutting chin, and thinning
hair. Some years ago, after both our spouses had passed, he
proposed marriage. But since I had no desire to be assigned
unassisted KP duty and appointed permanent latrine queen, I
declined.

Randall, a corpulent former hog-farmer who might be best
described as a less sophisticated Sydney Greenstreet (much less).

In the past, I avoided sitting next to him, or even just downdraft. He'd been out of the pig game long enough to lose his porcine bouquet, but he too had expressed marital intentions. Though he now leased his land, he still lived in the farmhouse and one thing those of us who live in the Midwest know is that the aroma of fertilizer carries.

Vern, who reminded me of the suave if vaguely villainous star Zachary Scott, particularly if I wasn't wearing my glasses. The retired chiropractor also had invited me to the altar, but he had a habit of cracking his neck, which would have gotten on my nerves, although the free adjustments would have been nice.

. . . and last but not least, **Wendell**, a doppelganger for Leo Gorcey (for those of you all Googled out at this point, Gorcey was the malapropism-prone star of a comedy team called the Bowery Boys, inexplicably popular with aging Baby Boomers like the ROMEOs). The onetime riverboat captain had his career cut short when he fell asleep at the wheel and T-boned a barge.

Now, I hadn't stopped by one of these informal get-togethers for some time – their services not needed in my intel-gathering – so there was a bit of a verbal bidding war over where I should sit, which, I admit, pleased me. But the army sergeant had the loudest voice – more of a bark – so I gracefully settled into the empty chair next to him.

A young waitress with tattoos and a pierced nose regarded the table of oldsters with boredom-tinged contempt. They were friendly to her – she was cute underneath – and called her 'honey' and 'kiddo' as she refilled their coffee cups. Her rolling eyes came to rest on me, and I requested an iced tea without the ice, as I was (I informed her) in need of a root canal, and the eyes rolled again as she retreated.

By the by . . . do you know what the most painful part of a root canal is? The bill.

Vern cracked his neck and said, 'Viv, we hear you've got yourself in the thick of a mystery again.'

Four pairs of rheumy, bespectacled eyes looked intently at me and eight bony shoulders moved closer. They perceived these meetings as give-and-take. The trick was to give them something small but juicy enough to satisfy their appetite without providing much of a meal.

'Yes,' Wendell said, with an alertness that would have served him well before he crashed that riverboat, 'what can you tell us?'

'Spill,' ordered Harold in his military way.

Randall, diplomat of the group, said, 'That is, tell us what you can.' The portly ex-farmer was the nicest of these old boys, but life with him would be mostly in the kitchen.

My ice-less tea had materialized in front of me, and I took a slow sip.

'What have *you* heard?' I asked, setting the glass down. Jowls were dropping, so I added, 'I don't want to needlessly cover old ground.'

'They're saying,' Vern reported, 'that Dolly Gambol was murdered.' Why was I suddenly thinking of *Mildred Pierce*?

'By Sally Wilson,' added Randall.

'Over some Peter-Mar arks,' interjected Wendell.

'And then Sally hung herself,' concluded Harold.

By the way, do you notice how I avoided repeating 'said' there? That's the mark of a skilled writer!

They knew quite a bit more than you might expect from their age group. The grapevine in Serenity had always been faster than fiber, but all of these oldsters were on Facebook, Twitter, WeChat, Nextdoor and what have you, which further fueled the speed of information, if not a degree of accuracy. Gossip had gone high-tech, but if you ask me, mean-spirited posting will never replace a conspiratorial whisper.

I sat back. 'Well, gentlemen, you certainly have the basics of the situation in hand.' True. 'But I'm afraid there's not much I can add.' False.

'Come on now, Vivian,' Harold growled in his drill-sergeant way. 'No holding out.'

Another sip of tea. 'Very well. As long as you fellas will keep anything I share to yourselves.'

Assurances and nods all around. Somehow I managed not to laugh in their faces.

Then I told them how Sally had killed Dolly with a pair of scissors because the woman had burned all the arks she'd won at the auction. Social media would soon be burning too, with *that* information. And what harm would it do?

The men let those details settle even as their Blue Plate Specials were doing the same.

Now it was my turn – I had given them a morsel in hopes of a meal. I asked the group, 'How did Doug Holden and Conrad Norris get along?'

They traded looks, then Vern tilted his head (neck cracking, of course) and said, 'Strained.'

'How so?'

'Word has it Holden thought Norris was pilfering goods that were part of the warehouse property.'

Could that have been the topic of the heated conversation between the developer and auctioneer I'd seen but not heard?

I asked, 'How about Ryan Dayton and Conrad? What was their business relationship like?'

Wendell shrugged. 'Smooth sailing, I'd say.'

No one contradicted the former riverboat pilot's assertion.

I followed with, 'What about Johan Larsen and Conrad?'

Everyone shrugged but Randall, who raised a thick palm. 'I picked up some scuttlebutt from my tenant. He's a friend of Larsen's.'

'Yes?'

'Maybe Larsen thought that phone bidder at the auction mighta been phony – a shill. Meant to boost Johan's bid.'

Which could explain the less-than-friendly exchange I'd seen between the button-museum owner and auctioneer.

No need to bring up Otto Berger, whose wife's affair with Norris was already a solid motive for killing the auctioneer (yes, that's what I had on the auctioneer). But I did ask about Conrad's spouse, Elizabeth.

'Oh, *her*,' Harold said. 'Yeah, well, I think she'd come to terms with Conrad's philandering.'

Vern snorted, 'Don't ask me to believe *that*.'

That was just how I liked it! My goal was always to get the ROMEOs talking amongst themselves.

'Then why else,' Wendell asked, 'would she stay married to the guy?'

'*Money*, of course!' Randall countered. 'That crook Conrad

Norris has been skimming merchandise from his auctions for years, and must've built up quite the tidy sum. All Elizabeth had to do was wait till Conrad's liver gave out.'

Unless Elizabeth grew tired of waiting and – believing the affair between her husband and Otto's wife had become too serious – took matters into her own hands and got rid of him before he could divorce her.

I had one last question: 'Any idea who the silent bidder on the buttons was?'

Shrugs all around.

Vern cocked his head – crack (*krak?*). 'What are you after, Viv?'

'Yeah,' echoed Harold. 'Why all the questions about Norris?'

Randall asked, 'What gives?'

The griller had become the grilled. Very well – time to secure my standing with the ROMEOs and demonstrate that social media was nothing compared to the investigative abilities and deductive reasoning of Vivian Borne.

I rose and looked down upon them. 'It is my belief that Conrad Norris was pushed down that elevator shaft *after* he was murdered.'

I left the slack-jawed gents to spread that rumor as they chose – fingertips, whispers, or a combination thereof.

Outside, I hopped on the Vespa and zipped the two blocks to the warehouse, where on the first floor I found Doug Holden in his usual colored T-shirt and frayed jeans, barking orders at several workmen in coveralls.

As I approached, the burly, sandy-haired developer snapped, 'Are you finally here for those lousy coolie hats?'

Correcting his insensitive language would be a waste of energy, so I merely answered, 'No. But I will be soon.'

'You better be, or out in the trash they go.' His eyes narrowed. 'If that's not why you're here, what do you want?'

'I was thinking,' I said pleasantly, 'about buying one of your condos.'

He already had a frown going and now it deepened. 'No, you weren't.'

I shrugged. 'Fine. Then I wasn't.'

'Well, what *is* it then? You can see I'm busy.'

His workers were.

But if he could be blunt, so could I. 'Did you kill Conrad Norris because he was stealing your property?'

Holden couldn't have looked more stunned if I'd thrown a pie in his face. Coconut cream is my favorite, but only if it's fresh. But I wouldn't have wasted one on this slice of unpleasantness.

Taking my elbow, the startled developer walked me out of his crew's ear-shot.

'Who says I killed him?' the developer asked, voice lowered. 'Who says *anyone* killed him?'

'I do. And the medical examiner will soon be conducting a more extensive autopsy that will bear me out.'

'That's a bunch of crap,' Holden said, only 'crap' was not the word he used. 'Norris fell down the elevator shaft because he was drunk on his behind.' And 'behind' was not the word he used, either.

'You had words with him before the auction, hot and heavy,' I said. 'I witnessed the confrontation. And I happen to know he was pilfering.'

'Yeah? And how do you know that, lady?'

'Well, if pilfering wasn't the issue, what was?'

Holden shrugged with his face. 'I told Norris I didn't like the way he did business. That I'd have no further use for his services.'

'Because of the pilfering.'

'No! Because he was falling down drunk! Even before the auction started, he was reeking of it. And *you* saw his performance – losing track of the bidding count, stumbling around, sweating, nipping at a flask. He was an embarrassment!'

I raised an eyebrow, Spock-like (science officer, not baby doctor).

Holden jerked a thumb at his chest. 'You think I care about a measly couple hundred dollars' worth of merchandise? You have any *idea* how much I'm worth?'

As it happened I did – over fifty million dollars, if my contact at the First National Bank of Serenity could be believed. And she could.

He was saying, 'Besides which, I was looking at another

property the afternoon Mr Falling Down Drunk fell down that shaft and died.'

I would leave it to Chief Cassato to check that out (I couldn't do *all* the work).

Holden went on, 'But if you think Norris was murdered, and want a good suspect, try Otto Berger. Everybody knows Norris was having an affair with his wife.'

Well, not everybody. Not Brandy. So my blackmailing Conrad – that is, the quid pro quo arrangement I'd made – hadn't really motivated him to do that wee-hours deal for the arks and the rest. He just wanted to pocket my money! Some people.

The developer was saying, 'Now, if you'll excuse me, lady, I've got work to do.' He turned to walk away, but over his shoulder said, 'Oh, and even if you *could* afford one of my condos, I'd give one away before selling to you.'

Well, at least *that* was an honest reaction . . . where it applied to the condo, anyway. I wasn't sure about any of the rest of it.

Leaving my ride at the curb, I backtracked a block to the button museum, which had once been the town's only locally owned department store. When business waned in the 1970s, thanks to the new mall, the owners had packed off to Florida while the getting was good, retiring before bankruptcy became the only option.

Even after all these years, not much had been done to the inside of the building – making me at once happy and a little sad. I'd bought Brandy her prom dress here, and my own long before that (never mind *how* long). Johan Larsen had retained the original wood flooring, tin ceiling, and mid-century light fixtures. Even the original wooden-slatted escalator in the center of the first floor could still take visitors (albeit jerkily) up to the second, where awaited an impressive photo gallery of Serenity's many former button factories, depicting workers (all women) at their stations, employing various equipment.

Salvaged real machinery was showcased on the first floor, along with a gift shop area with memorabilia for sale – books, jewelry made from pearl buttons, coffee cups, and the like. Also on display were several of the barrels Larsen had gotten, as yet unopened.

The museum owner materialized from behind a large hydraulic

button-cutting machine; he wore a pale blue button-down short-sleeve shirt with a navy bow tie and slacks. Other than a young couple heading up the noisy escalator, he and I were alone.

'Mrs Borne,' the blond, blue-eyed man said, pleasant but wary. 'Was there something you wanted to know?'

It didn't sound like he meant buttons. Why did everyone assume I wanted information from them? Was I in danger of being typecast?

I said, 'Oh, I just happened to be walking by, and it occurred to me I hadn't visited your lovely museum in some while.'

'Well . . . uh, welcome back. Let me know if—'

'What are you going to do with all your barrels?' That was just an opening gambit, because personally, I didn't give a hoot. He could roll out his barrels and have a barrel of fun, for all I cared.

'I'm not sure yet,' he said with a smile that appeared disingenuous. 'But I seem to have been shorted a barrel, according to the original count – you wouldn't happen to know anything about that, would you, Vivian?'

He was fishing, but I wasn't biting.

'Is that what you argued with Conrad about, after the auction?' I asked.

'I wouldn't say it was an argument, more like a discussion.'

I asked bluntly, 'Did you kill him?'

His expression, like his reply, was infuriatingly calm. 'Don't be ridiculous. My understanding is that his death was accidental.'

'There was nothing accidental about Conrad Norris's trip down that elevator shaft. Not that he would have felt it, as he was already quite dead.'

This flustered Larsen not a bit. 'If that's the case, I'm not surprised someone killed him. He was an unpleasant, unscrupulous man. But you'll need a better suspect than me, Mrs Borne. I do not go around killing people over a barrel of buttons.'

'I *saw* the confrontation.'

He shrugged, but his eyes had tightened – finally a reaction. 'I just wanted that crook to know that *I* knew he'd shorted me.'

A nice admission, but a flimsy motive.

I asked, 'Do you know who the phone caller was who was bidding against you?'

'No idea in the world.'

Maybe Larsen thought, as the ROMEOs had suggested, Conrad used a shill – enlisting a ringer on the phone (see what I did there?) – to drive the button bidding up, adding to the auctioneer's percentage of profits, and costing the museum owner a lot more money.

Now *that* was a murder motive. A better one, anyway.

I asked, 'What time did you pick the barrels up Saturday afternoon?'

'I didn't,' Larsen said. 'I paid a moving company to bring them here.'

'So you weren't at the warehouse any time after the auction on Saturday?'

'No. Mrs Borne, I've been patient with you. I've answered your questions as if you had a right to ask them, which you really don't. Now, if you're looking for someone who wanted to kill Conrad Norris, I would suggest Otto Berger. He had words with the auctioneer just before I did.' The museum owner paused. 'Or, you can find out who tried to break in *here* Saturday night. The police don't seem to be interested.'

'Break in?' My ears had perked up, much as do Sushi's when I open a bag of potato chips. 'When was this?'

'Around midnight. My security cam in the alley picked it up.'

'Did you report it to the police?'

He waved that off. 'I didn't bother. Something spooked whoever it was.'

'Was your would-be intruder male or female?'

He shook his head, already losing interest in this topic. 'Couldn't tell. The person wore a hoodie and ski-mask.'

'Could he or she have been after money?'

His chuckle was wry. 'I can think of better targets than a museum that relies on grants and donations.'

Otto Berger's retro-themed restaurant – At the Hop – was on the outskirts of town, near the fading mall and other fast-food chains. He had bought an old diner and refurbished it with all the '50s trappings: red vinyl booths, vintage Wurlitzer jukebox, long counter with round swiveling bar stools, and walls covered with authentic advertisements of the era, along with auto-graphed framed photos of celebrities of that period. The pièce de résistance was the front half of a 1957 pink Cadillac convertible protruding from one wall, the back half outside, as if the car had driven into the building and Otto decided to keep it that way.

Lunch hour and evenings, this joint was always hopping (how's that for a humorous touch?). Even now it was fairly busy, high-school and college-age kids spending precious time from their waning summer vacations to bask in nostalgia for an era they had not experienced at all. With 'Rock Around the Clock' blaring from the jukebox, someone vacated a stool at the counter, and I snagged it.

Half a dozen waitresses wore the same green vintage-style uniform: green dress with puffed sleeves and white trim piping, plastic imitation black patent-leather belt, and white hospital-style shoes (no Nikes here). The waitresses had '50s monikers, like Laverne and Shirley, Betty and Veronica, Lucy and Ethel. These, too, were mostly high-school and college students.

But a forty-ish gum-chewing woman behind the counter with hair ratted into an over-blown beehive (name tag: BETTY) asked, 'What'll you have, hon?'

'The High School Special,' I replied, after my eyes took a quick trip around the menu – vanilla ice-cream topped with chocolate sauce sprinkled with malt powder.

Betty guffawed. 'You may be special, but I got a hunch you been outa high school a while now.' She studied me. 'Hope you ain't diabetic, hon.'

This was part of the floor show. People came here – one of Serenity's top tourist draws – not only for the good food, but a good-natured ribbing.

'Merely on the cusp, dear,' I said.

She cracked her gum. 'Kinda like bein' a little bit pregnant, ain't it?'

'Then make it a *small* "High School Special,"' I said.

Betty's attention went to a thin older man seated next to me, who had pushed his half-eaten plastic plate aside, signaling he was done. I had to admit, cobalt blue Fiestaware would have classed up the dishware.

'Darlin',' she said, slapping his ticket down in front of him, 'if you don't finish those vegetables you won't grow up to be big and strong. Why do you think we add them to the dinners? Because they *taste* good?'

He smiled, picked up the ticket, tossed down a buck, and slid off the stool.

'Gee, thanks, Mr Rockefeller,' Betty said to his back, tucking the bill away in her neckline.

To me, she said, 'All right, I'll get ya that High School Special, but don't blame me if you go into insulin shock.'

'What's the ETA of that sundae?' I asked.

She turned toward the food window, where meals were lined up beneath warming lights. 'Twenty minutes.'

'Where's Otto?'

Betty jerked a thumb over her shoulder. 'Office.'

'What kind of mood is he in?'

The waitress dropped her act. Sotto voce, she said, 'Not so good lately.'

'Since when?' I asked.

She leaned forward. 'Since his wife left for the west coast last week for some time with her sister.'

'Better make that sundae to go.'

Back in character, Betty said loudly, 'Fine by me, sweetie. Rather you enjoy your seizure somewheres else.'

Otto's office was rather cramped – small desk, single file cabinet, one guest chair, the decor departing entirely from the *Happy Days* theme.

The pudgy middle-aged restauranteur was busy trying to make a dent in the paperwork scattered across his desk, and I had to fake-cough to get his attention.

'Vivian Borne,' he said flatly. 'I've been expecting you.'

So, had Doug Holden or Johan Larsen tipped him off that I'd be coming around? Or had my reputation preceded me?

I took root in the lone chair.

He said, 'Let's save us both some time.'

'Why don't we?'

Otto leaned forward, elbows on the desk. 'I did not kill Conrad Norris – if he really was pushed down that elevator shaft and didn't just take a tumble in one of his frequent drunken stupors. And, yes, I had words with him after the auction. I wanted to know if he was the one who had alerted the Homer Laughlin Company about the Fiestaware, which is why I lost that bid.'

'Is that what happened?' I asked innocently. 'And what did Conrad say?'

'He swore he hadn't.' Otto sighed, leaned back in his chair. 'And in the end, I was glad I didn't land the damn things. I've had to go to plastic plates after so much breakage over the years of Fire King Jadeite.' The restauranteur gestured. 'You know what happens when you drop one of those?'

I did indeed – a thousand little shards. Pretty little shards. But shards.

He was saying, 'Anyway, I left the auction and came here to work in the office. Any number of staff can verify that. I'd be glad to give you their names.'

'That won't be necessary,' I said gallantly. No sense making the man any more defensive than he already was. I could always check later with 'Betty.' She appeared reliable enough.

Meanwhile, Otto seemed to have lost his train of thought. But I needed to get him on a new track anyway and said, 'Now, if you'll forgive the indelicacy, I need to bring up the subject of your wife and Conrad.'

'So *that's* got around, has it?' He sat forward, neither visibly surprised nor annoyed. 'Brenda ended that a month ago. It was a way for her to . . . to get my attention.' He sighed. 'My fault. I was spending too much time here at the restaurant.'

'And now she's left you,' I said. I was extrapolating from the info waitress Betty had divulged.

His face reddened. 'That's a damn lie! Brenda went to California two weeks ago to be with her sister, who's recovering from surgery. Brenda'll be back in a few days.' He paused, then went on, 'Look, Mrs Borne . . . Vivian . . . that affair – if you can even call it that – has only brought the two of us closer together.'

'I'm so happy to hear that,' I said, doing my best to sound sincere. And, after all, I'm a trained thespian.

He smiled, but not in a friendly way. 'Now, I've been forthcoming with you, and it's your turn, Vivian, to answer a question. You wouldn't happen to know how the Homer Laughlin Company found out about the dishes?'

I jumped to my feet. 'Heavens! I forgot! I ordered a High School Special and it's probably melting right this second!'

And as I rushed out, Del Shannon's 'Runaway' encouraged me from the jukebox. Have you ever tried eating an ice cream sundae while steering a Vespa? Almost (but not quite) impossible.

Next up on my suspect list was

(*Note to Vivian from Olivia*: Since we do like to keep the chapter lengths relatively uniform, I suggest ending the chapter with 'Almost (not quite) impossible.'

(*Note to Olivia from Vivian*: With all due respect, that doesn't make for much of a cliffhanger – it certainly won't keep the reader reading into the night!)

(*Note to Vivian from Olivia*: With all due respect, Vivian, if you check your contract, you will note a clause limiting your per-chapter word count. I believe there had been problems with your previous publisher over excessive chapter length, disrupting the narrative flow. You may, however, continue on in the next chapter.)

(*Note to Olivia from Vivian*: Is Brandy subject to such a clause?)

(*Note to Vivian from Olivia*: You will have to take that up with your daughter.)

(*Note to Olivia from Vivian*: Three words – count on it.)

Vivian's Trash 'n' Treasures Tip

Vintage restaurant ware, also known as hotel china, remains very collectable. Airbrushed plates, saucers, and cups with Western, floral, or tropical settings and hotel logos are the most desirable. Of course, the holy grail would be china from the *Titanic*, as few pieces survived. I have a cup and saucer set from the Savoy in London, where Brandy and I had high tea a few months ago. Took some talking to get past Customs.

NINE

Huckle Buckle Beanstalk

Vivian, still at the wheel (metaphorically speaking – alas, my driver's license remains suspended). A brief summary: in the previous chapter, I interviewed three of five suspects for the murder of auctioneer Conrad Norris: downtown developer Doug Holden, button-museum owner/curator Johan Larsen, and retro restauranteur Otto Berger. The two yet to be interviewed were former warehouse owner Ryan Dayton and Conrad's widow, Elizabeth Norris.

I provide this scorecard by way of apology for the sudden and (in my view) unnecessarily weak conclusion of the previous chapter, a circumstance foisted upon me by the lingering injustice paid me by a previous editor, who felt I went on too long about things. And now a perfectly nice – and new! – editor is making assumptions based upon the opinions of someone who isn't even involved anymore. I mean!

One possible, perhaps even probable, result is that you have decided to set this book on your bedside stand and switched off the light; or perhaps wandered off into the kitchen to raid the refrigerator; or do some housework; or – heaven forbid! – select another novel to read, perhaps one in which all the chapter endings are nice and snappy.

(I will pause here to await a note from my new editor reprimanding me for what she may consider insolence. Hum something for a moment, if you would . . . I will choose 'Yankee Doodle Dandy' as it's in the public domain and requires no permissions or payments. *Dah da dah dah dah Dandy! Dah da dah dah dah do or die!*)

(Well, there being no reprimand . . . onward!)

(No offense meant to our brothers and sisters in the UK by humming this patriotic Revolutionary War ditty.)

Several blocks away from the center of downtown stood old

Firehouse Number One – a puzzling designation, as there never was a number two. The tan-brick two-story structure built at the turn of the last century had been saved from the wrecking ball by the Serenity Preservation Society (of which I was president at the time) and subsequently converted into four loft apartments by, yes, developer Doug Holden.

Virtually nothing had been done to the outside of the building other than tuck-pointing the brick and re-glazing the windows; in front, the three large garage-type wooden doors were also retained, the middle one modified into an entrance, the other two used by the loft-dwellers to park their cars where fire engines had once been at the ready. Perhaps a Dalmatian had once done dog duty here!

Only one vehicle was present at the moment, a late-model blue truck in which I'd seen Ryan Dayton tooling around town. The expensive pick-up, along with the upscale apartment, indicated the young man must have done well, selling Holden the warehouse property.

Consulting four mailboxes just inside the entrance informed me Ryan resided in apartment 2D. A central staircase took me to the upper floor (were one brave enough, exit was still possible via the brass pole left intact near the stairs), where I followed a hallway back to the rear of the building to the young man's apartment.

Behind the door I could hear two voices conversing, over salsa music.

(*Note to Olivia from Vivian*: Is using 'salsa' considered offensive? As a word, not a condiment.)

(*Note to Vivian from Olivia*: I will have to consult our editorial department. For now, just use 'music,' without differentiating what genre.)

(*Note to Olivia from Vivian*: But the genre of music one listens to is a window into their character – for instance, I prefer big band music, and dislike opera (both before my time, of course). Some rock 'n' roll I can tolerate while hard rock to me is like screeching cats, meaning no offense to the Stray Cats. Hola, Olivia? Are you still there? Should I hum again?)

(Apparently not.)

With no doorbell to ring, I knocked. Voices within ceased, then the music.

Most visitors will stand back from a peephole, gazing downward or to one side while the resident checks them out. But I believe in being up-close and personal, backing away just a touch and staring directly at the aperture, wearing a big smile, choosing to disregard the way the fish-eye lens might distort my face. (I just love those picture books of dogs with their huge eyes and noses, don't you?)

Footsteps approached as I continued to smile and stare; the footsteps came to an abrupt stop and someone said, '*Jeez!*' Then that someone revealed himself to be Ryan Dayton himself, his handsome, chiseled features taking on a peculiarly taken-aback aspect. The dark-haired man in his late twenties wore a black T-shirt and black jeans, feet bare, his only embellishment a gold chain around his neck, tucked down into his T-shirt.

'Vivian,' he said, returning my smile, if not as wide, 'how nice to see you.'

Well, wasn't that a civilized, even friendly greeting, for once.

'So sorry to arrive unannounced,' I replied. 'But if you can spare a few moments, I wonder if we might have a little chat.'

'Of course,' he said, then stepped aside, revealing who he'd been talking to. 'Vivian, this is my girlfriend, Maya Lopez. Maya, this is Vivian Borne.'

What a lovely creature she was! Tall with long jet-black hair, large dark eyes, straight well-carved nose, full red-rouged lips, and curvaceous figure. Perhaps in her mid-twenties, she was attractively attired in a colorful tunic top and black leggings.

'How delightful to meet you,' I said. 'Have you ever trod the boards, my dear?'

As director of the community Playhouse I am always on the lookout for fresh talent.

But Maya looked confused.

'Been on the *stage*, dear,' I explained. 'You have a natural beauty, perfect for theater or screen.'

Her giggle was adorable. 'Oh, no. I'd be too scared getting in front of people.'

'Well, you needn't be,' I said. 'We could work on that, so do think about it.' Even as a mere walk-on, she could definitely wake up men in the audience dragged to culture by their wives.

I followed my host further into the apartment, his girlfriend excusing herself, perhaps sensing the need to lend us privacy. She headed off to a bedroom, glimpsed as she went in a door off the big main room, open concept with a living-room area, dining room, and kitchen.

The walls were raw exposed brick, the ceiling revealing the original rafters, yet everything else was starkly modern. A graceful arched transom window allotted the only view of the outside, onto a backyard garden bursting with late summer flowers.

Ryan led me to a brown leather sofa, where we sat.

Refreshingly, he did not demand to know what I wanted or why was I here, instead waiting for me to talk.

'I suppose,' I said, 'you've heard about the deaths of Dolly Gambol and Sally Wilson.'

He nodded, sighing. 'Unbelievable. Terrible. I had no idea those women bore such animosity toward each other. And over some toy arks! It's sick. Absurd.'

'It is, particularly considered in the context of the rumor that Conrad Norris's death was no accident.' Which I'd circulated, of course.

The young man shook his head, frowning. 'I hadn't heard that . . . but I wouldn't be surprised.'

'Oh?'

A shrug. 'Norris certainly made his share of enemies over the years. It's long been said he'd would help himself to stock before his auctions.'

'If so, how did he stay in business?'

Another shrug. 'Perhaps because he never took more than just a taste. He was a good auctioneer, before his drinking got out of hand. Even then, he was able to draw large crowds. And he had a knack for putting listings together that attracted buyers. I think folks who hired him just, you know . . . looked the other way.' Ryan paused. 'But lately he'd been slipping. Other auctioneers, young ones, are on the scene now, and of course Conrad had made a fool out of himself, lately.'

'Letting his drinking get out of hand, you mean?'

'That, and . . .' His mouth twitched. 'Why speak ill of the dead?'

'You mean, why speak of him running around with Otto's wife, Brenda?'

His sigh was almost a surrender. 'Her and others.'

'Perhaps some jealous man or woman decided not to be so forgiving, regarding Conrad's foibles.'

For the first time, Ryan's eyes met mine; they were blue (his, I mean) (mine are too) (and beautiful) (his) (and maybe mine, but modesty forbids). 'Vivian, are you *sure* Norris was murdered?'

'An autopsy is scheduled, possibly being performed right now. This I believe will establish cause of death as a blow by a blunt object. Only then was he shoved down that shaft.'

The young man exhaled. 'Conrad was no saint, but who had reason to do *that*?'

'That's what I'm trying to determine,' I said. 'You had a conversation with Conrad just before the auction. Would you mind sharing the nature of that?'

Ryan frowned. 'I'd forgotten all about it. It wasn't anything pertinent in this context. I mean, wasn't even a conversation, really . . . more like a few words we exchanged.'

'And those words were . . .?'

'I told Conrad it was a relief to finally be free of the building, and its contents, and all the responsibilities that came with it. Wished him luck on the auction.'

This was the exchange the nature of which I'd not been able to deduce, as Ryan's back had been to me, blocking the auction-eer's face.

I asked, 'Just before you and Norris spoke, he and Holden had a conversation – did you notice that? Perhaps you overheard something.'

'Now that you mention it . . . yes, I saw them talking. But I have no idea what that was about – didn't hear a word of it – but Conrad did seem irritated about something. I guess that's why I went out of my way to say something positive to him. But that's just how . . . nothing.'

'What?'

He shifted on the couch. 'It's just that Holden can get pretty rough in his business dealings.'

Even though that was no surprise, I asked, 'How so?'

'He was always after Uncle Lyle to buy the warehouse, really hounded him about it . . . yet he was unwilling to pay what my uncle felt was a fair price. Holden was damn near harassing him.

Then, when I inherited the property, Holden started in on me. I guess that's why I held onto the building so long. I just didn't like his tactics.' He paused. 'But, ultimately, the warehouse started to cost me more than rent could bring in, unless I was prepared to do major rehab . . . and I couldn't afford that. Holden can be a jerk, but frankly, I'd rather see the old place used for a purpose than fall into ruin. Condos? Why not?'

I asked, 'Do you think Holden might have had something to do with your uncle's disappearance?'

Ryan looked startled. 'Good Lord, no! At least, I can't imagine he did. Honestly, Vivian, that never occurred to me, and doesn't really ring true now. Holden's a nasty businessman, but a murderer? No.'

Time to switch gears. 'Ryan, I understand that you were raised by your uncle.'

'Yes. My parents died in a car accident when I was five. As my only close relative, Uncle Lyle took care of me.'

'Adopted you?'

'No. It just wasn't necessary. He had no children, my parents were gone. It was a father and son relationship just the same.'

That seemed to be all he wanted to say on the subject. I moved on: 'When did you leave the auction on Saturday?'

'Pretty much right after.'

'Did you return to the warehouse that afternoon?'

He adjusted the gold chain around his neck. 'I had no reason to.'

'During the auction you were standing near Holden.'

'I was. We weren't there *with* each other or anything. Just . . . the former and current owners of the property standing together.'

He seemed to finally be sensing this chat was an interrogation.

I asked, 'Did Holden leave your side at any time?'

Just a shade irritated now, Ryan asked, 'Can you be more specific about when?'

'Just before the auctioning of the buttons.'

'I think he did . . . yes, I'm positive, because I remember turning to him to say Johan Larsen had a lock on the barrels, but Holden had disappeared.'

'There was a call-in bidder during that sale . . . do you know who that might have been?'

He shook his head. 'I don't know and really wasn't interested at the time. Or *now*, frankly. That auction didn't impact me whatsoever.'

Despite his growing irritation, I pressed on. 'Elizabeth Norris was standing near you, as well – while she was on the phone with the call-in bidder. Did you happen to hear her call the bidder by name?'

His manner was chilly now. 'I really wasn't paying much attention to her, Vivian.' He paused, adding, 'I guess I was just thinking Larsen was going to have to shell out more money than he expected, because of that bidder.'

'Could the phoner have been a plant? A shill, as it's called?'

He made a face. 'Vivian, I just wasn't that interested. Conrad Norris certainly would've been capable of something like that. So I suppose it did cross my mind.'

Mine, too.

'Well, I think that's all,' I said.

The couch was rather low-slung and I had some difficulty getting to my feet. Annoyed with me or not, Ryan rather gallantly helped me and escorted me to the door. Of course perhaps I'd overstayed my welcome enough to inspire such 'helpful' aid.

'Thank you for answering my questions,' I said, halfway through the portal.

'You're welcome, Vivian. Didn't mean to get testy.'

'Not at all. And please tell that stunning girlfriend of yours to come to the next audition at the Playhouse. I think she'd be a marvelous addition to our repertory company.'

Before dropping in on my last suspect, I paid a visit to George's Bakery on Main Street, where I picked up one of his specialties – puff pastry strudel with vegetables and cheese. With the box inside a plastic bag securely attached to my Vespa handlebar, I tooled toward West Hill and the oldest residential section of Serenity.

At the base of West Hill were homes of a modest size – including one housing our Trash 'n' Treasures shop – but as one ascended, the residences increased in grandeur, particularly those enjoying a panoramic view of the Mississippi. On the bluff an impressive array of mansions built in the 1800s by city founders

– lumbermen, bankers, and pearl-button makers – presented exquisite examples of Baroque, Queen Anne, Gothic Revival, and Greek Renaissance architecture, each determined to outshine the next, incorporating the finest materials from both home and abroad.

(*Note to Mother from Brandy*: I already covered the above in Chapter Three.)

(*Note to Brandy from Mother*: But not the architecture!)

I wasn't headed all the way to the top, however, stopping halfway, in front of a low-slung, sprawling structure with hipped roof, broad eaves, and long bands of windows providing indirect light. The house where Conrad Norris had lived with his wife Elizabeth displayed a quiet elegance in harmony with the woodland bluff, befitting its true Prairie style, form and function taking precedence over gloss and glitz.

Due to the steep angle of the street, I parked the Vespa between two cars, then removed the box of pastry – my excuse for dropping by – from its plastic bag.

Three wide cement steps took me to a short walk leading to three more steps, another short walk, repeat, rinse. The original owners had been mindful of a single high climb, thoughtfulness benefiting my double-replacements. The only porch was a concrete slab at a plain wooden door with a large brass knocker, of which I made use.

Front curtains moved, then a moment later the door was opened by Elizabeth Norris herself. Conrad's widow looked small in a simple black dress and sensible black flats, brown hair tinged with gray pulled back in a tight chignon.

Her face – somewhat plain but not unattractive – was devoid of makeup and, for that matter, expression.

I said, 'I thought perhaps you might be having company for the funeral, dear.' I held out the box, the pastry within visible through a cellophane window.

She took the offering. 'Thoughtful, Mrs Borne. My favorite.'

George at the bakery had said as much.

Elizabeth went on, 'But none of those people have arrived yet, so they won't be getting any.'

Since she and Conrad had no children, I assumed 'those people' must have been family members on her late husband's side. She did not appear to harbor warm feelings for them, whoever they were.

The woman made a little sideways gesture with her head. 'Come in.'

I did so, following her past a living room on the left, formal dining room on the right, both outfitted with antique Stickley furniture – beautifully austere, but I knew from experience that the chairs and couches were about as comfortable as a Puritan pew.

In the kitchen, where built-in Mission-style mahogany cabinets clashed with modern appliances and decor (perhaps the mistress of the house had tolerated her husband's severe taste only so far) – Elizabeth got us both mugs of coffee and we sat at a glass-topped table.

She opened the box, and tore off a piece of the puff pastry. She nodded for me to do the same, if I liked. I liked.

Yummm.

Plucking a paper napkin from a holder, I asked, 'When will the service be?'

'You tell me,' Elizabeth replied, mouth full. The words were harsh but the tone seemed barely concerned.

'Pardon . . .?'

'Whenever my husband's body is released, I'll deal with it.' She swallowed. 'I hear you think he was murdered.'

Social media or old-fashioned grapevine, word got around in Serenity. Those ROMEOs could be depended upon.

Elizabeth must have known that Conrad's body was being held for an autopsy due to the suspicious nature of his death. I told her that he had apparently been struck a blow, killing him, before he took that fall.

My hostess went on, between chews. 'Are you wondering if I killed my husband? Is that why you're here?'

'Did you?' I asked. My mouth was not full. I had lost my appetite.

Her laugh was a dry thing, like cracking cardboard. 'Why should I have bothered? There were plenty of others who might have been willing to. And somebody came through, it appears.'

A valid point.

'I know all about your strange hobby, Vivian,' she said, her voice cold but not icy. 'You fancy yourself a detective. No, that's unfair. You've actually solved some real-life mysteries – more than the local police, that's for sure.'

True. So true.

'Then perhaps you might indulge me,' I said, 'and answer a few questions.'

She tore off more pastry. 'Be my guest.'

'Were you aware of your husband's affair with Brenda Berger?'

'Yes.'

She didn't seem very concerned.

Then she went on: 'I know he had many affairs. We were business partners and we got along, but as his drinking worsened, I lost any interest in him in . . . in that way.'

And that seemed to be that.

I asked, 'What can you tell me about the call-in bidder for the button barrels at the auction Saturday?'

She frowned; this was a question she seemed not to have expected. 'Just that whoever it was wanted to stay anonymous.'

'Was the voice male or female?'

'It was mid-range and muffled, and could have been either.'

'Let's say, for the sake of argument, this was a man,' I said. 'Wouldn't he have to register like any phone bidder?'

'Not if he wanted his name withheld,' she said, then gestured with a hand whose fingers bore a few pastry crumbs. 'A while back Phillip Montgomery bought a valuable painting over the phone for his wife, and someone told her, spoiling the surprise. After that, Conrad changed his policy.'

Perhaps I should add Montgomery to the suspect list.

She was saying, 'From then on, anyone who requested to be anonymous, stayed anonymous, paying by cash or cashier's check, or through other parties.' She shrugged. 'Anyway, those requests are seldom, and there's never been any problem on those rare occasions. And who is to say the person bidding wasn't . . . well, doing someone else's bidding?'

'You have that cell number?'

Her shrug could not have conveyed less interest. 'I do. But chances are it was a burner phone.'

I did not disagree.

Elizabeth sighed. 'Anyway, what does it matter? Whoever it was didn't win the bid. More pastry?'

I declined, my appetite for anything but information still stunted. 'Did anything of interest happen after the auction?'

'How much after?'

'After you'd finished collecting the payments.'

She mulled that for a moment. 'Well, as usual, I put all the money and checks and charge-card slips into a bank bag. The main branch being closed, I used their overnight depository slot. Then I came here.'

'Did you return to the warehouse at any time in the afternoon?'

'I did not. My job was done. It was up to my husband to make sure everything got cleared from the building. In fact, I was having a nap when the police banged on my front door.' She paused. 'Vivian, I, uh . . . I heard you were the one who found Conrad.'

'My daughter and I, yes.'

'I'm . . . I'm rather relieved it wasn't me.' Her eyes welled with tears. Some feeling there, after all.

I handed her a fresh napkin. 'Do you have any plans, Elizabeth?' She'd used my first name and I took the liberty of using hers.

Dabbing at her eyes, Elizabeth said, 'I'll be selling the house. I have friends living in a retirement community in Florida who have been wanting me to join them. Now I have no reason not to.'

'You should get a tidy sum from this property,' I replied pleasantly, even though that was a murder motive. 'Especially in today's market.'

Housing was in short supply in Serenity, real estate listings often disappearing hours after going public.

I continued, 'Of course, the cost of living in Florida outstrips little old Serenity considerably. But then Conrad had such a successful business, I assume you'll be fine.'

A small smile pursed her lips. 'I know what you're getting at, Vivian. You want to know if *I* know about the side money my husband made on his auctions. Did he keep those funds separate, and secret, in a private account? Or was I his accomplice?'

'That hadn't occurred to me,' I lied. 'But now that you bring it up . . .'

'I knew all about it,' Elizabeth said. 'But unbeknownst to Conrad, I personally paid back anyone who came forward about his pilfering. He'd send them packing, very indignant . . . and then I would reimburse them with funds he was unaware I had.'

Dropping all pretense, I said, 'And where did those funds come from?'

'Well, from Conrad, of course. He just didn't know it – I did the books, you know. And he really was a poor businessman.'

Smart woman. Who'd had a drunken, terrible husband.

I asked, 'Did you make Doug Holden the same offer?'

'No. But if he were to come forward, I would.'

So the developer still had a motive.

She was saying, 'And you needn't worry about my finances, Vivian – I've salted away plenty for myself. My husband was very generous to me. He just didn't know it.'

'I like your candor, Elizabeth,' I said, 'and I like your style. And you have excellent taste in puff pastry.'

If not in men.

I rose, my knees, hips, and feet making a joint effort. 'I must be going.' I wanted to beat Brandy home.

At the front door my hostess turned to me. 'Thanks for the pastry, Vivian.'

'Thank *you* for the information.'

She paused, her expression reflective now. 'You know, I really thought Conrad *had* committed suicide. He was at a low ebb after Brenda Berger dumped him.'

'Perhaps he felt he really loved her,' I ventured.

'Oh, he loved them all.'

She closed the door.

The SUV was not in the driveway when I arrived home, which gave me time to find and remove the tracker from the little robot vacuum, stuck in a corner of the library.

While I was there, I pulled out the blackboard from behind the piano and erased the Prowler Suspect list Brandy had written, as that investigation had come to a close.

To the Killer Suspect list, I made a few revisions – eliminating

Dolly and Sally; the Unknown Warehouse Person (who had been Sally); but adding the mysterious button-barrel phone-in caller. Elizabeth had never been included, and I saw no reason to now; she had convinced me she had not done away with her husband.

The suspect list now appeared as such:

KILLER SUSPECTS

Name	Motivation	Opportunity: 2–4pm
Doug Holden	pilfered stock	?
Ryan Dayton	?	?
Otto Berger	wife's affair with Conrad	?
Johan Larsen	buttons	?
Button Phone-In	buttons	?

I needed to investigate the opportunity column. Holden, Dayton, Berger, and Larsen all claimed they were not at the warehouse during the afternoon hours when Conrad met his death; but a claim was not a fact. That meant contacting every auction winner who'd been on hand to collect their purchases, and find out when they had seen the auctioneer last. Or, if they had seen any of the suspects.

Then there were the women Conrad had dalliances with over the years, and the husbands of any married women that included, which would have required a much bigger blackboard.

A car door slammed outside, signaling the return of Brandy and Sushi. I busied myself in the library corner where the vacuum had been, pretending to rearrange books on a shelf.

'Did you have a nice time?' I hollered as Brandy came in the front door. She said nothing and approached, entering the library with a wary expression.

She eyed the bookcase, then me. 'Yes . . . and you?'

'Most relaxing. I should stay home more often. Housework allows one to think, to really go over things.'

'Yes, you *should* stay home more often,' she replied, in a way that made me wonder if I'd missed a second tracker.

Then she informed me she had a dinner date with Tony at his

cabin this evening, and, since she was going to pick up some food at Salvatore's – Serenity's most popular Italian restaurant – I would have to fend for myself this evening.

Which was fine with me, as 1) she wouldn't be sitting around here getting increasingly suspicious about what I might really have been up to today, and 2) I could try out a new casserole recipe I knew Brandy wouldn't like: rusks layered with chicken, ham, and mushrooms, covered with bearnaise sauce.

Sorry. Much as I'd like to share that recipe with you, no can do.

The following morning, Brandy, Sushi, and I piled into the SUV for what I hoped would be a lucrative Tuesday at the shop, our coffers getting low. While Brandy put our three flags out on the porch, I – under Sushi's watchful eye – started the cookies baking and got the coffee percolating in our vintage coffee maker.

I much prefer the sharp *pop pop* of a percolator to the dull *drip drip* of modern coffee makers. Plus it's entertaining to watch the hot dark liquid shoot up into the little glass dome. Don't you agree?

Kitchen duties done, I returned to the entryway where Brandy was putting the finishing touches on the Halloween display in the curio cabinet. Although it was late August, it's never too soon to put out spooky holiday items – always good sellers – and we still had another box to distribute throughout the shop. She was pulling things out onto the floor when our first customer of the day came in.

This was not one of our regulars, rather an attractive, fortyish, well-dressed woman who looked like she had money to spend. Perhaps she was one of the many out-of-town tourists who came to enjoy Serenity's antique shops, boutiques, and bistros, although most traveled in packs. Possibly her husband was in town on business. If I were the nosy type, I might have asked.

Brandy, quickly gathering strewn-about decorations, made her apologies for the mess.

'Oh, that's all right,' the woman said, adding, 'You know, Halloween is my *favorite* holiday!'

Which was good to hear; perhaps we could recoup some of

our investment, especially the vampire cookie jar for which Brandy had overpaid.

Brandy said, 'It's really starting to rival Christmas in popularity.'

'Candy and costumes,' our new patron said. 'What's not to love?' Her eyes traveled to the barrel of buttons. 'Oh! Look what you have! I had wanted to attend the auction, but couldn't. Although I understand one person got all the barrels of these precious things, which let me out, anyway.'

I asked, 'Are you new in town?'

She crossed to the barrel. 'Yes, my husband has just started a job here.' She bent at the waist and read the sign. 'Ten dollars a scoop? I'll take one scoop. I can make a collage of my cat – she's as white as these buttons!'

Not a cat person, personally, but I'm not one to judge. Anyway, ten dollars is ten dollars.

The woman picked up the scoop, dug deep into the barrel, then withdrew it.

And from within the heaping pile of the pearly buttons, came a bony pointing finger.

'Oh, how clever!' she exclaimed. 'You love Halloween, too! You've put plastic skeleton bones inside!'

While Brandy and I exchanged wide eyes and slack jaws, our new customer pulled the finger (never a good idea) and the skeletal digit came out with the rest of a bony hand attached.

She dropped the scoop, and screamed.

Now *that's* how to end a chapter!

Vivian's Trash 'n' Treasures Tip

Genuine Halloween collectibles (not reproductions) remain highly popular and a good investment, depending upon material, maker, and condition. Especially sought after are early illustrated post-cards, even when inscribed. For twenty-five cents, I bought a vintage card depicting a black cat wearing a witch's hat, an item that had been passed over by many a collector due to its poor condition. But its real value was the 1909 one-cent green stamp of Benjamin Franklin, worth one hundred and thirty dollars.

TEN
Tic Tac Toe

B randy here – two chapters in a row from Mother is quite enough, don't you think?

After the shock of a bony surprise in the barrel of buttons, the spooked patron abandoned the skeletal scoop and fled the shop, unlikely to become a regular customer. Or, for that matter, ever to think of Halloween as her favorite holiday again.

I admit to standing there, staring, startled, a wrist bone poking from the sea of buttons, the dropped button scoop's white finger pointing accusingly in my direction. Meanwhile, Mother was on her cell, coolly notifying the police department of what had been found, instructing the dispatcher not to bother sending para-medics, or the coroner – 'Just the forensics team, dear.'

'Brandy,' Mother said, 'take down the flags. I'll put the "Closed" sign in the window. We don't want any Trash 'n' Treasures *habitués* tromping on the evidence.'

I numbly followed her command. Then I got behind the counter, just to put something between me and that barrel. Mother was just standing there, hands on hips, near the thing, looking quite pleased.

'Surely, Brandy, you've intuited whose skeleton this is,' she said, eyes gleaming as if buried treasure had been uncovered.

Actually I did feel I knew who that disturbing digit belonged to, and agreed that the bony rest of what went with it was down in that barrel, drowning in buttons.

'Lyle Dayton,' I said, my voice hushed. 'The Liquidator. Ryan's uncle.'

'Explains where the man's been all these years,' she said, quite self-satisfied.

'But *not* how he got in there,' I said. 'Assuming the rest of him is in that barrel.'

And here I was, back in the thick of it, my respite from

Mother's sleuthing short-lived. Not that I ever believed she'd hung up her deerstalker. She hadn't fooled me into thinking she'd stayed home, not for a moment – I'd tucked a second tracker inside her scooter's headlight next to the bulb. The app on my cell had told me everywhere she'd gone while I went to Tina's.

(*Note to Brandy from Mother*: You've become quite the little sneak, haven't you? Still, I must applaud your resourcefulness.)

Also, the books on the shelf she purported to have rearranged still had dust on them, *and* the blackboard suspect list had been revised.

(*Note to Brandy from Mother*: Bravo!)

Mother said, 'You look a trifle pale, dear. Why don't you go pour yourself some coffee and let me handle the unpleasantness with the authorities.'

Though her concern should have made me suspicious, that sounded like a thoughtful suggestion at the time. I'd been through quite enough, after all, and didn't know how much more I could take. It had been one grisly discovery after another. First, Conrad Norris dead on top of an elevator, Dolly Gambol stabbed with scissors, Sally Wilson hanging from a beam, and now skeletal remains submerged in buttons. Prozac could only take the edge off of so much.

On wobbly legs I made it into the kitchen, poured myself some coffee, and sat at the table. My cell vibrated.

'Is this on the level?' asked Tony. 'A skeleton in a barrel?'

'Of buttons. Yes. And I wish it were otherwise.'

'I bet you do,' he said, and I could almost hear his eyes rolling.

He signed off quickly and I sighed at the phone.

Before long I heard the little bell over the front door jingle and it wasn't Christmas, not hardly. Rather the ding signaled the arrival of the forensics unit. Soon came the voices of two men and Mother, which I tuned out.

I figured Sushi would keep me company, especially since there was a possibility I might eat a cookie (though I had no intention of doing so). But she preferred to stay out there where the action was, possibly in anticipation of Tony's arrival. Soon she'd be dogging his heels, trying to catch a scent of his manly mutt Rocky.

When Tony's voice was added to the mix, I considered going out there, but somehow couldn't rouse myself. Twenty minutes, another cup of coffee and, yes, a cookie transpired while Tony spoke with Mother in the outer room. Finally I heard the forensics officers grunt as they hefted the barrel to carry it out the front door.

Mother's voice echoed shrilly: '*I'll be wanting each and every one of those buttons back!*'

Sigh.

Shortly after that, Tony came into the kitchen with Mother, where they joined me at the table, Sushi settling by the chief's feet.

Mother said, 'Dear, I think it best we come clean about how we acquired that barrel.'

'*You* did the acquiring,' I corrected.

'Well, you aided and abetted,' she said.

'Aided maybe. Abetted, no way.'

Tony, his eyes closed, raised a hand. 'Let's not lay blame. Just please explain.'

Mother said, 'You haven't read us our rights.'

His eyes opened. 'You have the right not to remain silent.'

Mother leaned back, clasped her hands primly beneath her chest, and said, 'Very well, *I* shall shoulder the blame.' To me, she said, 'Though you might at *least* have tried to stop me.'

I shook two fists in the air. 'You woke me up in the middle of the night! I had no *idea* what you were going to do!'

'Well, how was *I* to know a skeleton was in that barrel?'

The chief rubbed his forehead. 'Please . . . I'm not looking to lay blame on anybody. Please just get to it. The barrel.'

'Always eager to help our first responders,' Mother said, and recounted our wee-hours rendezvous with the auctioneer.

Tony asked, 'Did Norris *select* the barrel he gave you?'

Mother gave that some thought. 'Actually, Sushi did,' she replied. 'I took the one she'd been sniffing around.'

I said, 'She must have detected the . . . *ick* . . . human remains within.'

Tony sat back, arms folded. 'So Norris didn't steer you at all? He didn't appear to know the special contents of that particular barrel?'

'Or if he did,' Mother said, 'he took the opportunity to rid himself of the thing and get it out of the building.'

I said, 'It *was* the barrel nearest to us. Which would have been convenient.'

The chief said to Mother, 'I'm going to assume you've been out investigating.'

'Glad to be of help,' Mother said.

'Please don't. But, like Sushi, you do have occasion to sniff things out. Have you come up with a motive for Norris killing Lyle Dayton?'

'I have not,' she admitted. 'I've been focusing on rather more recent events. But that doesn't mean there isn't a motive dating back to when the Liquidator went missing. We'd have to determine what the relationship between Conrad and Lyle was back in the day.'

I made a face. 'Tony, do you mean Lyle Dayton has been in that . . . that *thing* . . . all this time?'

Tony seemed uneasy about answering. 'Brandy, obviously we haven't identified that, uh, skeleton as Lyle Dayton's.'

Mother supplied the rest of the answer. 'If Lyle Dayton had been prematurely interred in that Edgar Allan Poe-ish manner, the contents would be quite putrefied, the Liquidator liquified, the buttons caked in dried gore, and, oh, the *smell*—'

'OK, OK!' My palms were up in surrender. 'I get the picture.' The coffee in my stomach was close to going back out the way it came in.

'Vivian's colorful description aside,' Tony said to me, rather gently, 'it's clear those remains were put in that barrel recently.'

Roll out the barrel, we'll have a barrel of bones . . .

'I concur,' Mother said with a nod. 'After all, it takes a good eight years for a body to decompose in soil.' She raised a finger. 'And, as I noticed dried dirt on some of the bones, I would say poor Dayton – if our assumption about the victim's identity is correct – had been buried somewhere . . . since his "disappearance" . . . and then dug up.'

Stay down coffee, stay down . . . you too, cookie.

Tony gave Mother a frown. 'You *disturbed* those remains?'

She tossed a hand. 'I just dug around a little. I wanted to see if the whole skeleton was there. Second, I must point out that those buttons are my property.' She glanced at me with a tiny smile. 'Well, *our* property.'

The chief's frown deepened. 'Vivian, that barrel is evidence in what is very likely a murder!'

Mother responded childishly, 'Well, *I* didn't start it. That woman dug around in there first!'

Tony already had been told that we did not know who our hapless customer was, other than the wife of someone who'd recently taken a job in Serenity.

I asked, 'Could we move to a more pleasant topic?'

'Splendid idea, dear,' Mother said, then looked at Tony. 'What have you learned from Conrad's autopsy?'

That was a more pleasant topic?

'You know very well,' the chief said somewhat testily, 'those test results won't be available for several weeks.'

'Come, come, now,' Mother chided, 'I'm not asking about the BAC test – I *know* he'd been drinking. Surely you've learned *something* else.'

Tony's sigh started somewhere down in his Florsheim shoes. 'Norris died from head trauma. The fall was post-mortem.'

'Ahhh! My supposition was correct.' She leaned forward conspiratorially. 'In the spirit of cooperation, I will share something else with you.'

'In the spirit of law enforcement,' Tony said, 'I will remind you that obstruction of justice is a serious crime.'

That just made her chuckle. 'I've done nothing of the kind. But I may have given you the false impression I considered it a strong possibility that Sally killed Conrad. Actually, I found proof by way of her receipt book that she was in her shop all that afternoon.'

Which explained why she'd continued investigating.

Tony said, 'So you were withholding evidence. That's a crime, too.'

'I didn't withhold anything! I left that receipt book right where I found it. It's not my fault if you and the sheriff overlooked it.'

'We didn't overlook it,' Tony said. 'We have already ruled Sally out in the Norris murder.'

Mother was livid. '*Now* who's withholding evidence!'

Coolly, Tony said, 'Vivian, you need to let us do our job. If you know anything that might be helpful, you have a responsibility to share it. Otherwise . . . back off.'

He got up and stalked out through the shop. He was boiling – even Sushi didn't tag along. But I caught him at the door.

I clutched his arm and said, 'Tony, I'll do my best to keep her in check.'

'You need to,' he said. 'It's looking like we have two murders over a ten-year period, probably by the same hand. If Norris died because somehow the earlier murder was discovered, that indicates a killer in a panic. And who has been out there stirring up the waters? Vivian!'

'But the murders may not be related. It may be *two* killers.'

'Oh,' he said. 'And that's comforting how?'

And he was gone.

Shortly after Tony left, Mother found me turning the CLOSED sign to OPEN in the window.

'What on earth are you doing?' she asked.

'What does it look like?' I asked testily. 'Opening back up. Put the flags back out, would you?'

'Absolutely not,' she said and came over to turn the sign back to CLOSED. 'Dear, when word gets out about our barrel of bones, we'll be wading in gawkers and media.'

She was right about that.

'Besides,' Mother continued, 'I have somewhere to go.'

'Where?' I asked, alarmed. 'You heard Tony.'

She made a calm-down gesture. 'I would just like to confer with Tilda.'

'Whatever for?'

'Possibly she might be able to hypnotize me into revisiting the auction and remembering where people were standing, and other significant details I may have overlooked.'

'Oh. OK.'

That seemed harmless enough.

Matilda Tompkins – Serenity's resident New Age guru, who taught a range of classes out of her house – had from time to time used hypnosis to assist Mother in our investigations. This included regressing a witness to remember a detail, or to help Mother recall something she had seen unconsciously.

Sometimes when Mother was 'put under,' however, out popped a former life, and so far Tilda and I have met such former incarnations of Mother as Iras, handmaiden to Cleopatra, the Egyptian queen's asp-handler; Matoaka, the younger sister of Pocahontas, and true love (or so she claimed) of Captain John Smith; Myles Carter, personal attendant to King George III, who convinced the monarch that any talk of revolution by the colonists was empty 'poppycock'; and Madame Curie's cook, Helena Kowalski, who claimed *she* (not madame) had come up with the idea of radioactivity. Anyway, these characters, once revived, were often reluctant to leave, and it took both the guru and myself, working together, to send them back into the past.

For that reason, I thought it best to accompany Mother.

I gathered Sushi, set the shop's alarm system, and we proceeded out to the car. Mother was rather quiet on the ride, which should have triggered my own alarm system . . .

Tilda lived across from Serenity's cemetery in an old white two-story clapboard house of the type often called shabby-chic, thanks to its timeworn outdoor furniture and flowering greenery. Originally more shabby than chic, the house had seen enough repairs and remodeling to put the emphasis on latter, thanks to an ongoing interest in New Age and the occult, which had increased the guru's clientele.

As we pulled up to the curb, I commented, 'I'm surprised Tilda's willing to see you after what happened last time.'

So as not to have to issue a Spoiler Alert, I'll simply say Tilda's first session as a death doula, in which Mother played an integral part, was not a heavenly success (*Antiques Carry On*).

Mother said, 'On the contrary, after word of that, uh, embarrassing incident got around, Tilda had to add several more classes. Which just goes to show that there's no such thing as bad publicity.'

'That's ridiculous,' I said, turning off the engine. 'And in this case, ghoulish.'

'How short-sighted you can be, my dear,' she replied. 'Even something apparently unfortunate can prove fortunate. Those who come as cynical thrill-seekers may leave as the idealistically enlightened.'

'Just the other day,' I said, 'I saw someone in a T-shirt that said, "I Survived Tilda's Death Class." Which category does *that* fit in?'

Mother shrugged. 'Enlightened, obviously.'

'How do you figure that?'

'Tilda doesn't sell the T-shirts till *after* class.'

She led the way along the flower-lined, cracked sidewalk with me following, carrying Sushi, then up two creaky wooden steps to a wide slanting porch with wooden railings and latticework.

Tilda was waiting behind the screen door, which she opened for us with a lovely smile but wary eyes. She knew us well.

Forty-something, slender, with long golden-red hair, translucent skin, and a scattering of youthful freckles across the bridge of her nose, she wore Bohemian attire no matter the season – today, a white peasant blouse with flowing sleeves, colorful full patchwork skirt, and brown suede Birkenstock sandals.

We moved past Tilda's gracefully gesturing hand into a mystic shrine of soothing candles, healing crystals, and swirling mobiles of plants and stars, incense hanging in the air like a fragrant curtain. From somewhere drifted the tinkling sound of New Age music.

But enjoying the comforting ambiance was made difficult by her ever-growing horde of cats. Cats, cats, cats everywhere, on the floor, windowsills, couch, and chairs. Cats sitting on matts. Cats sitting on cats. Big cats, medium cats, small cats, too, brown fur, yellow fur, gray fur – AH-CHOO! (From the unpublished work by Dr Seuss, *Allergic to Cats I Am*.)

These were no ordinary felines, however: they were reincarnations, and not of other cats, either.

Spirits from the cemetery across the street who still had issues and hadn't 'moved on' often returned to earth in the form of a cat. Or so Tilda believed of the felines showing up on her doorstep, somewhat regularly after a burial.

I knew most of these felines by name, or that is, by the names they'd had in their human forms; I'd met many of them in real life (their previous real life). But it was getting harder and harder to keep track.

'Is that a new one?' I asked Tilda, pointing to a white Persian climbing a curtain.

'You have an excellent eye, Brandy,' the guru answered. 'That's

Franklin Ellis Upshaw.' She referred to each cat by its entire
name.

'Oh, dear!' Mother said. 'That's unfortunate.'

Tilda frowned (which she rarely did). 'Why do you say that,
Vivian?'

'I knew Franklin. And he was a dedicated dog person.'

'Ah,' Tilda said. 'That explains why he's been having a hard
time adjusting.' She paused. 'Also, he's a "she" now.'

Mother made a *tsk-tsk* sound. 'And here he'd been such a
confirmed, woman-hating bachelor. Perhaps he's doing penance.'

'Poor Franklin Ellis Upshaw,' I said, as the cat came back
down the curtain. 'He looks anxious to be moving on – even if
the direction is down.'

The two women looked at me. Was I mocking them? I'll never
tell.

Sushi squirmed, and I let her jump to the floor. She'd always
gotten along with Tilda's cats, and if any newbies gave her a bad
time, Eugene Lyle Wilkenson – a fat yellow tabby, a bank guard
in a former life – would be there to protect her.

Tilda was saying, 'I only have an hour before my Tantric Sex
class, so I'm afraid there's not time to explore any past lives
today, Vivian.'

Like me, the woman assumed she'd be hypnotizing Mother.
But you know what they say about the word 'assume.'

'Oh, I'm not here to be put under,' Mother replied. 'No, dear,
I want you to give me a psychic reading on an object.'

Tilda's eyes saucered. 'Having to do with a crime? Not a
murder?'

'Well, yes . . .'

Tilda's translucent face paled further, and when she replied
her tone was uncharacteristically sharp. 'I don't do that kind of
thing anymore, Vivian.'

Mother had told me that before I returned to town Tilda
occasionally had been called upon to help the police. Her
cryptic readings, which she declined to interpret, had led to
finding a lost child and, later, locating the body of a man
assumed (accurately) to have been drowned. But when she was
asked to help find a missing person by handling a scarf found
where the woman had last been seen, her reading – or writing,

because she used paper and pen – came out so cryptically, the police deemed it worthless. The woman later turned up alive in an amnesiac state, in a manner consistent with Tilda's reading, but not before police statements in the media had damaged the guru's reputation.

A reputation it had taken years to rebuild, Mother said.

'It will be for my eyes only,' Mother was saying. 'Not a soul will know about your reading except you, me, and Brandy.'

And the horde of reincarnated cats, who fortunately had not brought along the ability to speak in this life.

Tilda sighed. 'Very well.'

We followed her back to the kitchen, off of which was a small, dark, claustrophobic room.

The single window had been shuttered, the only source of light a table lamp with a revolving shade whose cutout stars sent its own galaxy swirling on the ceiling. In addition to the small table were a chair and red-velvet Victorian fainting couch, the latter taking up most of the space. Clients would recline on the couch to be hypnotized.

Tilda moved the chair to the table and sat. Mother, having thought ahead, produced a blank sheet of paper and, from her tote bag, a pen she handed to our mystic hostess.

'A few ground rules, first,' Tilda said. 'You must not pronounce this person's name or gender, and if the object you have brought is too *old*—'

'Define too old,' Mother cut in.

Tilda shrugged, her flowing sleeves shimmering. 'If the person has not had contact with the object for several years.'

By now I had deduced: (1) the reading was for some object connected to Lyle Dayton, meaning (2) Mother had brought along something of his, and (3) since he'd been dead for a lot more than several years, the item could hardly be of any use.

'No problem,' Mother said. 'What I have was definitely with this person this morning.'

Had Mother found something else in the barrel? A scrap of cloth, perhaps, or piece of jewelry?

Tilda held out a hand, and Mother placed a small white object in her palm.

I leaned in. 'What is *that*?'

'I don't know the precise term,' Mother said. 'Call it a toe bone.'

I jerked back. 'You mean, you . . . you snapped it *off*?'

'Just the little one,' she replied. 'I thought taking a finger might be missed.'

Tilda, seemingly nonplused, said, 'This will do.'

She adjusted herself in the chair and, with the toe bone clenched in her left hand, her right hand held pen to paper. The guru closed her eyes and began breathing in and out, slowly and deeply.

For a moment, nothing happened.

Then the pen began to move across the paper rapidly and with purpose, as if the implement had a life of its own. Then the pen dropped from Tilda's hand, as if it had suddenly become too hot to hold.

Her eyes flew open. 'That was . . . *potent*,' the guru said.

Mother and I moved in to peek over her shoulder and read what she had written, but Tilda quickly folded the paper several times.

'Don't look at this until you're home,' she instructed, handing the message to me, not Mother.

'We won't,' I promised.

'Now, please leave me,' Tilda said, looking completely spent, a hand to her head. 'I must have time to recover before my class. Tantric Sex can be quite demanding.'

On the ride home, an impatient Mother – Sushi in her lap – badgered me for the message, trying to get it from my hand grasping the wheel; but I managed to fend her off without hitting any parked cars. Soon, she and I were at the dining room table where I unfolded and smoothed out the paper.

We bent over, to see what Tilda had produced. Written in cursive was:

Princetonian thinks they're great but to hot

'What the heck does that mean?' I asked.

'It's cryptic, dear – like clues for a crossword puzzle.'

'Shouldn't "to" be "t" double "o"?'

'Perhaps it's a homophone, dear.'

'A what?'

'Never mind. Fetch your laptop.'

I went off, grumbling, 'Homophone, shmonophone. I *hate* crossword puzzles.'

When I returned with the computer, Mother had found a notebook and pen, and we sat next to each other in front of the screen.

'Let's deal with the first part of the clue,' she began. 'Start with famous people who attended Princeton.'

'I'll ask Google,' I said, and did. 'John F. Kennedy seems to top the list. And he thought movie stars were "great" . . . but some were "too hot" like Marilyn Monroe. Is that something?'

She put a finger to her lips. 'Hmmm . . . J.F.K. Are those the initials of anyone who may have been associated with Lyle Dayton? Someone included on our suspect list?'

Hereafter came a discussion of whether or not to use all the suspects from various lists, since any one of them might have had a history with Lyle. Mother concluded, 'The more the merrier . . . Who else famous attended Princeton?'

'Well, there's a ton of them,' I said, looking at the screen. 'Michelle Obama, F. Scott Fitzgerald, Jimmy Stewart, Jeff Bezos . . . even Brooke Shields. But those are only the *really* famous ones.'

For a more extensive list of notable alumni, I consulted Wikipedia. While I was doing that Mother had written down in alphabetical order:

    Otto Berger = OB
    Ryan Dayton = RD
    Dolly Gambol = DG
    Doug Holden = DH
    Johan Larsen = JL
    Conrad Norris = CN
    Elizabeth Norris = EN
    Sally Wilson = SW

A half hour later, we had matched only one suspect, Sally Wilson, with two prominent alumni: Steven Weinberg and Susan Woodward.

'Who are *they*?' Mother asked, clearly unhappy she'd heard of neither.

'Weinberg won a Nobel Prize in Physics,' I said, 'and

Woodward is a respected Political Science professor.'

'Nobodies! That gets us nowhere.' Then she added, 'This is going to take forever.'

(*Note to Vivian and Brandy from Olivia*: Would you like some assistance? Cryptic crosswords originated in the UK, and although the US seems to have its own set of rules, I might be able to sort it.)

(*Note to Olivia from Brandy*: Yes, please!)

(*Note to Vivian and Brandy from Olivia*: I believe 'Princetonian' is referring to the general rather than the specific. That is to say, anyone who had attended Princeton, whether they are famous or not. According to the university's website, their mascot is a tiger. Now, my little girl's favorite cereal is Frosted Flakes – 'Frosties,' we call them – and Tony the Tiger 'thinks they're great.' Finally, 'to hot,' is written correctly, being an anagram for 'tooth.' So there you have it. Tiger tooth.)

(*Note to Olivia from Brandy*: Thank you very much!)

(*Note to Olivia from Vivian*: Cheers.)

'You could have been nicer,' I told Mother. '"Cheers" isn't exactly "thank you," and you could at least have used an exclamation mark.'

'I could have figured it out,' she said sullenly.

'Really? Maybe so, but whatever "it" is, "it" doesn't make a heck of a lot of sense. What does a tiger tooth have to do with anything, anyway?'

No wonder the police had discarded that reading of Tilda's.

After a dinner of some left-over rusk concoction Mother had made yesterday – containing mushrooms, which she knows darn well I don't like, washed down with the lemonade we always kept on hand in the fridge – her attitude had improved.

We'd planned to watch a movie on TCM together, but by eight o'clock neither of us could keep our eyes open. So off to bed we went, Mother crawling under her covers wearing her clothes. I followed suit in my bedroom, equally spent. It *had* been a long, eventful day.

What I recall next was Sushi barking, sounding far away, yet right there licking my face, smelling like filet mignon . . . or maybe, in my stupor, that's what I *wished* we'd had for dinner.

Then Sushi started biting my hand with her sharp little teeth.

Why was she doing that? I tried to open my eyes, but couldn't, like when I was a child and my lashes got stuck together from sleep crust.

Plus, I couldn't seem to move.

Near the edge of the bed, I willed myself to roll off, thinking the thud onto the wood floor would jar me from a horrible nightmare that seemed all too real.

When I belly-flopped onto my stomach, my eyes popped open, taking in a dark shadow filling the open doorway. Hands with curling fingers extended from the apparition, and seemed to stretch as it moved slowly toward me, coming closer, closer, finally entering my mouth and nose, making me gasp for air.

I knew I couldn't reach a window, let alone have the strength to open it . . . but an air-conditioning floor vent was only a few feet away, and like a slug I inched my body along to reach the grille, pressing my face against it, breathing in sweet, cool air.

I woke up in a hospital bed.

Tony was sitting next to me, his face wan and grim.

'M-mother?' I managed.

'She's all right. In the next room.'

'And Sushi?'

'Her too. She's with Rocky at my cabin.'

At least someone was happy right now.

'What happened?' I asked.

'A fire in your kitchen.'

So one of those vintage electrical appliances had short-circuited, again. We really needed to upgrade . . .

'How did we get out?' I asked.

'Sushi woke a neighbor, who called the fire department.'

I never thought when we installed a doggie door it might save our lives.

'Help me sit up?' I asked.

He did, adjusting the angle of the bed.

Tony's demeanor seemed off. His relief was obvious, but something else was mixed in. Anger? Resentment?

'Let's have it,' I said.

His steel-gray eyes searched my face, as though he were wondering if I could handle it.

'The kitchen door had been jimmied,' he stated.

Absurdly, I was somewhat relieved by this news. It seemed better than thinking my fiancé was about to call off our engagement – not that I would blame him.

He went on: 'A sleeping aid showed up in both of your blood tests. Had you taken something last night?'

'No. But after dinner we were both very drowsy.'

'What did you eat?'

'Left-over casserole Mother made yesterday.'

'And to drink?'

'Lemonade from the fridge.'

Tony said, as if to himself, 'So it could have been either. Although the drug would have dissolved better in liquid.'

I sat up straight in the bed; as straight as I could, anyway. 'We were *drugged*?'

He nodded. 'Was there anything left of that dinner?'

'Just the lemonade. And since I didn't eat much of the casserole, I think you're right about the drink being doped.' I paused. 'Would the fire have destroyed the lemonade if it was in the fridge?'

'Possibly not. I'll get forensics over there as soon as it's safe.'

'Is the house . . .?'

'The kitchen's a total loss. Everything else is fine. Some smoke damage, but fine.'

We fell silent.

Then I said, 'Whoever did this took an awful chance with Sushi on the loose. Wait! She had dog food in her dish from this morning, which she never eats until after dinner, hoping for something better. But Mother had finished off the casserole, yet Sushi *still* didn't touch her food. And she's starving by then.'

'If the drug had been added to her bowl,' Tony said, 'she probably smelled it.'

Maybe, but Sushi had gone on hunger strikes before.

'Even so,' he went on, 'the arsonist might've figured the little dog wouldn't be able to rouse you or Vivian, anyway.'

Though Sushi sure did try, biting my hand. Bless her.

The chief was asking, 'Were you at your shop in the afternoon, after I left?'

'Only for a little while . . . but we closed up because Mother thought the media might come around asking about Mr Skull and Crossbones. So we went to visit Tilda Tompkins for a while.'

Thankfully, he didn't ask why.

'Then at some point,' Tony said, 'when you weren't home, someone came in through the kitchen, saw the lemonade in the fridge, added the medication to it – possibly the dog food, too – and booked it. And, after dark, he or she returned to set fire to the kitchen, assuming it would be mistaken for an electrical malfunction.'

Nice.

Tony went on, 'It'll take a while to establish the exact cause of the fire, but it's arson all right. In the meantime, this killer is still very much at large.'

I reached for his hand and squeezed it. He squeezed back.

Then he stood, looking down at me. 'Until you're released, I'll assign some protection in the hallway.'

'But *can* we go home?' I asked, clarifying, 'Is the house habitable?'

'Wouldn't you rather stay somewhere else?'

'No. I won't be chased out of my own house!'

'All right,' he sighed. 'I'll talk to the fire chief. If he thinks it's safe, and the smoke smell isn't too overwhelming, a contractor could seal off the kitchen.'

Tony leaned in and kissed me. Not on the forehead, either – full on the lips. Something he's rarely done while on duty.

After he'd gone, I checked my status. No catheter, just an IV.

I wanted – *needed* – to see Mother, and make sure she was all right.

I eased out of bed. With my legs a little shaky, I secured the back of my thin gown, got into my slippers, and, wheeling my pole along next to me like my best friend, made it slowly into the hallway.

I asked a passing nurse, 'Where's Vivian Borne?'

She nodded to the room on my left and continued on. The door was closed. With some difficulty I opened it, and entered.

'Mother?' I called out, my voice cracking. I was on the verge of tears.

But the bed was empty, IV dangling from its pole, hospital

gown discarded on the floor, the door on the little closet open where her clothes from last night should be hanging.

And weren't.

A Trash 'n' Treasures Tip

Valuable antiques and collectibles should be insured against fire. But Mother refuses to do so, believing that things such as her shoulder pad that Frank Sinatra had autographed could never be replaced. Even by a lot of money.

ELEVEN
Truth or Dare

Yes, my loyal followers, you are blessed with another chapter written by Vivian! How lucky can the readers of one book be?

After discharging myself from my room – I've become quite adept at removing an IV without leaving any telltale scarlet evidence – I did not exit the hospital. Rather I proceeded directly down to its most subterranean floor (basement sounds drab, don't you think?), where the morgue awaited. There I found Tom Peak at his little desk, writing up his latest autopsy report by hand.

To spare the sensibilities of delicate readers, and in consideration of those who may have consumed a recent meal, I will dispense with a description of the half-covered-for-decency late male on the stainless-steel table, including what was in the organ pans, and what had drained into troughs below. You're welcome.

Tom looked up, startled to see me (not an unusual reaction, I admit). 'You've been released already?'

'We detectives call it taking a powder.'

The pathologist stood as I approached. 'I heard what happened,' he said. 'And was relieved to hear everyone's all right. The last thing I need is more customers.'

He seemed sincere. If he wasn't, he might have just the acting chops needed for the lead in my *Dr Kildare* musical. Plus, think of the free, authentic props!

I gestured behind me. 'I hadn't heard that (*name withheld for privacy*) had passed away.'

'Late last night. Cirrhosis of the liver.'

I shook my head. 'When I think of all the times I told that man at Cinders bar to lay off the Wild Turkey . . . not that a more expensive brand of libation would have saved him from a pickled demise.'

For a moment Tom paused, eyebrows up, as if that simple statement required parsing. Then he said, 'I suppose this visit is about the skeletal remains found in that barrel of buttons.'

'A *full* skeleton, I'm going to guess.'

'Almost. All but the fifth phalanges of the right foot . . . the little toe.'

'Imagine that.'

'Would you like a look?'

'Very much!'

I followed him to a corner cordoned off by screen, which he rolled aside.

On a gurney, the bones had been carefully reassembled. It was as perfect a specimen as might be displayed on a stand in a doctor's office, but for a cracked cranium.

I asked, 'Have you made an identification?'

He nodded. 'We've confirmed that this is indeed Lyle Dayton. I received the man's last dental X-rays earlier this morning.'

'Have you been able to learn anything?' I asked. 'Not that there's much to base an autopsy on here.'

'Well . . . he'd been buried in dirt long enough to decompose, then dug up and put into the button barrel.'

Just as I'd thought.

I asked, 'Were you able to get a sample of the soil?'

He nodded. 'Enough to be sent off and analyzed.'

'Do we know what killed him?'

A blow to the skull, I thought.

'A blow to the skull,' he said.

Now the Sixty-Four Thousand Dollar question (in my day that was considerable moolah) (and a very popular television show) (rigged, unfortunately). 'Would you say Lyle Dayton's injury was similar to that of Conrad Norris's?'

'I would, Vivian.'

'Similar enough to have been caused by the same weapon?'

The doctor hesitated. 'That's not for me to say. That's a more appropriate question for a forensics specialist.'

'But,' I pressed, 'would you say it was *possible* both injuries *could* have been made by the same weapon?'

He frowned in thought. 'Off the record?'

'With me, Tom, it's always *way* off!'

That made him smile for some reason. Then he said, 'Yes, it's possible.'

I leaned in, eyes narrowed, and whispered, not that there was anybody in here to eavesdrop, 'And if you had to make an educated guess, what would that weapon be?'

'I don't make guesses, not even educated ones.'

'Call it way-way-way-off-the-record speculation. Just between you and me.'

'The problem is, Vivian, nothing ever seems to be way-way-off enough to *stay* just between you and anybody.'

'This time it will,' I promised. But the second and third phalanges of my right hand were crossed behind my back.

When he didn't budge, I worked up some tears.

'Tom! I was almost *killed*. And Brandy! How many more lives is this fiend going to take before he's stopped?'

The pathologist inhaled, held it as if for a CAT scan, then exhaled. 'All right. Just between us, if I had to guess, I would say the weapon was the underside of a shovel head.'

'Thank you!'

I was nearly out the door when he called to me, and I turned.

'Be careful, Vivian,' he said. 'I would hate to meet you in this room under less than ideal circumstances.'

'Tom,' I said, 'I've already tried out one of your lockers, and did not find the accommodations accommodating at all.'

With going home not an option – where either Tony or Brandy might show up to impede my efforts – I exited the hospital through the basement door, then stood in August sunshine to consider my options.

Since I didn't have my Vespa, I made my way to the side of the building where public transportation was available; the old reconverted-to-gas trolley car was due on the hour, its arrival imminent, judging by the little group waiting on a bench inside the covered Plexiglass booth.

The trolley was the brainchild of the Downtown Merchants Association to bring shoppers back to them after the mall went up on the outskirts of town. The free-to-all ride had a hitch, however, which was that the trolley always wound up downtown.

I had been banned from riding the trolley after the driver swerved off the road and hit a electrical pole, tipping it over onto a dry-cleaning establishment whose roof had burst into flames. That the blame for this freak accident landed at my feet was most unfair! All I had done, from my seat behind the man at the wheel, was – in a moment of euphoria (it *had* been lovely out, much like today) – suddenly burst into song. Specifically, and appropriately, that song was 'The Trolley Song,' as memorably performed by Judy Garland in the film *Meet Me In St Louis*. Apparently, my enthusiastic rendition of clanging and dinging and zinging was enough to startle said driver, who had quit after the 'incident,' unsuccessfully suing the Merchants Association over his nervous breakdown.

Anywho, the Association found a new, less easily rattled driver, Mary McBride, who'd stayed in the job longer than anyone – coincidentally, coming on about the time I began using my Vespa for most of my local transport.

The trolley arrived, and the door swished open, and I waited for the other passengers who were ahead of me to embark.

'Well, hello, Mary,' I said sweetly, climbing the few steps. I knew her only slightly, as I was not a terribly frequent user of the trolley, post-Vespa.

She was a bottle blonde somewhere in her forties, her undeniable attractiveness marred by an abundance of makeup that could smear in the heat of the non-air-conditioned trolley, despite the lowered windows.

Eyeing me warily, Mary asked bluntly, 'Aren't you banned from riding, Mrs Borne?'

I splayed a hand across my chest. 'Me? Heavens no! You must be thinking of my daughter Brandy. She's the one who dressed a chimpanzee up like Shirley Temple and brought it onboard to challenge the no-pet policy.'

Actually, it was yours truly who pulled that protest, the chimpanzee borrowed from a friend with a penchant for owning exotic pets. My friend had bought the monkey after her python escaped, causing a panic until the serpent was found wrapped around a flagpole outside City Hall. Unlike the snake, the chimp – named J. Fred Muggs after the long-ago mascot on the *Today Show* – had been content to stay close to his new home.

I headed toward the rear of the trolley, leaving Mary in a state of confusion, which was her own fault – if you can't deal with the public, why drive a trolley? Finding an empty seat on a nearly full bus, I settled in for the short trip.

I'd forgotten how much I'd enjoyed riding the trolley. Such fond memories! There was the time Billy Buckley, the town's little person, was seated in the back when the driver suddenly hit the brakes, and Billy (the following phrase best sung) flew through the air with the greatest of ease (end singing), landing quite unexpectedly in the lap of the recently widowed Stella Snodgrass. (Coincidentally, Billy came from a long line of acrobats who had traveled with the Barnum and Bailey Circus.) Well, after getting acquainted, so to speak, the widow and Billy started dating and were married a year later. Isn't that a lovely story?

Then there was the time two visiting and competing high-school girls soccer teams both boarded the bus, and the melee that followed led to . . . Oh, the details will have to wait! We've arrived downtown.

Everyone disembarked in front of the courthouse, a beautiful limestone Grecian structure reminiscent of a giant layered wedding cake, if it had had a man and woman perched on top (or man and man or woman and woman) and not a belfry with literal bats and a busted clock that hasn't worked since Harry Truman was president.

From there I hoofed it four blocks to ye olde fire station lofts, hoping to catch Ryan Dayton at home. Again, as luck would have it, his truck was inside, establishing his probable presence.

In the hallway, I encountered his girlfriend, Maya, who had just left his apartment.

We paused.

'Has Ryan heard about his uncle?' I asked the attractive young woman, her long dark hair shimmering beneath a ceiling light. She was wearing another colorful tunic with white leggings.

'Yes,' she said somberly, nodding.

'How is he taking the news?'

'Not well, I'm afraid. I'm off to get some groceries, and probably will stay over a few days. And keep an eye on him.'

Until now I hadn't been sure of their living arrangement.

'Good idea, dear. Men are such delicate creatures.'

She blinked at that, then nodded with a small smile, moved past me, and moments later I pressed Ryan's bell, respectfully keeping my distance from the spy-hole.

Ryan opened the door. He really *had* taken it hard! He looked simply terrible, face puffy and drawn, dark hair matted, and atypically sloppy in a well-worn gray sweatshirt and baggy fleece pants.

Without a word, he stepped aside, and I entered. He headed slowly for the couch and I followed.

When we were seated, I asked, 'When did you hear about your uncle?'

He was hunched forward, hands clasped between his legs. 'The coroner called a few hours ago.'

Hector Hornsby no doubt, not Tom Peak.

I said, 'I am very sorry for your loss.'

'Thank you. It's difficult to process. He's been missing for such a long time. Still . . .'

'It's always better to know.'

'I suppose . . . I heard you had a fire.'

'Oh? Has that got around already?'

He nodded. 'Someone posted it on Facebook.'

I shrugged. 'Well, it was a relatively minor conflagration. I'm fine, as you can see. Brandy and even our dog, Sushi, too. Nary a singe.'

'I'm relieved to hear it.' Ryan frowned. 'The coroner also said my uncle was found in . . . a barrel of buttons you had in your shop?'

'Yes. That's why I thought I owed you a personal visit. Otherwise I wouldn't intrude.' Wouldn't I?

The frown deepened. 'I don't understand. I thought Johan Larsen bought the entire lot of those barrels. So how did you end up with one?'

I wasn't anxious to get into that, so I just said, 'I managed to obtain one before the auction,' adding quickly, changing the subject, 'At least this brings you closure, regarding your uncle.'

Actually, I don't believe there's any such thing as closure. The past can come after you and slap you around any time it feels like it.

Ryan sat back, with a sigh. 'I always thought my uncle would eventually turn up. But not like *this*.'

Of course, who *would* have figured a missing relative might turn up a skeleton in a barrel of buttons?

'At the time Lyle disappeared,' I asked, 'did he have any enemies?'

His eyes tightened. 'I'd have to think about that. I was a few years out of high school when he disappeared, but I'd worked for him since I was fifteen.'

'You mentioned he was like a father to you.'

'He was. Of course, as I maybe mentioned, Doug Holden had been hounding my uncle about buying the building. This was after Holden had bought up the rest of the block, *except* for the warehouse. I think it really bugged the guy that he couldn't have it.'

'Did you ever see them arguing?'

'Oh, yeah! Plenty of times. Holden started out sweet enough, but it could get sour fast.'

'How contentious had it been?'

Ryan hesitated.

'Enough to come to blows?'

He raised a palm. 'Hey, I don't want get Holden into any trouble. It wasn't a one-sided thing. My uncle had a pretty bad temper himself, and didn't get along with plenty of people.'

'Including Johan Larsen?'

Again, hesitation.

Then: 'Larsen wanted the warehouse, too. For his museum. But he wound up having to buy the building it's in now, from Holden, for big money. I think Larsen held a major grudge against my uncle over that.'

'What about your uncle and Otto Berger? Any animosity there?'

Ryan shook his head. 'No, I don't recall him having any dealings with Uncle Lyle.'

I tried a long shot. 'How about Elizabeth Norris? Conrad's wife – now widow.'

And that hit home! He shifted on the couch. 'I'd . . . rather not go there.'

'Why?'

'I just . . . don't.'

'But you're going there right now, in your mind, aren't you? Best get it off your chest. I'm a good listener.'

Well, I am.

He took in a breath, let it out. 'All right. As I said, I'd started working for my uncle weekends, when I was in high school. This one Saturday, I was supposed to pick up some merchandise with his van – I'd just gotten my driver's license – but the seller wasn't home. Anyway, I went back to the warehouse to tell Uncle Lyle, and barged into his office, where . . . well . . . he and Mrs Norris were, uh . . . you get the picture.'

I certainly did. Norris wasn't the only one who strayed from his marriage vows. Elizabeth had found her way back on the suspect list.

Ryan said, 'If you don't mind, we need to put a halt to this. Before you came, I took a sleeping pill to try to just get away from all this, and it's kicking in.'

Until this moment, I had eliminated Ryan Dayton as the killer, but now I wasn't sure. Brandy and I had been drugged last night with sleeping pills! Still, who *didn't* have them in their bathroom cabinet?

'I'll see myself out,' I replied.

I had just closed the door behind me when it opened again.

'I just remembered something about Otto Berger,' Ryan said. Not asleep yet!

'Yes?'

'My uncle sold him an expensive, original Wurlitzer jukebox that didn't work, and then refused to refund Otto's money, or even pay for repairs. Is that helpful?'

I hadn't answered when the door closed.

From there, I power-walked – albeit on low voltage – to the warehouse, where I found the front door locked, with nary a sign of the new landlord nor any construction workers.

But Doug Holden had an office on a side street nearby, in a small building that used to be a barber shop, after local hair salons brought about the demise of all but a few survivors in the red-and-white-striped-pole trade.

I entered the former-shop/current-office, surprised by how

shabby the digs were, the old linoleum floor showing the mark-
ings of where barber chairs had been ripped out, sinks pulled
away from the walls, the ghosts of big mirrors. Was this a ploy
Holden devised to make people think he wasn't as rich as he
was cracked up to be? Or had the man seen no benefit in sinking
money into something he wasn't renting to someone else? Could
be both.

He was seated behind a cluttered desk, shouting at his cell; in
his usual colored T-shirt, he might have been one of his blue-
collar employees (not to imply the T-shirt had a collar, although
it was blue). The conversation ended, and he tossed the phone
onto a pile of papers in disgust.

'Contractors!' he barked. 'When they say one week, they mean
one month. I'm at their mercy like everybody else.'

'Problems at the warehouse?' I asked.

'What do you want?' he said by way of a non-answer.

I got to the point. 'I want to know about a fight you had with
Lyle Dayton that came to fisticuffs.'

Scowling, he studied me. 'I hear you found that louse stuffed
in a button barrel. Not a bad place for him. You accusing me of
putting him in there?'

'Not at all. But did you?'

He grunted what may have been a laugh. 'I didn't kill the bum
over that building, if that's what you think. I knew I'd eventually
land the thing, either from him or his nephew. So I went on to
other things.'

Which was certainly true – Pearl City Plaza had been born, a
tourist destination of bistros and boutiques and antique stores
that breathed life into a downtown that could use resuscitation.
(Thank you, Margaret Atwood's MasterClass in creative writing!)

Holden was saying, 'You won't live long enough to question
everybody who came to blows with that S.O.B.'

Was that a threat?

Something crossed his face, taking away the negativity. 'I hear
you had a fire at your place.'

'Yes. Destroyed the kitchen.'

'Everyone all right?'

'Tickety boo.'

'What does that mean?'

'It means we're fine. Thank you for asking.'

He nodded, then snorted, 'Good luck getting a contractor you can count on.'

I was heading for the door when Holden said to my back, 'Those coolie hats you haven't picked up yet? Linger at your own risk, lady, or their next stop is the alley Dumpster.'

That was Douglas Holden – a boon to the downtown and as charming as a bad cold.

I backtracked to Main Street.

Visitors at the museum were non-existent at the moment, and I located Johan Larsen in a rear storage room, where he was unpacking some Button Museum swag on a table, specifically T-shirts with the facility's name and button logo. Rather attractive, though I doubted the youth of today would be lining up for them.

His demeanor seemed disgruntled even before he noticed my presence.

'Vivian Borne,' Larsen said, as if through a bad taste in his mouth. 'So *you* had my missing barrel.'

'Yours?' I asked innocently.

He approached to face me. 'That's right. It *should* have been mine – it was included in the inventory number I'd seen several weeks before the auction.'

That was at odds with Conrad's claim that it had been an extra.

'I was unaware of that,' I replied, which was actually the truth. Then: 'Is that what you argued with Conrad about, after winning the bid?'

He didn't reply.

I continued, 'And is that why you were so vexed when you didn't get that barrel, because you knew what besides buttons was inside?'

'What are you inferring?'

'Nothing. I'm *implying* that you killed Lyle nine years ago when he wouldn't sell you his building for your museum, which led to you having to pay a much bigger price for this one. You buried him somewhere – the warehouse basement perhaps? And when the building finally sold to Doug Holden, you had to dig him up – how awful that must have been! Then you emptied a barrel, placed Lyle's sad remains within, and returned the buttons as packing material. After you won the bid on the barrels, what a shock it must have been to not find Lyle among them.'

'You're crazy,' he said.

I shrugged. 'That rather overstates it. I think "eccentric" might be more fair. I prefer, "One of a kind."'

'Are you finished with this nonsense?'

'Only at the halfway mark, I'm afraid. You see, you also killed Norris. He suspected what the contents of that missing barrel might be, implied by your desperation to lay hands on it. So you returned to the warehouse after the auction, waiting until no one was around, and hit him with the very shovel you employed to dig Lyle up. Then you threw the already late auctioneer down the elevator shaft.'

'I'm going to stick with "crazy,"' he said. 'Even if this were true, you haven't a shred of evidence. Get out before I call the police and inform them you're harassing me. Next, I'll be seeing about getting a restraining order against you.'

'It'll go easier on you if you turn yourself in,' I said. 'They say confession is good for the soul.'

'A defamation lawsuit would pay better,' Larsen said, and reached for his cell on the table.

As a trained actor, I recognized my cue to get out of there.

Without my Vespa to whiz me to At The Hop, I ducked into a doorway recess between buildings and called Otto Berger's personal cell number.

His gruff voice answered, the noise of the popular eatery in the background.

'What *now*, Vivian?'

'Lyle Dayton once sold you a dysfunctional jukebox, then refused to repay you.'

A long pause. 'He did and he was unpleasant about it, but it turned out the thing *wasn't* badly broken. A wire had come loose when I moved it. I was able to fix it myself.'

'Oh.'

Then he hung up on me! Can you imagine? No mention from him of having heard about the discovery of Lyle, or my kitchen fire.

I was feeling increasingly frustrated. Was I just spinning my wheels?

Never before had I felt so stymied. Never before had Vivian Borne questioned her native sleuthing abilities. Even the time I'd been chased by a killer through the county fairgrounds at night, and had to resort to setting the old wood stadium ablaze to attract attention, I had not lost my sleuthing mojo. (Happy ending: killer caught; new state-of-the-art stadium. Can't tell you which prior book without ruining it for you.)

Was it time I be put out to pasture? By the end of her stint playing Miss Marple, actress Margaret Rutherford seemed so pitifully befuddled. Was that me? A born detective becoming a Borne self-parody?

Say it ain't so, Viv!

I had one final shot at investigative redemption – Elizabeth Norris. When the woman didn't answer her door, I went around the house and found her in the backyard, on her knees, digging up irises.

A word about these plants. While they produce beautiful flowers in the spring (and fall, if double-bloomers), they're quite high maintenance, bulbs growing in tight clusters that must be divided every few years. And I am not in the habit of dividing *anything* – particularly the caramel pecan turtle cheesecake at the Cheesecake Factory.

With the assistance of her shovel, Elizabeth got to her feet; her face looked puffy – perhaps she'd been crying.

Gently I asked, 'You've heard about Lyle?'

She nodded.

'I understand you were . . . *close*, once.'

She got my meaning. 'Briefly.' Dropping the shovel, Elizabeth then gestured toward her back porch.

We sat on a step next to each other.

'Lyle and I had an affair ten years or so ago,' she said. 'I guess I'd had enough of my husband's running around, and wanted to strike back. I'd hoped it might help me regain some self-esteem, but all it did was leave me cold and empty. Anyway, I wound up breaking it off. When Lyle went missing, I thought it was because of me. That he'd picked up and left town to find a new life. That he couldn't bear seeing me, should we run into each other in this small town.' She laughed humorlessly. 'Now I know different. Which in a way, I suppose, is a relief. Small solace.'

'Could your husband have found out, and killed Lyle over it?'

Elizabeth's eyes widened. 'No! Not in a million years. No. I don't imagine Conrad would even have *cared*. He had his own flings, one after another. Besides, the "affair" lasted barely a week. I doubt he knew.'

It certainly hadn't got around town. Or I would have known.

'There's another possibility,' I said.

'What would that be?'

'That you killed Lyle.'

If I'd expected to get a rise out of her, I was mistaken. All she said was, 'Whatever for? Like I said, I ended the relationship. If you could call it that.'

'Perhaps he began harassing you. Or threatened to tell others?'

She shook her head. 'If you want to know who I think murdered Lyle, it's that nephew of his. Lyle was always on that poor boy's back. Humiliating him in front of others.'

Was this an attempt to throw suspicion onto Ryan because the young man had once caught the lovers together?

I said, 'I understood it was a father-and-son relationship between Ryan and Lyle.'

'Yes, an abusive father-and-son relationship.' Elizabeth stood abruptly. 'I'm done talking about this.'

She went inside, leaving me on the steps.

A trolley ride later I arrived back home, where a furious Brandy greeted me in the foyer, demanding, 'Where the devil have you been?'

'Not now,' I said, hobbling past her to the Queen Anne couch, where I kicked off my shoes. 'My hammer toes are killing me.'

The windows had been thrust wide to get rid of the acidic smell from the fire, the breeze doing a good job.

Brandy, to her credit, sensing my mood, backed off. She sat next to me and asked, 'What is it?'

I sighed. 'Have I . . . have I *lost* it, dear?'

She smirked. 'You never had it to begin with.'

'I'm not talking about my mental stability. I mean my powers of deduction. My prowess with detection.'

I told her where I'd been, whom I'd seen, and how little of substance I'd discerned.

'Speaking of Holden,' Brandy said, 'he sent some contractors around while you were gone – to cover the back roof with tarp, and seal off the kitchen.'

I hadn't noticed, as distracted as I was. Did the developer have some humanity, after all? Or was he trying to play me like a kazoo?

Brandy stood, helped me off the couch, and took me by the hand to the doorway of the kitchen, where a plastic curtain had been hung.

Parting the curtain, we entered the black, charred husk of what had been a shrine to the sometimes questionable culinary delights of the 1950s.

'I was thinking,' Brandy said, 'we could reboot this baby, gear it to the '70s. After all, the '70s are the new '50s.'

That applied to age, as well.

I felt a tingle of excitement. 'Avocado, gold, and brown appliances.'

'Fondue pot,' she said.

'Bun warmer.'

'Presto Hot Dogger!'

So what if the gizmo that electrocuted hot dogs had never gotten the Good Housekeeping Seal of Approval. And had burned down more kitchens than our prowler.

Suddenly, I felt better, my little gray cells receiving a jolt of electricity, too.

'I *know* how to catch that killer!' I announced.

Brandy frowned at my non sequitur. 'What? How?'

'Elementary, my dear Watson. We'll set a trap.'

'What will we use for bait?'

'What do we have handy? Me!'

Vivian's Trash 'n' Treasures Tip

Collecting memorabilia from the psychedelic '70s has given the fabulous '50s and swinging '60s a run for the nostalgia money.

Some hot items are Fisher Price toys, *Sports Illustrated* board games, Pyrex casserole dishes, Happy Meal toys, the original Sony Walkman, and Talking Busy Barbie. Was that among Brandy's dolls I threw out? I'll never tell.

TWELVE
What Time Is It, Mr Wolf?

The following morning in Tony's office at the police station, Mother and I sat facing the chief as he leaned forward on his elbows at his desk, hands folded, expression impossible to read as she pitched her plan.

I, course, had been fully briefed. And while the basic idea of the trap Mother proposed to set was not original – it had been seen in books and movies before (she credited Rex Stout as her primary inspiration) – her plan nonetheless displayed a unique vision and flair that was pure, unadulterated Vivian Borne. Even I had to admit it rivaled the Presto Hot Dogger.

Her 'sting' was based upon texting each of the five prime suspects – Doug Holden, Johan Larsen, Otto Berger, Elizabeth Norris, and Ryan Dayton – the same message from Vivian Borne:

I have proof that you killed Lyle Dayton and Conrad Norris. Meet me at the warehouse tonight at midnight. I will be alone. I know that you are not a bad person, and that in both instances you were put into an untenable situation.

I can help.

After reading a handwritten note of the proposed text, the chief sat back in his chair. 'Well, I have to hand it to you. That's might just be dumb enough to work.'

Mother beamed. 'Thank you!'

I said to her, 'Not really a compliment.'

Tony, nodding as his eyes again traveled over her draft, said, 'This sounds just wacky enough to make the guilty party believe you.'

Mother pressed her hands together and lowered her head, salaam style. 'Many thanks.'

'Again,' I said, '*not* a compliment.'

'Well, *whatever* it is,' she huffed, straightening, 'I'll take it.'

The chief sat forward, leaning on his left elbow, gesturing with the note in his right hand. 'All right, Vivian, here's what I want you to do. Go ahead and send the texts. Then, today, you and Brandy keep your regular store hours. After that, go home . . . have dinner, and relax, as best you can. Watch a little TV maybe, keeping tabs on incoming texts. And wait.' He paused. 'If you get a response from anyone, call me on my cell.'

We waited for more instructions. When none came, Mother asked, 'That's it?'

'Yes. Make it just another unremarkable day in the lives of Vivian and Brandy Borne.'

Was there such a thing?

I asked, 'What if the killer is watching us?'

'Officers will be tailing each suspect throughout the day and on till midnight,' he said. 'In plain clothes in unmarked cars.'

'Ah,' Mother said, liking the sound of that. 'So we'll know where the suspects are at all times.'

'*You* won't,' Tony said, eyes hard and dark and unblinking. '*I* will.'

Mother sat forward, her expression suddenly indignant. 'Hey! Just whose plan is this, anyway?'

'Mine, now,' he said.

That did not sit well with her, but I was still reeling somewhat from Tony going along with her latest nutty notion. She needed his approval and help to pull this thing off, but now he'd commandeered her scenario, which threatened to reduce her from star to supporting player.

I said, 'So what happens after a suspect gives himself or herself away? What happens at the midnight meeting?'

'I'll let you know in due time,' he said.

'What's wrong with *now*?' Mother protested.

Tony stood, gestured to the door dismissively. 'What's wrong with *now* is that I have a lot to organize.'

Neither of us budged.

'You're not using my mother as bait,' I said, 'unless you can guarantee her safety!'

Oddly, this did not seem in the least to trouble Vivian Borne, who asked excitedly, 'Will I be wearing a wire?'

He pointed to the door, as if we were two wayward children being cast out into the cold, cruel world. 'Go! You'll hear from me later.'

We went.

We returned home briefly to collect Sushi, then headed back downtown to open up the shop. To start that unremarkable day in the life of the Borne girls that Tony had spoken of.

But for me it was difficult to conduct business as 'usual.' The Halloween displays that seemed so innocuous before – invoking playful, fun, exciting childhood memories – now took on a sinister cast. Masks grinned manically, hunched-back cats poised to hiss threateningly, paper skeletons took on an altogether new dimension. At least no actual bony fingers were pointing accusingly at us out of a sea of pearl buttons.

And Mother? The grande dame of the Serenity Playhouse was in her element, lost in her greatest role – herself – hamming it up as she jabbered incessantly at the occasional bewildered customer, sharing the fascinating history of even the most insignificant item, dumbfounding regulars witnessing an over-the-top self-portrayal of the co-proprietor of an antiques shop on a just another day, with the reviews running from 'Huh?' to (whispered to me) 'Have they changed your mother's medication?'

She was flittering around dusting (which she never did at home) when I interrupted to say, 'You need to dial it down a notch.'

'Whatever do you *mean*, dear?'

'A kite just called and said you were flying higher than it was. Get a handle or when you take that meeting tonight you'll give yourself away.'

Her eyes flared behind the magnifying lenses. 'Who are *you* to suggest—'

'I'm your daughter and I don't want to see you hurt or even killed. Quit trying to be heard in the back row.'

Her brow creased in thought and a finger went to her chin. 'A more *filmic* performance, then?'

'Yes. Go for understatement.'

'Oh, I am very good at that. Not to worry.'

She flittered slower after that and, to give her credit, did seem her normal self with subsequent customers. Normal being a relative term.

We sent out for lunch. Then, with customers infrequent and Mother 'going for understatement,' an interminably long afternoon stretched before us.

So far, Mother had not gotten a response back from any of the suspects. And 'the plan' hadn't even been mentioned since Tony stepped in and took over. Which frankly both surprised and relieved me, because what she was suggesting seemed pretty half-baked.

But finally I said, 'You'd think Doug Holden would've at least protested you using his building.'

Mother glared at me, as if I'd breached the fourth wall in a play, or knocked down the scenery or something, compromising her performance.

She responded in a whisper, 'Had he done so, he'd only have made himself look guilty. Even if he were innocent.'

I guessed that made sense. Anyway, it was the last either of us said on the subject.

There had been one bright spot in the afternoon – I finally sold that yellow smiley-face wind-up alarm clock that I'd paid too much for and had been trying to get rid of since the beginning of our antiques business. A good omen? The Smiley-Face Gods looking down on us? Time, like the smiley-face clock, would tell.

At last, five o'clock finally happened, and we closed the shop and departed. On the way home, since our kitchen was unusable, I went through the McDonald's drive-up, getting us burgers and fries, and chicken nuggets for Sushi. Who was it that asked which part of the chicken was the 'nugget?' In any case, it was an option, her dog food having burned up in the fire.

Once inside the house, however, the thought of eating anything – especially fast food – made my stomach lurch. We'd aired the house out, but a faint scorched ambience lingered.

So I lay down on the Victorian couch to rest, which – as uncomfortable as the thing was – made sleep unlikely. In our current situation I thought it best to stay awake and alert. And, of course, I dropped right off to sleep, no drugged lemonade necessary this time.

When Mother roused me, I didn't know where I was for a moment.

'Tony's here, dear,' she said.

He came into focus standing next to her, and I sat up. The front drapes behind them had been closed.

I yawned, stretched. 'What . . . what time is it?'

'A little after ten,' he said.

'That long? Did I miss anything? New house fires, break-ins, murder attempts?'

Mother, of course, took the question seriously. 'No, it's been quiet. No new developments.'

My fiancé, in his work shirt and tie, took my arm gently and helped me from the unforgiving couch. 'Let's move into the dining room.'

He and I sat at the Duncan Phyfe table while Mother got everyone cups of coffee from the little station we'd set up on the Mediterranean buffet.

I gulped the strong, hot liquid; I could swear I felt it coursing through my veins.

Tony, very much in chief mode, spoke. 'We've had eyes on the suspects since noon. Officer Munson has been tailing Doug Holden, Schultz was assigned to Johan Larsen . . . Kelly to Otto Berger . . . Cordona, Elizabeth Norris . . . and Monroe, Ryan Dayton.'

Of course, over time Mother and I had encountered all of the officers: Munson, the Herman Munster look-alike; Schultz and Kelly, an affable Mutt and Jeff pair; Cordona, the PD's only female detective, my one-time friend who now never missed a chance to come down hard on Mother and me; and Monroe, of course, was Shawntea, another friend who might now be an ex- after we'd enlisted her help loading up Mother's blackmail-discounted merchandise in our SUV.

Tony took a sip of coffee, then continued: 'We've logged where the suspects have gone, at what time, and how long they stayed, continually monitoring them throughout this undercover operation.'

'*Oh!*' Mother yelped, startling Tony and me. 'What are we calling it?'

'Calling what?' Tony asked.

'The undercover operation! It has a name, doesn't it?'

Reluctantly, he said, 'Operation Warehouse.'

Mother frowned. 'Well, now that's just terrible! Has no ring to it, whatsoever. We can do better! Remember Operation ABSCAM, Overlord, and Serpico.'

The chief said, 'Serpico was a man's name, not an "operation."'

Her eyes glittered as she leaned toward him. 'How about . . . Operation Going Down. For the elevator? No. Try, Operation Skeleton! Oh, Operation Vivian Borne!'

He just looked at her. And I was looking at him from between the fingers covering my face.

'It's already in play, Vivian,' he said. 'Operation Warehouse.'

'You may be a fine chief of police,' Mother said, 'but you have no literary flair whatsoever. Much less any sense of drama!' Then she whispered to me, 'We'll change it in the book.'

'No we won't,' I said. Then, to keep my fiancé from strangling his future mother-in-law, I asked Tony, 'Have any suspects gone near the warehouse?'

'No,' Tony said.

Mother asked, 'Where are they now?'

He shrugged. 'Last report, all in their homes.'

I asked, 'Where does that leave us?'

From beneath the table, Tony produced a black duffel, which I hadn't noticed, placed it on the table, then unzipped the bag.

Mother and I leaned in for a look. Assorted electronics stared back at us.

'I *am* going to wear a wire!' she said, excitedly. 'Goodie!'

Note to all readers over the age of seventy, particularly of the female gender: saying 'Goodie' at your age is decidedly undignified. Make that all readers. Of any age.

'Not a wire exactly,' Tony replied, remarkably patient I thought. He withdrew a small transmitter that had a thin transparent wire running to a tiny earbud.

Mother clapped her hands. 'How *very* James Bond. You know, I just *love* Daniel Craig – "Stop touching your earpiece!" Especially that last installment of his . . . but that ending . . . Spoiler alert – it's a tear-jerker!'

'Mother,' I said, 'you need to get a grip.'

'This is not a play, Vivian,' Tony said sternly. 'This is real, and it's dangerous.'

For a moment I thought he might call off Operation Warehouse. Mother must have, too, because her voice was soft and absent of excitement when she promised, 'I *will* behave.'

'I'll pull the plug,' he said, 'the moment you don't.' They locked eyes, she nodded, and he went on: 'My officers are already equipped with earbuds. I'll be wearing one, too, as will you, Vivian. Everyone will be able to hear and talk to each other.'

'What about me?' I asked. Despite my trepidation, I was feeling left out.

'You'll have one too,' Tony said, 'but you'll only be able to hear.'

He didn't want me yap yap yapping at him, huh?

Reading my mind, he said, 'There's no need for you to communicate, since you'll be with me, and one less voice means less chance of cross-talk.'

Mother stiffened. 'I don't think there's any need for cross talk. Aren't we all friends here?'

'Not that *kind* of cross-talk, Vivian.'

I said, 'It's fine, Mother. Or would you *like* me talking in your ear?'

'No! No, we'll do it Tony's way. This time.'

He went over a few more details before attaching Mother, me, and himself to our surveillance gear, and testing it with the officers in the field.

Satisfied the electronics were working properly, Tony and I left via a window in the library – the one he'd surreptitiously come in, so as not to be seen from the street – and walked through back yards and around to his unmarked car parked a few blocks away.

Mother was to remain home, until 11:30, when she would go to the warehouse on her Vespa.

We rode in his car in silence, except for Mother occasionally coming through our earpieces, going, 'Testing one, two . . . testing one, two, can you hear me now, can you hear me now?' Finally Tony asked her to stop, saying she was coming through loud and clear, and to keep the channel open.

Downtown, in the dark alley behind Main Street, a block away from the warehouse, Tony parked his car in back of the Shamrock, a bar that had been a fixture in town for nearly a century. We got out and I followed him down some crumbling cement steps to the basement door of the old Victorian building, which was unlocked.

What were we doing here?

Soon it became clear. While I'd lived in Serenity all my life, except for the years spent with my ex in Chicago, the town still had secrets it had never shared with me.

But I'd long heard rumors of underground tunnels running from some taverns to the warehouse that, as a lucrative sideline to food products, supplied them with illegal liquor during Prohibition. Until now I'd never seen proof any such tunnels existed.

But here one was, a passageway in the basement of the bar, allowing Tony and me to enter the warehouse unseen; a precaution, I deduced, in case the killer had someone *else* watching the building for him or her.

The tunnel's entrance had been sealed with bricks, but enough had been removed – quite recently, judging by the brick dust persisting in the air – to enable us to squeeze through.

With Tony in the lead, following the beam of his flashlight, we made our way along a surprisingly well-preserved passageway encased in bricks from level flooring to arched ceiling, wide enough to walk side by side. Other than clawing through an abundance of cobwebs, and ignoring the occasional sound of a scurrying rat, we reached the other end unscathed.

The tunnel's exit was covered by a sheet of plywood, which Tony lifted and set aside, and we came out behind an ancient boiler, a huge metal octopus whose tube-like tentacles stretched along the high opened-beamed ceiling to carry heat to various parts of the building.

Mother and I had explored the warehouse, but not the basement with its dirt floor and dank, musty smell. The place would have given me the heebie-jeebies any time, but that jumpy feeling was heightened by the uncertainty of what lay ahead.

We crossed to the wooden stairs, then ascended to the first floor. There, Tony extinguished his flashlight while we stood allowing our eyes to adjust to the fathomless darkness. Tony moved forward, with me right behind him, so close I occasionally stepped on the back of his Florsheim shoe. Light from streetlamps filtered in through the bank of windows on our left, aided by a nearly full moon, and finally I got my bearings.

This where it had begun – the area where Mother had

attended the auction that was the prelude to Conrad Norris's death.

Tony whispered for me to stay put, then disappeared for what seemed forever and was probably a minute and a half. He returned with a folding chair, which he placed in the center of the room, facing the glass-paneled front door. He turned on the flashlight, positioning it on the floor a few yards away, washing the beam over the chair.

The trap was set, awaiting only the bait.

Mother.

When Tony pointed to the rickety staircase hugging the far wall and leading to the second floor, I raised my eyebrows. But his nod was assertive, and I obeyed it. Together, navigating missing steps, we climbed to the landing, halfway up to the second floor, and he gestured for me to kneel at the railing there.

From this high vantage, we had a view of the cavernous room, including the front entrance and rear area. I could even make out the mound of Mother's conical-shaped straw hats that had been gathered by the back door.

Tony, in a crouch, whispered, 'Report.'

For a second, I thought he was talking to me – but what did I have to report? Then voices came through my earpiece.

'*Munson. Holden still at home.*'

'*Shultz. Larsen at home.*'

'*Kelly. Berger home.*'

'*Cordona. Norris, too.*'

'*Monroe. Dayton, also.*' Then Shawntea said, '*Wait. He's getting into his truck.*'

'Don't lose him,' Tony replied.

'*Copy that.*'

Mother's voice came through. '*Isn't this simply* too *exciting?*'

'Viv-i-an,' Tony said, as if she were a naughty child.

'*Oh, right! I mean, affirmative. Keep the channel clear! Roger, Wilco, over and out.*'

Tony looked at me, thin-lipped, and I smiled back weakly. I whispered, 'Are we all going to die?'

'Could be.'

Naturally, I had left my cell behind, but being one of the few

Gen Xers who still wore a watch as a fashion statement, I could keep track of the time – and it was nearing eleven.

Fifteen minutes later, Shawntea reported in.

'*Monroe. I've followed Dayton to a bar called the Golden Spike.*'

A rough dive a few miles north of town.

Tony asked, 'Do you need eyes inside?'

'*No. I'm parked close to his truck, and can see him through the window playing pool, clearly visible in the same red shirt and black baseball cap he's been wearing all day.*'

'All right. Keep me posted.'

At eleven-thirty on the dot, Mother said, '*Vivian Borne, leaving the house.*'

'You recall my instructions?' Tony asked.

'*Park my Vespa at the curb, and go in the front entrance.*'

'Yes. It's unlocked.'

He had probably taken care of that when he'd gotten the chair.

Over the putt-putt of the Vespa motor, Mother was saying in my earpiece: '*What is my motivation?*'

Tony's voice was tight. 'Consistent with your plan. You say you want to help, but this is really blackmail.'

'*It's a stretch . . .*'

Not much of one.

'*. . . so am I threatening? Am I evil?*'

'No! Just act naturally.'

'*Well, I might naturally whistle. Or hum. Show I'm not afraid. Keeping it casual.*'

'No whistling, no humming. We have to hear each other.'

'*Ah, Roger that.*'

A few minutes later, Tony asked the team for another report.

Holden, Larsen, Berger and Norris remained in their homes; Ryan Dayton was still playing pool.

My earpiece went quiet, but for that faint putt-putting of Mother's scooter as she rode to the warehouse.

At exactly eleven forty-five, my earpiece seemed to explode as the officers began talking over each other, reporting that Holden, Larsen, Berger and Elizabeth were all leaving their homes – the men in cars, woman on foot!

Holy . . . was this a conspiracy? *Could all four be involved in one or both of these murders?*

Tony hadn't heard from Shawntea, and barked, 'Monroe, report.'

'Still playing pool, Chief.'

That seemed to put Ryan Dayton in the clear. But he still had time to get here . . .

I heard the front door open, then shut. Slowly a figure moved in the semi-darkness toward the center of the room. I gripped Tony's arm as he knelt beside me.

Mother stepped dramatically into the beam of his flashlight, like it was a stage spot and she about to reprise the dramatic opening of Libby Wolfson's one-woman show, 'I'm Takin' My Own Head, Screwin' It On Right and No Guy's Gonna Tell Me That It Ain't.' She'd gotten raves for that. Not rave reviews – just raves.

'Where are you?' Mother whispered, shading her eyes as if peering into the audience to see if anyone important were there. Or anyone at all for that matter.

'Don't look for us,' Tony said softly.

She dropped her hand and said in a normal tone of voice that nonetheless echoed, 'Oh, right. I might inadvertently disclose your position.'

Tony moaned a little.

Mother sat in the chair he'd provided, primly placing her hands in her lap.

'Officers, report,' Tony said, admonishing, 'In order, one at a time.'

'Holden is in his car, in the lot across from the front of the warehouse.'

'Larsen is in the alcove of his button museum.'

'Berger's in the all-night diner at a window seat.'

'Elizabeth is standing across the side street under a tree.'

From their positions, all four had a view of the front entrance of the warehouse. What was this, *Murder on the Orient Express?*

Shawntea sighed, *'Ryan is still playing pool,'* as if disappointed her subject wasn't in play at the scene.

Midnight came and went.

Twelve-fifteen.

Twelve-thirty.

The suspects seemed to be just waiting.

But for what?

Suddenly, Mother whispered, 'Someone's here.' She was in character and in the moment, her words audible only in our earpieces and not in the big room itself.

'Report,' Tony whispered to his team.

They did; none of the surveillance subjects had moved!

Alarmed, I got on my knees, peering over the wooden railing into the darkness surrounding Mother in her flashlight halo, listening for any sound.

Shawntea: '*Ahhh, Chief? Point of information. Is Ryan Dayton gay?*'

'Not that I know of,' Tony said, adding quickly, 'Why?'

''Cause every guy in that place has been hitting on him.'

I whispered to Tony, 'Mother says he has a girlfriend.'

'Monroe, make contact,' he instructed urgently.

I could hear her car door open, and slam, then heavy breathing as she ran. The din inside the bar and country western on a jukebox filled my ears.

'*Chief! It's a woman in Ryan's clothes!*'

Behind Mother, the beam of the flashlight caught the glint of a shovel blade above her head.

I screamed.

Mother reacted, twisting in the chair, half-rising, managing to grab the handle of the tool to deflect the blow.

Tony flew down the stairs, his .38 revolver in his hand, firing a shot in the air as he came. The muzzle flash caught Ryan, all in black, dropping the shovel, then fleeing to the back to escape . . .

. . . running right into the mound of conical-shaped hats and tripping and landing with a crunch – not of bones, but straw.

Tony reached the young man, whose arms were flailing in a desperate attempt to extricate himself from the pile of hats; then my fiancé pulled the killer roughly to his feet, and slapped hand-cuffs on in back.

I had remained on the landing, gripping the railing, watching the tense scene below unfold. Somehow I made it down the sketchy stairs and ran to Mother, wrapping my arms around her.

She seemed almost serenely composed, but I could feel her heart beating as fast as mine.

'Quite the happy ending, right, dear?' she said, drawing back slightly.

Wiping away tears, I managed to croak, 'Well, it's an ending, anyway. I'll let you know when we get to the "happy" part.'

Tony hauled Ryan by the arm back into the central area and deposited him on the floor, on his knees, head bowed, sobbing.

The chief moved to an electrical panel, flicked some switches, flooding the first floor with light, and I could see Ryan clearly. From a gold chain around his neck dangled a tiger-tooth pendant. Tilda's cryptic reading alluding to Lyle Dayton's killer had been correct.

Soon, one by one, the officers arrived with their subjects in tow, Shawntea last to arrive, Ryan's girlfriend, Maya Lopez, in Ryan's clothes, looking scared, and the only one cuffed, hands in back.

Tony instructed Officers Munson and Monroe to take Ryan and his apparent accomplice to the station in separate cars. When they had gone, he lined up Holden, Larsen, Berger, and Elizabeth Norris and asked one question that applied to each: 'What were you doing here?'

Holden answered, 'That text, of course. I was curious to see who showed up.'

Larsen and Berger reiterated as much, while Elizabeth Norris said quietly, 'Is it a surprise I wanted to see who killed my husband?'

Tony, studying them for a moment, said, 'All right. You can go, all of you . . . but I'll be interviewing each of you tomorrow. You'll hear from my office in the morning.'

With a swagger that would have been well served by a spit of tobacco, Mother added, 'So don't even *think* about leaving town!'

Officers Schultz and Kelly were dispatched to secure the outside of the building, and to keep back any gawkers.

Tony then turned to Mother and me. 'Are you both OK?'

'Right as rain,' she chirped.

Me? I was still recovering from a downpour, but nodded.

Mother pointed to the shovel on the floor. 'That may be the very weapon Ryan used on Lyle and Conrad.'

'And *almost* on you,' I couldn't resist saying.

'I noticed it in the basement a week ago,' she continued, 'when I attended the auction.' She paused. 'And, speaking of the basement, if I were you, I'd start digging for evidence.'

'Thank you, Vivian,' Tony said. 'What would I do without your advice?'

She shrugged. 'I'm not about to criticize a man who came to my rescue.'

'That's appreciated. But Brandy's scream accomplished more than I did. Anyway, we'll talk in the morning. Go home, girls – get some rest.'

Mother yawned. 'I *am* a trifle knackered.'

As she headed out, I took Tony's hand. 'Thank you, darling.'

His stony mask dropped, steel-gray eyes softening, revealing the relief he felt, and his hand squeezed mine. 'We'll get some alone time soon,' he said. 'I promise.'

Outside, a small crowd was gathering on the periphery, bar patrons mixed in with men and women with robes over nightclothes, a few kids in jammies, too. Other downtown dwellers were visible watching from apartment windows.

Mother climbed on the Vespa, and I got on behind her.

'You know, dear,' she said, starting the putt-putt of the scooter, 'there's one thing you can't deny.'

'I'll bite. What's that?'

'Those hats turned out to be a wise investment.'

A Trash 'n' Treasures Tip

While there are some exceptions, buying fad collectibles like Beanie Babies, Limited Edition plates, and Coca Cola products is a bad bet, as these items are plentiful, and easily accessible. Another drawback can be when the collectible – say, a wind-up smiley-face alarm clock – no longer has popular appeal. (I did recoup my money from a smiley-face cookie jar, because, hey, who doesn't still need a place to store cookies?)

THIRTEEN
Mother May I

The following day, Tony's office informed us that the chief could not (stand to?) meet with us until mid-afternoon, which miffed Mother, because she'd been up and dressed since dawn. In her latest Breckenridge ensemble, she paced in the living room like a prosecutor before a jury of one, me, sitting cross-legged and barefoot on the uncomfortable couch in my knotted floral-print top and jeans, reading in *Elle* about luxury spas I'd never go to.

Mother was muttering, going over all the points she intended to make later today. I didn't pay any attention, although when we caught lunch at the Big Cat Café I was subjected to her summation. It was a pretty good one, a combination defense of her actions and the case against Ryan Dayton. I really didn't think she needed to bother – a guy about to club her with a shovel made its own convincing case.

Finally we were sitting in the conference room at the PD, the chief at the head of the oval table, Mother and I across from each other. Tony looked so tired, he might still have been up, post-Operation Warehouse; that he wore the same clothes as last night seemed to confirm as much. When an antsy Mother opened her mouth to speak first, he raised a silencing palm.

'Ryan Dayton has given a signed statement,' the chief said, 'confessing to killing his uncle . . . *and* Conrad Norris. He also admitted to setting fire to your house, and attempting to kill Vivian last night.'

Mother stiffened. 'Was he coerced?'

Blind-sided by that, Tony snapped, 'Certainly not. See for yourself.'

He handed the document across to her and she read it for perhaps two minutes. She offered me a look and I shook my head.

After returning the single page, she continued her own interrogation. 'Did he have a lawyer present?'

'No,' the chief admitted. 'He declined legal representation.'

'Then his statement *could* be withdrawn.'

A vein on Tony's temple was throbbing. 'It could,' he said flatly. 'What are you up to, Vivian?'

She ignored the question. 'When is the young man's arraignment?'

'Tomorrow morning.'

'I would like to see him.' She pushed back her chair, and rose. '*Immediatamente*, if you please.'

'Mother!' I blurted. 'What are you up to?'

She gazed down at me. 'What I am *up to*, dear, is taking steps to make sure the scales of justice aren't overly lopsided.' Back to Tony. 'Well?'

Tony stood and met her gaze with his own, although hers was wide-eyed and his slitted. 'You can see him, Vivian . . . but only *if* he wants to see you.'

'Fair enough.'

The chief stormed out of the room.

Mother said, 'My, but he can move fast for a man of his size,' and sat back down.

'I *do* know what you're up to,' I said through tight lips.

'Dear, if you think I'm trying to drive a wedge between you and that man, that's simply not the case. I have come to feel he has several good points.'

'Never mind the soft soap. You just want to make sure Ryan Dayton goes to trial! So you'll get to testify – feed your ego by being a star witness.'

Mother seemed genuinely hurt. 'Brandy, that was harsh. I'm shocked you think so little of me.'

'What, then? Whip up a courtroom conclusion for our book?'

She raised a defiant chin. 'Are you quite finished?'

'Oh, I'm *finished*, all right.'

Her head drew back as if I'd slapped her. 'I'm not sure how to take that, dear.'

'Here's how to take it,' I said. 'I'm finished with watching you put yourself and me and everyone and everything around us, from Sushi to our kitchen, in harm's way.'

That hung in the air a while before she responded.

'Would it be unkind of me to remind you,' she said, no theatrical delivery in it at all, 'that my efforts, and yours, were due to a *child* being put in harm's way? Through no fault of my own?'

Be-Be.

And it was the ark I'd given her that really started this whole mess. You may not believe it, but I couldn't think of a thing to say.

Tony reappeared and said tersely, 'Dayton has agreed to see you.'

Mother rose; I remained seated, having no intention of going with her. My words had stung her, and hers had stung me. But when she reached the door, with her back to Tony, he bobbed his head to me to follow.

I sensed at once why: he wanted a report on what was said between Mother and her would-be assailant. And honestly? Part of me was curious to know, as well.

Ryan was being kept in a holding cell pending arraignment, at which time he would be charged and moved to the county jail facility next door.

Tony brought the suspect – hands cuffed in front now, feet shuffling in chains – to a small interview room, all but filled by a bolted-down rectangular table where Mother and I were already seated in plastic chairs.

With no windows – not even the one-way viewing variety – the room was as claustrophobic as a closet, adding to my discomfort of being so close to this admitted murderer.

Tony seated Ryan across from us, shackled the foot-chain to a metal ring at the bottom of the concrete wall, then left.

Ryan, in the same black T-shirt, jeans, and running shoes he'd been captured in last night – minus belt, shoelaces, and tigertooth necklace, of course – looked defeated, skin sallow, eyes haunted, dark stubble. He seemed almost to have aged years in a single night.

Mother's voice was kind, with nothing phony in it, when she asked, 'Are they treating you well?'

The prisoner nodded, his eyes wary.

'I've read your confession.'

He said nothing.

'But if you don't mind,' she said, 'I would appreciate some clarification on a few matters.'

A shrug.

'I have heard that your uncle was abusive. You don't mention that in your statement.'

He came alive a little. 'Abusive. I guess you could put it that way. Uncle Lyle used to beat me with his fists when I was a child. He didn't stop till I was old enough to fight back. Sometimes it was so bad he'd have to take me to the hospital, where he'd say I fell down the stairs. He let me know if I contradicted him, he'd just beat me again.'

'I'm sorry you had to endure that,' she said. And the sympathy in her voice sounded genuine, too. 'No one should have to. But you weren't a child when he . . . disappeared.'

'You want to know how he died,' Ryan said. 'That's why you're here.'

'If it's not too difficult,' she replied.

Either this was Mother's finest acting performance, or she was actually sympathizing with someone who had murdered two people and nearly killed her, as well!

Ryan took a deep breath. His voice came soft and his words matter of fact, as if from a distant place. 'I was in the warehouse basement that day, nine years ago, trying to fix the old boiler, when my uncle came down. Like I told you before, I'd been working for him since I was fifteen for minimum wage, and he'd always promised to hand over the liquidation business to me when he retired.' He paused. 'But I always suspected he was just stringing me along for the cheap labor.'

Ryan halted, as if he'd lost his place.

Mother softly prompted, 'Your uncle had come down to the basement.'

'To the basement, yes. Uncle Lyle stood there and said he was selling the business, but he'd done me a big favor – he'd arranged for me to stay on . . . at minimum wage. We argued, and he started pushing me. There was a shovel leaning against the wall, and I just . . . grabbed it, and hit him, hit him on the side of his head. When I realized he was dead, I panicked, and buried him in the basement, knowing as his only relative and being over eighteen, I'd inherit the building.'

Silence took its time before Mother broke it.

She said, 'You should not keep this to yourself. A jury could understand how this happened, after what you'd been through. It might even be considered self-defense.'

He looked at her, his eyes strangely placid. 'No, it's you who don't understand. I'd wanted to kill that monster for a long time. I'm not sorry. Not one little bit. I'd do it again. And if asked, that's what I'd say in court.'

'Before say anything else,' Mother said, 'I'd like to tell you a story. I'm an author, after all . . . co-author.'

Ryan's half smile was wholly bitter. 'Are you kidding?'

'Just listen. Suppose a young man who had killed his abusive uncle in self-defense had buried the body in the dirt-floor basement of a certain warehouse. Suppose, after the sale of the building, the nephew saw the advisability of disinterring his uncle's corpse and removing the remains elsewhere for disposal. The same shovel that had killed the uncle years before unearthed him now. The nephew emptied a barrel of buttons – there were a number still in storage at the warehouse – and placed the skeletal remains in that barrel and refilled it with buttons.'

Ryan said nothing.

Mother continued. 'Now let's say the nephew decided that the best way to remove this newly significant barrel was to bid on the entire lot and dispose of the key barrel at his own pleasure and discretion. He bid through a proxy but unexpectedly lost to the local pearl-button museum. This was a setback, but not without recourse – he could break into the museum and help himself to the button-packed bones. With me?'

'Some story,' he said.

'The afternoon of the auction, the nephew had overheard the museum curator complaining that thirteen barrels of buttons had been listed but the lot contained only twelve. The somewhat sleazy auctioneer assured the museum curator that this was a mere inventory flub. Unbeknownst to either the museum curator or the nephew, the barrel with the uncle's remains in it were in the possession of a local antiques shop, a midnight transaction having been made with said sleazy auctioneer.'

'You had the barrel,' Ryan said.

'Yes. And yet the nephew's attempt on my life was due not to that fact but to the insistent questioning I'd undertaken. But back to our story . . . The afternoon of the auction, the nephew went back for something. It had occurred to him that, even after nearly a decade, some forensics evidence might have clung to that shovel, so he returned for it – it hadn't been among the auction items, and was last seen in the dirt-floor basement where it had been left during its recent use in an exhumation. Now I'm afraid I must get a bit fanciful.'

'Sure. Why not.'

'The nephew collected his shovel and on the first floor ran into the auctioneer, who I will guess was stepping off the elevator, perhaps taking a final pass through the building. The nephew took the opportunity to confront him about the possibility of a thirteenth barrel, and . . . I admit I'm speculating . . . the auctioneer reacted to the nephew's fixation on the barrels, took one look at that shovel, and put the pieces together. Perhaps he offered not to share his suspicions elsewhere, for a sum . . . he was a sleazy auctioneer, as I say. At any rate, a swing of the shovel, a trip up a few floors, an elevator lowered, and a corpse took a long fall . . . What do you think of my story, Ryan?'

'Sounds kind of far-fetched.'

'The truth often does.' She shifted position. 'The tale may be improved by some finishing touches I need to put on. Like whether the nephew's girlfriend knew about the two killings . . . the uncle and the auctioneer.'

He lurched forward and I jerked back; but Mother didn't move at all as he said, insistent, desperate, 'Maya didn't know *anything* about either *one* of them!'

I broke my silence: 'But does she know about you drugging us and your arson at our home?'

He hung his head; shook it, his voice was soft and tinged with shame. 'I stole Maya's sleeping tablets to put into that lemonade. And I told her to wear my clothes last night because I wanted to play a joke on someone.'

If that panned out, and she *was* innocent, about the only thing Maya could be accused of was being too trusting.

His eyes came up, his expression oddly shy. 'Look. Both of

you. I'm sorry about setting the fire in your kitchen. That got more serious than I intended. I only meant to scare you . . . stop you from investigating.'

Now I lurched forward. 'You weren't trying to scare my mother last night at the warehouse. You tried to take her out with that shovel – your favorite murder weapon!'

He stared at the floor. 'No reason for you to believe me, but . . . I wouldn't gone through with it. Everything just got out of hand, and that was . . . you know, my breaking point. It's why I gave the police my statement.' He shifted in the chair. 'You see, in my mind, I could justify everything else I did – my uncle was the cruelest man I ever knew. Conrad Norris was a drunk and a liar and a thief. You could say they had it coming. But Mrs Borne . . . Vivian . . . *you* didn't.'

'Thank you, dear,' she said.

I couldn't believe her! I was not about to go easy on this two-time murderer – *at least* two times!

I demanded, 'Did you have anything to do with Sally Wilson's death?'

Taken aback, he said, 'Of course not. Why would I? And stage a . . . a hanging? What kind of monster do you think I am?'

'Like uncle, like nephew?'

'Brandy!' Mother said scoldingly.

Then Ryan said, very quietly, 'But she's not wrong, is she, Mrs Borne? As much as I hated my uncle, however cruel he was . . . he at least was not a murderer.'

'You did kill two people,' Mother replied. 'And you endangered our lives when you burned down our kitchen. Of course, we're fully insured . . .'

'Mother!' I said.

She ignored me, saying to Ryan, 'At tomorrow's arraignment, I'd advise that you plead not guilty.'

He goggled at her. 'I can't do that. I *am* guilty. Of everything.'

'If that's how you feel, plead no contest.'

In the past, whenever Mother was presented for arraignment, that's what she would plead, just to be contrary. Except she used the Latin term: *nolo contendere*.

Ryan frowned. 'How is that different from a guilty plea?'

'It implies mitigating circumstances.'

When his frown deepened, she clarified: 'It means you may have some justification for your actions. Would you like to hear them? You may find them useful.'

He shrugged. 'Why bother?'

'Because there's a big difference between first- and second-degree murder, regarding sentencing and the amount of time you'll spend in prison.'

The sound he made was only technically a laugh. 'Either way, I'll be an old man when I get out.'

She nodded. 'However, the *degree* of old age has significance. Or does dying behind bars appeal to you?'

That seemed to have some effect on Ryan. 'All right. Tell me the mitigating circumstances.'

'Regarding your uncle,' Mother began, 'he frequently abused you, and there will be records at the ER which can substantiate your injuries.' She paused. 'If Norris tried to get money from you, that makes him a blackmailer, and an accessory after the fact in the murder of your uncle. As to your attempt to break into the museum . . . according to the security tape, that's all it was – a misdemeanor.' She paused. 'Now, as to Brandy and myself. Yes, you laced our lemonade with sleeping pills, and set fire to the kitchen. By the way, did you doctor our dog's food, as well?'

'No. I thought she'd go for help out that little door.'

I said, 'I'm surprised Sushi didn't attack you in the kitchen. Surely she heard you.'

'Yes. The dog did come down. But she was friendly.'

'Because you fed her steak,' I said, which explained the whiff of filet mignon. The little Bene-dog Arnold.

'And we did make it out of the house, as you hoped,' Mother said, adding, 'basically unharmed.'

Really? What about the trauma of going through that ordeal? Not to mention the damage to our house!

I said to Mother, 'OK, then, what about him taking a swing at you with that shovel? What are the mitigating circumstances in that?'

She replied calmly, 'When you screamed – and thank you for that, Brandy dear – I turned and grabbed the shovel's handle with both hands, as you may recall.'

'Oh, I recall, all right. And as I *recall*, it was coming down on your head!'

'Ah, but it wasn't, dear.'

I frowned. 'Wasn't what?'

'Coming down. There was no resistance from Ryan, no struggle. The blade had come up, yes, but hung in the air as if a freeze frame in a film.'

Ryan said, 'I told you both . . . I couldn't do it.'

'And perhaps subconsciously, dear,' she said to him, 'you wanted to get caught. You had to know you were likely walking into a trap. If in fact you dropped the shovel and ran, perhaps some part of you thought you might take a bullet in the back and end the madness.'

Ryan hunched over and buried his face in his cuffed hands. His sobs were enough to finally make me feel some sympathy for him, too. Mother produced some tissues from a pocket of her Breckenridge slacks, leaned forward, and pressed the tissues into his hands.

He wiped his eyes, blew his nose, and – somewhat composed now – said, 'Mitigating circumstances or not, I have to ask myself . . . why put everyone through the ordeal of a trial? Why put myself through the public shame and humiliation?'

Mother smiled benevolently. 'To get the truth out, dear. People crave closure. And that includes yourself. Might I suggest, if you and Maya are really serious, getting hitched? For one thing, spouses cannot be made to testify against each other. For another, conjugal visits can enliven prison stays nicely . . . In the meantime, I'll be glad to help you line up a good defense lawyer.'

They'd be lining up to take this case on, for the publicity alone.

'Now, remember,' Mother said as we were going out, 'plead no contest tomorrow at your arraignment.'

By the time we'd left the interview room, Tony had been called away from the station, so I'd have to give him a report later. He wouldn't like it, not the report or that I'd come to believe Mother had Ryan's best interests at heart – in spite of her exclaiming on the way to our car, 'I can't wait – that trial is going to be a *doozy*!'

I hated being caught in the middle between Tony and Mother, two of the handful of people in this world I really loved. Which is why, on the drive home, I said to her, 'I'm thinking of getting married soon.'

It sounded like I was asking for her permission, as if that might assuage my guilt for abandoning her.

Mother, in the passenger seat, barely turned her head. 'When, dear?'

'I've been picturing a winter wedding,' I said.

'Splendid idea! Summer nuptials are a dime a dozen, don't you think?'

'Outdoors, in the gazebo at the park.' Which looked just like the one where Bill Murray and Andie MacDowell danced in *Groundhog Day*.

Mother was saying, 'The snow sparkling! Icicles hanging from the roof . . .'

'Me, in white faux fur with matching hand-muffler instead of a bouquet. Tony wearing a black wool topcoat, hat, and leather gloves.'

She sucked in air. 'I could play "Wonderland By Night" on my cornet!'

'Or maybe just the recording by Charly Tabor.'

'*Or* I could sing "Winter Wonderland."'

'Or maybe the recording by Michael Bublé.'

Mother clapped her hands. 'What a magical wedding it will be! Right out of a fairy tale.'

'Let's make it Hans Christian Andersen, not Brothers Grimm.'

'Of course,' she began slowly, 'it *could* be twenty below, with a blizzard, everyone shivering . . . my lips stuck to the mouthpiece of the cornet like that poor child's at the flagpole in that Christmas story, whatever it's called.'

'*A Christmas Story*.'

'Yes, it's a Christmas story. But what is it *called*?'

At least Mother had helped me visualize beautifully the best-case scenario before pointing out a bad idea's obviousness.

At home, Sushi was all over us, sniffing to determine where'd we'd been without her, no doubt smelling Tony, and by extension, Rocky.

While I was giving the traitorous little furball some extra

tummy-scratching attention in the living room, Mother retrieved the mail.

'Anything?' I asked.

'Junk, junk, junk, junk,' she reported, fanning through.

But Mother surreptitiously pocketed a small white envelope, making me suspicious enough to go looking for it later, when she was busy.

I found the letter upstairs in her bedroom, tucked in the back of her art-nouveau nightstand drawer.

The envelope was addressed to her, written in block letters, like a child might, with no return address. Inside, a torn slip of paper, similarly printed, read:

YOU DESTROYED MY LIFE, AND NOW I WILL DESTROY YOURS.

What kind of happy ending is that?

A Trash 'n' Treasures Tip

'New' dead stock doesn't always mean the item will be in mint condition. In the case of clothing, damage can come in the form of dust, mildew, pests such as moths, unstable dyes, breakdown of plastic, and knits whose shoulders have been stretched from hanging too long. As Joan Crawford famously once said, 'No wire hangers!' And I thought *my* mother was a handful!

BARBARA ALLAN

is a joint pseudonym of husband-and-wife mystery writers, Barbara and Max Allan Collins.

BARBARA COLLINS made her entrance into the mystery field as a highly respected short-story writer with appearances in over a dozen top anthologies, including *Murder Most Delicious*, *Women on the Edge*, *Deadly Housewives*, and the bestselling *Cat Crimes* series. She was the co-editor of (and a contributor to) the bestselling anthology *Lethal Ladies*, and her stories were selected for inclusion in the first three volumes of *The Year's 25 Finest Crime and Mystery Stories*.

Three acclaimed collections of her work have been published – *Too Many Tomcats* and (with her husband) *Murder – His and Hers* and *Suspense – His and Hers*. The couple's first novel together, the Baby Boomer thriller *Regeneration*, was a paperback bestseller; their second collaborative novel, *Bombshell* – in which Marilyn Monroe saves the world from World War III – was published in hardcover to excellent reviews. Both are back in print under their joint byline.

Barbara also has been the production manager and/or line producer of several independent film projects.

MAX ALLAN COLLINS was named a Grand Master by the Mystery Writers of America in 2017. He has earned an unprecedented twenty-three Private Eye Writers of America 'Shamus' nominations, many for his Nathan Heller historical thrillers, winning for *True Detective* (1983), *Stolen Away* (1991), and the short story 'So Long, Chief.'

His classic graphic novel *Road to Perdition* is the basis of the Academy Award-winning film. Max's other comics credits include 'Dick Tracy'; 'Batman'; his own 'Ms. Tree'; and 'Wild Dog,' featured on the *Arrow* TV series.

Max's body of work includes film criticism, short fiction, songwriting, trading-card sets, and movie/TV tie-in novels, such as the *New York Times* bestseller *Saving Private Ryan*, numerous *USA Today* bestselling CSI novels, and the Scribe Award-winning *American Gangster*. His non-fiction includes *Scarface and the*

Untouchable: Al Capone and *Eliot Ness & the Mad Butcher* (both with A. Brad Schwartz).

An award-winning filmmaker, he wrote and directed the Lifetime movie *Mommy* (1996) and three other features; his produced screenplays include the 1995 HBO World Premiere *The Expert* and *The Last Lullaby* (2008). His 1998 documentary *Mike Hammer's Mickey Spillane* appears on the Criterion Collection release of the acclaimed film *noir*, *Kiss Me Deadly*. The Cinemax TV series *Quarry* is based on his innovative book series.

Max's recent novels include a dozen-plus works begun by his mentor, the late mystery-writing legend Mickey Spillane, among them *Kill Me If You Can* with Mike Hammer and the Caleb York western novels.

'BARBARA ALLAN' live(s) in Muscatine, Iowa, their Serenity-esque hometown. Son Nathan works as a translator of Japanese to English, with credits include video games, manga, and novels.